THE SEA FILE

THE SEA FILE

A Novel of Suspense

by Jack Denton Scott

N.G

Thorndike Press • Thorndike, Maine

Library of Congress Cataloging in Publication Data:

Scott, Jack Denton, 1915–
The sea file.

1. Large type books. I. Title.
[PS3569.C63S4 1981b]   813'.54   81-9089
ISBN 0-89621-306-4   AACR2

An excerpt from "A Fear of Pheromones" in *The Lives of a Cell* by Lewis thomas. Copyright 1971 by the Massachusetts Medical Society. The essay originally appeared in the *New England Journal of Medicine*. Reprinted by permission of Viking Penguin, Inc.

Large Print edition available through arrangement with McGraw-Hill Book Company

Cover design by Christy Rosso

FISHERMAN. Master, I marvel how the fishes live in the sea.

FISHERMAN. Why, as men do aland; the great ones eat up the little ones.

William Shakespeare

Appreciation for the two who made this book possible: My editor, Curtis Kelly. She not only is that rarity, a creative editor, but offers encouragement and enthusiasm when it is needed. My wife, Maria Luisa, for always giving me everything a writer needs – her gifts to me much too long to list.

JDS

TOP SECRET*

*EYES ONLY: CICAF, PRESIDENT U.S.A.

SUBJECT: *Imminent World Famine*

SOURCE: *Office Special Operations, Counter Intelligence Agency*

The Department of Agriculture reports that of the 500 insect species that cause most damage to world crops, 430 have built up complete resistance to all insecticides. The remainder are rapidly developing immunity.

Integrated Pest Control reports that rodents have also become immune to all known poisons.

World scientists and chemists have scraped the chemical barrel clean. U.S. entomologists and agricultural scientists are attempting to create biological controls, but this may take at least a decade.

To compound this critical situation, leading meteorologists report that climatic changes are shortening summer months, lengthening winter. Result: We have lost two growing months per year, and this loss may be doubled in less than three years.

World population is approaching 4 billion. Food stockpiles are vanishing; current crops are sparse. It has been conservatively estimated that by 1990 full world famine will be upon us.

FAIL-SAFE: The sea. It can feed the world until insect biological control is perfected and patterns of food production reestablished.

Problem for the U.S. Japan annually nets 1,205,604 metric tons of fish off our coasts. The Soviets, 1,100,520. Ten other countries also heavily fish our waters. Result: U.S. fishermen catch less than half the fish taken near our shores.

Coast Guard activity must be substantially increased to guard our 200-mile zone.

Attached is a 285-page Aramco report outlining the importance of marine life to human survival. This leading oil company concludes: "Protein from the sea is much more valuable than oil."

Respectfully,

Chester Morgan

Chester Morgan
Admiral, USN, Retired
Director
Counter Intelligence Agency
Langley, Virginia

Starred PTFN addenda: Recommend full communicative blackout be maintained. D/OSP/CIA

N.B.: No copies. CICAF Eyes Only.

PROLOGUE

A dawn sea off Cape Cod. Twenty fathoms down bluefish marauded among a school of tiny herring, slashing them into pieces, gulping them whole, wasting more than they swallowed. Bits of the carnage floated to the surface. Swooping, banking, herring gulls, sparkling white adults and dusky brown young, dove for the mutilated herrings, or darted down to gobble the live fish driven to the surface. The birds screeched and fought over the feast, some landing on the water to gulp the little fish in faster. In minutes it was over. The gulls floated away, their poetic flight belying their greed and savagery.

The lobster had come up from thick green

water at forty fathoms, working its way through kelp where it had caught and eaten a small squid. Not the complete scavenger it was believed to be, the big shellfish could live anywhere on the ocean floor, in clay, silt, cobble or sand, but it preferred rocky ledges, burrows, the underwater growth where it not only found shelter but prey.

Reaching the edge of a bed of rockweed, the lobster flushed eight herrings that had fled the school and hidden when the bluefish attack began. It caught one with a fast swipe of its big right claw, then closed its pincers, killing the fish. Using the slender scimitar left claw, the lobster sheared the herring into pieces, then with its antenna-like jaw attachments pushed the pieces of fish down its narrow gullet. Its four pairs of legs took the lobster in a slow spiderlike walk across the ocean floor, the feathery gills on the bottom of each leg sieving water to give it oxygen.

Like most offshore lobsters this one was constantly aggressive and did most of its hunting during the night and early morning hours. It had a daily range of about ten miles. Its armored shell made it invulnerable to most marine predators, but sometimes during a molt big bottom-dwelling fish could attack and eat the then-soft lobster. This was a large specimen of *Homarus americanus,* the American or Maine lobster found off the North American coast from Newfoundland to North Carolina. Ten years old, weighing over five pounds, this was a male that had molted its shell sixteen times during its first year.

Transparent hairs, alternating between the protective stiff row of guard hairs on antennae attached to its head, contained cultivated senses of smell and touch and telegraphed information to its brain. Now, suddenly agitated by the information it was receiving, the big lobster flexed its tail muscles and fan. It spurted backward.

Again using that powerful tail, the lobster went swiftly backward, spinning in a circle. Then it lay almost motionless, only its antennae moving, working like a radio receiver getting a signal.

The message it received made it again flip its tail and swing around. It began moving jerkily, erratically. As if being pulled by an invisible wire. Beneath its tail the feathery swimmeret flaps that gave it motion were in frantic action, propelling the lobster nearer shore. It was not hungry. The squid and herring filled its stomach. It was moving, being drawn shoreward, against its will.

Swiftly it swam in a half mile. Still in deep water, it came to a square object on the bottom. Two long, fragile, meshlike funnels reaching from either end rose and fell with the motion of the water.

Diffused light fell diagonally in long greenish stripes on the object. It was a thirty-six-inch-long, slatted, semi-cylindrical box of oak. Floating from the box to the surface was a main cedar buoy, and a secondary bottom toggle buoy.

Slowly, in a hypnotic state now, all aggression gone, the big lobster went through a long nylon mesh funnel. Trapped inside, it ignored the bag of bait. Docilely it closed its claws. It stood upright. Rhythmically, with the movement of the sea, it began a slow, bouncing dance. A ballet.

Harry Paucek had moved out of Maine and was moving out of lobstering in stages. Martha had nagged at him so steadily about the long hard winters with their bone-chilling cold and deep snow that he had finally, against his better judgment, left York County and come here to the coast of Massachusetts. He knew nothing but lobstering. But he knew that well.

It was his life. He loved the sea, the time when he was on the water in the early morning, the long stretches of silence, the freedom of being alone in the boat. He was not a philosophical man. But he knew deep inside that if you were lucky enough to work at what you liked, you had won one of life's most bitter battles. So he sadly contemplated that soon perhaps Massachusetts would also become too cold for Martha. Then what could he do? Move to Florida. Maybe run a party boat for tourist fishermen. On a tame sea that was too warm and full of fish he didn't know.

Tall, lean, with sharp blue eyes, leathery skin always covered with a little fuzz of gray beard that his razor didn't get, Harry Paucek was a prototype of the legendary Maine fisherman. Laconic, he was simple and direct in language and in thought. But unlike most of his taciturn tribe, he was flexible. His being here was proof of that.

The lobstermen here amused him, as a professional among amateurs is amused. Too many were "set-over" lobstermen. Checked their pots only every two or three days. A good man pulled his pots every day. No matter what the weather. Paucek also had contempt for the greedy ones who used otter trawls. Fished in water of several hundred fathoms, dragging for the big lobsters. This offshore dragging was depleting the lobster supply. Interfering with lobster larvae. It stopped their natural movement inshore on the current. Pared down the inshore population, where most lobster-men fished.

But he was able to jump that problem. He had a rugged thirty-five-foot inboard that for twenty years he had run in all kinds of weather. Twice the craft of those clinker-built dories around here, it would have to be filled with cement to sink it. With that boat he went out into water of thirty-six fathoms where the large lobsters often came. He had the equipment and the know-how for this kind of lobstering. It put him above the others. A hydro-slave, a hydraulic winch, enabled him to send his pots down to the depths. He used Double Header pots, oak-slatted box traps, floored with cement to get them to the deep bottom where the big ones were. These heavy pots could not be hauled up by hand, the method used by his competition. But even with Paucek's equipment and expertise, this hadn't been a great season. He had had only two hundred haul days this year. Four hundred lobsters from each trap. Lobster prices were up and going higher as everything was. But you had to fish harder. They weren't as numerous here as in the Maine waters. And he suspected that the sea was being soiled too fast these days to keep fish and shellfish healthy and at a population peak. But he wasn't an expert on that aspect of the sea. He tried not to think about it.

Dawn was red on the water; wisps of mist floated before him as he put out to sea from a cove just below Jacob's Landing Oceanographic Institute. He could hear the gulls way out raising hell. Probably working with the blues butchering a school of herring. He could hear other boats chugging away in the mist, going out to haul their pots. Way out, the foghorn of a big boat going to one of the islands bleated like a great beast in pain. These were the sounds that began his working day. He mentally ticked them off as routinely as he did the solid hammering of his old boat's motor, a reassuring sound for him over deep water. Like most professional fishermen, he didn't know how to swim. He let his boat do it for him.

As he headed toward his pot buoys another mile away, he lit an old briar pipe. He enjoyed the smell of the sweet tobacco even more than he did the taste. He was glad it was a mild morning. As he thought about that, he grudgingly agreed that maybe in a way Martha had something about his trade being too rugged. In winter — maybe.

At the sight of his buoys bobbing in the sea he smiled, always excited about what he would find in the pots when he brought them up. The anticipation, the surprise, were a strong part of the satisfaction his job held for him.

He found two eels and a pretty good sea bass in the first pot, but no lobsters. He still had twenty-three pots to go. The next two pots brought lobsters in each, three in the first, two in the second, all chickens, all about a pound or a little better. Carefully he took his metal rule and measured the length of each carapace. Though the legal limit for keepers was three and three-sixteenths of an inch, he was keeping only three-and-a-half-inchers. He thought it was good for the industry. He also examined each lobster closely, making sure he didn't have a female with eggs attached to the swimmerets under the tail. If he did, he also put that lobster back into the sea to reproduce. He despised the greedy lobstermen who kept everything they caught with no thought to the future.

The taking was disappointing until he got to the tenth pot. Winching it up spouting water, he opened its hatch and saw what he had. A big one, five pounds at least! No need to measure that one. But he'd look under the tail to make sure it wasn't an eggy female. He hoped it wasn't. This was a beaut.

Even before he lifted the lobster out he saw the white lettering on its carapace, "Vaughn, 50, JLOI." It was an identification for lobsters that were to be studied by the Jacob's Landing Oceanographic Institute. The name was the scientist conducting the test; the "50" was the amount of dollars paid to any fisherman returning the lobster.

The scientists were always running tests on everything from tuna to oysters, and the "tags" told a story for them. As lobsters molted their shells periodically, the lettering was effective only for the lobsters that were in what was called a "short release," or a tank release. For long release, a long, spaghetti-like tag was fastened to their stomachs and was unaffected by the shell molt.

This was a strong lobster, but Harry Paucek was surprised at its lethargy. It wasn't snapping its claws at him, and he didn't have to place the thick rubber bands on the claws to close them in order to examine it. But to be on the safe side, he did it anyway.

In another hour and a half, when he had brought his twenty-four pots in by hydraulic winch and tabulated his take, Harry Paucek was stunned. Nothing like this had happened in his three decades at sea. From those two dozen pots he had trapped seven big male lobsters, all weighing at least five pounds, and all bearing the white lettering of the institution. Three hundred and fifty dollars!

The laws of happenstance didn't go this way. But there it was. The lobsters were in his baskets, healthy and sound. Except there had been a strange thing about them. They were all docile. All let him handle them as if they were clawless. Were they sick? He hoped not. At least until he got them into the hands of that scientist at Jacob's Landing and got his money.

Something else puzzled Harry Paucek on the way back to his landing cove. The bait in his pots wasn't his. He used racks. Ocean perch racks; in his opinion the remains of those fish after filleting were the best lobster baits.

But what he found in all twenty-four of his pots after a careful examination were bags filled with bluefish heads, some big chunks of sea bass, and some racks — but they weren't Harry Paucek's racks. There was too much of the ocean perch's flesh attached to them. He, himself, filleted skillfully and frugally, leaving little more than skin and bones.

And then those big offshore lobsters. All males. And all acting dopey. Fierce critters that would normally shear a finger off given a chance, or eat one another. Seven from the sea in one haul-day. It just didn't happen. One of that size, maybe; if you were lucky. Two would be a record.

But he wouldn't worry about it. Take what you get from the sea. No questions. The money he'd pick up for these seven would be almost enough for that remote-control Zenith color TV Martha was hankering after.

THE SEA FILE

CHAPTER ONE

It was a moist May night. Rain had fallen lightly all day, and a fine mist still hung in the air, giving a cobwebby texture to the thick darkness. From the distant Merritt Parkway sparse late-hour traffic hummed like a strange night bird.

Although there was a moon, it was pale and lusterless; a few stars floated dimly. Out of the darkness, beside the building, a shadow stirred, falling on the bottom of a window. A watcher might have seen the window opening as if by itself. A black-clad arm in dark night has little shape and almost no dimension.

Now the moving shadow was inside the building; it pushed open a door marked "Mail

Room." Seconds later the window opened and closed, again as if by its own volition.

Clouds obscured the moon; the city of Stamford Connecticut, slept. The Janis Chemical Company building stood in morguelike silence.

Facing the monster first thing every morning made Arthur Lundberg squeamish. It was sometimes all he could do to retain his breakfast cup of coffee and slice of Pepperidge Farm Very Thin toast and not spray it on the Basra Ghiordas prayer rug, the latest status symbol in the world of the big corporation. It used to be two phones, a bigger desk, maybe an English secretary; now it was brilliantly hued Oriental rugs and your own Xerox and computer. Arthur Lundberg had recently reached the rug stage.

He saw that infernal creature in dreams nearly every night, stuck against the inside of the tank of water, black tail moving like a drowned man's finger, its round, multi-lipped mouth suctioned to the glass, the ghastly mouth lined with one hundred and fifty sharp, conical teeth arranged in concentric rows. Arthur Lundberg had actually had to count those teeth, and examine them microscopically, one by one.

Although eellike, only thumb-thick and eighteen inches long, it could suck the blood and life from a fifteen-inch whitefish in fourteen hours. Sometimes it hung onto a big lake trout for two weeks. Pressing its mouth against a fish's hide, it rasped away the scales, then penetrated the flesh with its toothed tongue, sharp as a blade. Simultaneously it spit into the wound a saliva containing a chemical that prevented coagulation of the fish's blood and actually dissolved tissue. An associate had named the chemical "lamphredine" after *Petromyzon marinus,* or the sea lamprey, that had nearly wiped out the fish population in the Great Lakes. The sea lamprey was of the *chordate* family, primitive as a blowgun dart and as deadly, solid cartilage, not a bone in its body, one of the oldest links in the sea's evolutionary chain of life. It had taken scientists six years working through six thousand chemicals until finally a watersoluble chemical compound was found, toxic only to sea lamprey larvae. Arthur Lundberg was grateful to be engaged in more important experiments than rescuing fish.

Walking past the tank, which was placed in his office because of cramped lab space, an old forty with bristly gray-blond hair, eyes a life-less pale blue behind black horn-rimmed glasses, limping from a skiing accident that broke his left leg in three places, Arthur Lundberg sank sedately into the chair behind his desk. It was a rare plain Regency pedestal desk with drawers in front and cupboards in back of the pedestals where he kept locked notes of his secret experiments. The desk went everywhere with him, from chemical company to chemical company, as did the desk chair, a *chaise à bras,* a heavy, not especially comfortable sixteenth-century Renaissance armchair.

He had a passion for antiques. Not only did their elegance of craftsmanship and design give him pleasure, but he had discovered that they also gave him instant stature. When the movers had brought the pieces to Janis from Renn Chemicals, the company he had left over a year ago, the secretaries very nearly sprang to their feet and saluted. But that was only fleeting security. Arthur Lundberg was rest-less in his occupation, wasn't by nature a team man, and couldn't operate without a challenge. Right now he had one too many.

The sea lamprey. He was studying the creature's mysterious chemical that mascerated fish flesh and halted the normal function of the fish's blood, trying to turn the chemical around to benefit man. Except for the blind-worm, seven-year-living-in-the-mud ammocoete period, Lundberg had observed this lamprey in most stages of its predatory life, even from the moment it left its spawning stream to begin its twenty-month parasitic existence. And he was sick of it.

Charlie Levy had gotten the experiment that Lundberg wanted – wanted so badly that he had actually gone to Bolk, the president of the company. But because he had long ago restricted his research to marine subjects, Lundberg had been turned down. It was a weird assignment really, but no telling where it would go, and whoever pulled it off would probably win the Nobel.

The goal was increasing man's longevity through the study of frogs. Frogs and man reproduced somewhat similarly, with one of several exceptions being that frogs always produce exact duplicates, perfect twins. Charlie Levy's aim was to learn how this was done chemically and adapt it to man. Thus, man could reproduce doubles at will. The projection was that one twin would be allowed to function normally; the other would be kept in perfect condition in a latent state in a special bank. When the normal twin grew old or became ill, he could call upon his banked duplicate for spare parts, tissue, eyes, kidneys, heart. As they were identical twins there might never be the complication of rejection.

Once Charlie Levy had called him in to watch a pair of frogs breeding, like people, frenzied, the male on top, holding on with front feet that looked like freckled hands, the female participating in the action, grunting loudly. Arthur Lundberg could almost see the sweat pour off them. As soon as they had finished, Charlie dissected them alive, taking samples of blood serum, ovaries, testes, sperm. Arthur Lundberg could still hear the frogs' cries as the knife probed the abdomen.

But Lundberg consoled himself with the thought that Levy's experiment was too weird to work. And he was doing well enough with a couple of his own assignments. He had almost perfected one he called "Pseudomonas," a bacterium he had created through genetic engineering that was capable of devouring oil spills by breaking down several components of petroleum as it floats on the ocean.

The other experiment he kept to himself. He did not permit himself to think about the psychological ramifications of the enjoyment he derived from it. He excused that pleasure by rationalizing that what he was doing each day to the lamprey was an important part of his secret experiment, even though the constant repetition wasn't scientifically necessary.

He went into the next room, the laboratory proper, returning to his outer office with a small glass vial of colorless liquid. He stood beside the tank where the lamprey lay as if dead, suctioned against the glass. Using an eyedropper, Lundberg drew up a small amount of the liquid. Smiling, he delicately dropped one gleaming globule into the lamprey tank. It always took exactly six seconds for the creature with its marvelous senses to react. He counted, *one, two, three, four, five, six.*

The lamprey fell backward into the tank. Writhing, it raced back and forth with unbelievable speed. It twisted as if trying to break itself in two, frantically smashing against the glass sides of the tank. It zoomed to the surface and stuck its ugly head out of the water, then fell to the bottom, scraping the entire length with its head. Finally, in a tormented S-shape, it fell exhausted in the far corner of the tank.

The lamprey had proved once again Lundberg's mastery of the psychobiology of smell and taste, of chemically reproducing and using the ultrastructure of chemoreceptors. It was driven mad searching for what it thought was a fish in its tank, a female fish lush with blood from breeding.

Breathing heavily, Lundberg went to his desk and sat, staring at the exhausted lamprey on the bottom of the tank. He didn't move again until the creature recovered its strength and returned to its favored position, suctioned against the glass side.

Lundberg finally got out of the clumsy embrace of the old chair, looked at the painting on the far wall, an early Harold von Schmidt, capturing the green fury of the ocean and the fragility of the boat battling it. The artist's genius clearly showed the sea master, manipulating man. Arthur Lundberg had always loved the sea, although he couldn't swim a stroke, didn't like to fish, hated beaches and knew nothing about boats. Now, as a marine biochemist, he felt himself a part of that vast, mysterious world, in some ways master of it, but worried about whether he was happy.

He suspected that happiness was simply an artificially enforced and reenforced state of mind. Now that Joan had left him, he told himself he had achieved it. She was a big blonde, a lamprey of sorts, the way she drained him of everything, emotion, house, car, bank account. Small price to pay for no more nagging about his spending eleven hours at the lab.

He gazed out the window at the land beyond, the broad sweep of lawn green as golf-putting grass. Three years ago this company had moved from Manhattan to Stamford, to these beautifully landscaped acres that were a credit to both Janis Chemical and this Connecticut community forty miles from New York.

Peace came through the window. Sun. Bird-song. Quiet. The silver maples waving like friendly people. Old John Morley, the gardener, with the perfect simian head, even to the sagittal crest, hoeing around the emerald spikes of iris in the moist May earth that soon would be aflame with color.

Before going into the lab, Lundberg automatically picked up his pipe and filled the bowl with honey tobacco. He had taken off the dark blue, double-knit Blass jacket that he had gotten on spring sale at Barney's and slipped into a mole-gray cotton lab coat. As he tamped the aromatic tobacco into the burled black walnut pipe bowl, the knock came.

It was Harry Murphy from the mail room, an aggressive gray sparrow of a man, a sour North Irishman who sent money for the Cause and was always taking up collections. Lundberg didn't like Harry much, but everyone should have some kind of cause; living, working, retiring wasn't enough.

Harry wanted to chat up Ireland, but Lundberg held his hand out for the letter and the old man got the message. It was special delivery, in a plain white number 10 envelope, his name and the company's inked rather than typed. As he examined the letter he wondered why there was no return address if it was important enough to rate special delivery.

He went back to his desk and picked an ebony wood opener with a leering East African head that he had gotten on a Pan Am tourist charter trip to Kenya. As he slit the letter's flap the ink instantly faded. Lundberg saw it. He stopped. It was too late.

The charge was enormous. The explosion tore his head cleanly from his body and propelled it, geysering blood, into the lamprey tank. The force of the entry was so great that the splash it sent up shattered on the floor like a shower of crystal.

When they finally found Arthur Lundberg's head the lamprey had fastened its suctioned, tooth-spiked mouth onto the tattered right cheek. It took an enormous pull to get the tenacious creature off.

Local police found it disturbing that Arthur Lundberg's entire cheek was torn off with the removal of the stubborn lamprey.

CHAPTER TWO

Eiko Adachi, ever conscious of his image as president of Morimoto, Japan's largest industrial complex, did not permit the shiver that ran up his spine to telegraph its presence to his eyes. Dabbling with death, toying with it with his chopsticks, his friend Tokura sat there benign and ageless as a Buddha statue, not a wrinkle on his face, the soft lights shining on his bald head. He had removed the one concession he made to his age, heavy, tinted wraparound glasses that somewhat masked the old wisdom in his eyes, large glasses that gave him the look of a marine creature from the depths. The glasses lay beside Tokura's dish on the table. The overhead light picked out pinpoint reflections in them. In the dish were thin slivers of fugu that looked like sliced onions. Beside it was a rice bowl of sauce in which the raw fish was dipped, a searing blending of soy, red pepper, lemon juice, scallions, and spices. Once the fugu was dunked into that sauce no tongue, no matter how knowing, could tell if the diner was about to die from eating it until the telltale tingle that began in the lips, then spread to the mouth, and finally to the fingers and arms.

Tokura was speaking softly as he ate his fish. His voice was surprisingly young and vibrant. "If you have been unlucky and the poison has not been properly removed from the fugu's liver, ovary or testes, skin, flesh, and intestines, soon the tongue will become paralyzed, your veins will grow large, blood pressure will drop. The stomach contracts, breathing becomes labored."

Adachi watched as Tokura elaborately pincered a sliver of fugu, dipped it lightly into the sauce, and chewed it meditatively. "The mind remains lucid, but response is not possible. It's like one of those nightmares, I am told. When a man comes to you in the night, puts his big strangler's hands around your throat. But you are frozen in fear and can do nothing about it. In two hours the man who

37

ate the wrong fugu is dead."

Eiko Adachi nervously poked his chopsticks into his bowl of *yaki-meshi;* the rice mixture of chopped onions, carrots, pepper, and eggs was a favorite. But he had no appetite; his hiatus hernia was beginning to burn. From the tension, not the food, he was sure.

Tokura, he knew, was toying with him. It was a favorite sport. Drama of one kind or another was Tokura's stock in trade.

Tokura had arranged this meeting in his usual manner. First the phone call and a meeting place, the lobby of the Imperial Hotel. At the hotel Eiko Adachi was identified by a bellboy and told he was wanted on the phone. On the phone, a male voice told him to go to room 1150 in the hotel. When he arrived there, his knock was answered by a cheery, aging Japanese woman whose fading elegance marked her as a former geisha. She told Eiko that at exactly 11:45 he was to be at the phone booth beside Hara's shop in the Ginza and wait for the phone to ring three times. Annoyed, but knowing the cautious, almost paranoic, routine from old, Eiko followed instructions. The voice on the phone was the quavery one of an old man. "Shintaro's fugu restaurant is on the street you are on. Go there immediately. In the window there should be prominently hung the framed fugu license of chef Hajime Kono, signed by Masaru Kainuma of Tokyo's Bureau of Health. If the license is not in the window, leave the vicinity immediately. If it is, enter."

Tokura was waiting at a small table in the rear of the restaurant. There was no one else in the place. A fishnet hung beneath the ceiling, four large starfish, an outsized cod, a sand shark, a stingray, and a huge jewfish were spaced on the walls. As in all excellent seafood restaurants there was absolutely no odor of fish. Eiko Adachi could smell the pleasant aroma of peanut oil from the kitchen. As usual with this strange old man he felt like a bumbling schoolboy. It made him angry. He snapped, "Can't we meet like normal friends? This is getting ridiculous."

"We are not normal friends," said Tokura, not getting up. Then softly, "This might prove to be the most important meeting we have ever had."

When the waiter arrived, bowing, Tokura tried to convince Eiko that he should order fugu. "They are famous for their fugu here," he said with a faint smile. "Never has a customer died. At least on the premises." He turned to the waiter. "Isn't that so?"

The waiter did not smile. "It is so. Hajime Kono is Tokyo's fugu master. Second to none."

"You see." Tokura turned to Eiko.

Eiko shook his head. "I do not share the fugu fan's death wish. Frankly, you surprise me."

"It's the only way to take sake. Sake without fugu, fugu without sake is sacrilege."

Declaring his desire to get down to business Eiko raised his hand, summoning the waiter. They ordered.

Tokura started his fugu sermon as soon as the fish arrived, sipping sake warmed several degrees above body temperature. He began by asking if Eiko knew the fugu.

"No, not well," Eiko said wearily. "Must I?"

"It is pertinent to the meeting," Tokura said, firing facts. Thirty species were found in the waters around Japan, but only twelve eaten, thus recognition was a problem. Fugu had thick, scaleless skin, some of them had spines, all had parrotlike beaks and two strong teeth enabling them to crack shellfish. "When caught on our fugunawa long lines baited with shark meat, the fugu blink their pop eyes and shed tears."

Tokura ate his fish silently for a while. Eiko poked at his rice.

Finally Tokura raised his cold black eyes. "The fugu is my friend. Not only on the table. The fugu has helped me eliminate various enemies and hostiles."

The shiver that had never left the base of his spine raced to Eiko's brain. He wanted to say, Do not tell me any of this. My world is commerce. Yours is intrigue and violence. Let us keep them separate. But he knew that this was not possible. Tokura was doing much to help Morimoto win its economic war. Not only was he respected by Keidanren, the governing body of the Japanese business empire, but at this point Tokura had become indispensable to Morimoto.

At first Tokura had pointed out some industrial plums that needed plucking, and after he had Eiko's approval and financial backing had put his people to work. But lately Eiko himself had ideas. He didn't imagine that he was masterminding the industrial espionage that was bringing Morimoto so much extra profit. But he considered himself a partner in the planning, conferring with Tokura on many of the early steps of the important targets and operations. The hugely successful electronic fish net that Tokura had managed to take from the Americans had been Eiko's idea. Of course Tokura was the one who cleverly brought the net to Japan. It was catching hundreds of thousands of metric tons of fish before the Americans even knew that their plans had been taken.

Eiko's partnership with Tokura wasn't exactly secret. But neither had Eiko pointed out to the Morimoto Board of Directors that he worked closely with the master spy. He simply let the profit do the talking. If it was brought up that he was dabbling in industrial espionage he would not deny it. But neither would he make it a corporate conversation.

"I will spell our situation out clearly," Tokura said finally. "It is only fair that you should be fully informed. You have been more than generous to me and my operation." He bowed his bald head briefly. "I am grateful."

Eiko bowed back. "You have also been our benefactor. We too are grateful."

"To bring this all into focus, I have a question. Do you know the little fish *E. ringens?*" Tokura's stare was unblinking.

"No."

"The anchovy. Tonnage caught in Peru in a normal year outweighs the combined fish catch of any other nation."

"Yes. I remember. It is the anchovy used for fishmeal and fish oil. We blend it with cattle and poultry feed. It is rich in protein —"

"Do you know how much that little fish earns Peru annually?"

Eiko shook his head.

"Three hundred forty million. Dollars. Not yen."

Eiko felt his skin tighten. He knew he showed surprise, but he restrained himself from vocalizing it.

Tokura stared at him. "It is the world source for this protein you mention. Especially for cattle. Last year these fish vanished from Peru. From the waters around Pisco, to be precise. No one knows why. There still were no anchovies off Pisco when a certain American arrived. In three days he had quite a number returning. Not the usual huge schools. But enough to prove a point to me."

"He actually brought some fish back?" Eiko asked incredulously.

Tokura nodded. "What does that mean to you? If he could do it with large numbers?"

"Millions!"

"Nothing more? You mean millions in profit by bringing the fish where we want them?"

"Of course," Eiko said impatiently.

"Yet, if we had the power to make the fish reappear, doesn't it follow that we could also make them disappear? At least for as long as we wanted them to disappear?"

"To what point?"

"How long would it take Morimoto to control the soybean market?"

Eiko stared. "We are into it deeply right now." He pushed his chair back. "I understand," he said quietly. "I have been dense. Soybeans are the substitute for fishmeal as a cattle and poultry feed. No anchovies. Soybeans would soar."

"I won't go into more detail," Tokura said quietly. "That American who brought the fish back in Peru was bought by us. But either he didn't know enough or he was holding back. We believe that he lied, that he didn't have enough information, at least scientific information, to make him valuable. He doubled his price but not his information. So I decided to make him a message."

"A message?"

"Yes. He was teamed with another marine scientist who I suspect has the answers I need. So we eliminated the lesser scientist to convince the other that we were ready to come to terms. There is a small problem, however. That scientist has disappeared. But we'll find him."

Eiko Adachi frowned. "I have asked you, my friend, to please forego all of the fine points of your profession. I have no need to know."

Tokura smiled. "But perhaps I have the need to tell. I have covered our trail in Peru. It was our only overt move. If anyone gets that far they will not live to further unravel the twisted thread to the truth."

"Is what you are after involved with more than fish? Also perhaps oil?"

"I don't know." Tokura's gaze was serene. "But I do know that for the first time man is looking at the oceans as real estate. Right now we are in a period much like the opening of the American West. Everybody is trampling over everybody to stake a claim in the oceans. As yet there are no laws telling us who has legal title to that wealth. The Nations' Conference on the Law of the Sea in Caracas got nowhere. The one in Vienna didn't either. There is too much greed, and in our case, need, at work for men to sit down and be magnanimous."

"Tokura, I know these things. Already Russia is at our throats on the offshore oil discovery in the Sea of Okhotsk."

"True, Eiko, but in my view, without some kind of law, nations will now form bilateral agreements on ocean use, stirring up a jumble of jurisdictions that will make rational development of ocean resources impossible. Or it could lead to unilateral decisions that could cause war."

"What you are saying I do indeed realize as truth. To survive Japan must stay ahead in the sea."

"I am going to muster all forces to secure this American secret. If it is what I think it is we can use it on other nations as our own law of the sea to get whatever we want. Oil territory, offshore rights, exclusive swordfish sectors, anything. I am going to summon the Brothers of the Night."

Eiko Adachi sat back in his chair, stunned. The old man is becoming senile, he thought sadly. "The ninja? The sect of assassins? Tokura, they were wiped out of existence several generations ago."

"They are reborn," Tokura said calmly. "You might even say that I have established a chapter in America."

CHAPTER THREE

This was an excellent tape, clear, no background noises, the tempo slow.

"I am sending Spargo to you. Norikura started him with *aikido* –" An assured, cultured British voice.

"Aikido? What is aikido?" This voice was slightly overlaid with a Middle-European accent.

"Then I sent Spargo into our own style karate class. He was born to it. With a slight problem for us. Norikura reported that Spargo is such a natural he is unintentionally injuring other students in practice sessions. I instructed Norikura to graduate Spargo ahead of schedule. He tells me in another month

Spargo would be nearly as good as he is."

A clock softly ticking in the background. The tape clicked off.

One of the four men who had been listening to the taped conversation rose from his chair and faced the other three.

"That soft English voice you heard is Gore, once director of the Company's training center near Langley. The other, with the slight foreign accent is Josef, a Hungarian, an instructor in armed and unarmed combat, one of the best men in the world with the knife, and almost as good at *tirer la savate*, fighting with the feet —"

The cathedral-ceiling living room in the rented Maryland house was raftered with old beams, furnished with two small chintz-covered sofas, four beige club chairs, a red, well-burnished leather chair, and two stately rose wing chairs. A Tabriz rug of scarlet and jade hues faded with age covered much of the polished random-width oak floor. A bright sun shone through leaded windows on the east wall.

It was late May, but the seasons had been changing abruptly and summer had leap-frogged spring, coming in with a sudden blast. The house was not air-conditioned and the men were uncomfortable. The one who was standing left the room and returned with a tray of Labatt ale, the bottles beaded with moisture. He expertly poured the ale into thin-stemmed wine glasses, collaring each with foam, and passed the tray around. The three men accepted the cold drinks gratefully, casting quick, puzzled glances at the silent tape player.

"That it?" the admiral said. A former fleet admiral, accustomed to being in charge, he had taken a belligerent tone since his intelligence organization had been placed in a weakened position. Bald, short, muscular, dapper in a double-breasted blue blazer, he had a ramrod stance and subdued fierceness about him that was disconcerting.

The man who had poured the drinks shook his head, crossed the room, and reactivated the tape player. It hummed. Again the soft British voice came into the room.

"Because you are relatively new, Josef, I assume that you are unacquainted with Buddha. He is an innovation of mine. A Japanese sumo wrestler on whom I am testing all graduate karate students. Three hundred pounds. Solid as a block of ice. When Buddha gets through with them, student agents quickly realize they are not invincible. Keeps them sharp.

"In any event, Spargo slipped into Buddha's room, feinted karate, set Buddha up, then kicked him in the balls. A deadly kick. Even with the heavy jock Buddha wore. Had the old boy on sick call for a week."

A noise like a pencil tapping on a desk.

"The reason I sent for you, Josef, must be obvious. I admire your mastery of two arts. I'd like you to finish Spargo's training. He may be the best we will graduate. I don't want him to leave with his education incomplete."

The tape automatically clicked off.

The admiral was amused. He seldom was these days. "I suppose the consensus is that this Spargo is brainy because he kicked that Jap wrestler in the balls."

He stared thoughtfully at William Pryor, the man who had set up this meeting. The youngest in the room, Pryor's prematurely silver hair covered his head like a helmet, giving him a deceptively gallant air. The eyes were an almost opaque gray, the nose straight but too long, the lips too thin, the six-foot body trim as that of a professional tennis player. He should have been handsome, but he was not; there was something coldly restrained about him, as though he belonged to a race apart, regarding all others with a sardonic, almost contemptuous air.

The admiral peeled back his coat sleeve and glanced at a Rollex Oyster. "I've got to be at the White House in exactly two hours."

Arthur Means, gangly, seemingly with two extra elbows, stood up and took a pipe out of his mouth. The stem was scarred with toothmarks, proof to the admiral that Means wasn't as much in control as he seemed. As a former professor of political science at Cornell, Means had difficulty speaking simply; his inclination was to lecture.

"Admiral," Means said, "I know you are bitter and so are all of us who have given our best years to this organization. The Company may be reduced to a skeleton, but we want you to know that we still have some of our old skills intact."

He paused, contemplating his approach. "Question. What kills most Americans on our highways?"

The admiral snapped, "Drunks."

Means nodded. "As we are all aware, our banker president is almost paranoid about industrial espionage, and has given its prevention top priority. To that end we have been stretching ourselves pretty thin. It is physically impossible to place men in all sensitive areas. But we had a lucky break. We've had a man on the engineering staff at General Motors Technical Center in Warren, Michigan, keeping his eye on a unique development."

The admiral raised heavy black eyebrows. "It involves drunks?"

"Yes," Means said, "and led, indirectly, to this meeting. At the Center they are testing a steering wheel that controls a needle on a dial in the instrument panel. When the ignition is turned on, the needle begins fluctuating. The objective is to steer well enough to keep the needle in a shaded area on the instrument panel. This permits the driver to start the engine. If the driver's reactions are impaired, the needle swings back and forth outside the designated area. A red 'reset' button lights and the starter is immobilized."

"Now if we could only come up with something for idiots."

Means chuckled on cue. The admiral expected his wit to be appreciated. "We caught an engineer photocopying a complete set of the working plans and specifications. We let him deliver and got the contact man. Ryal. Dublin Irish. Working for the Japanese. If he had been Japanese I doubt that we could have broken him. We used a technique perfected by interrogation teams in Vietnam. A drug, anectine. It temporarily paralyzes the respiratory system. Makes it extremely difficult to breathe. We told Ryal that unless he cooperated he would drown in oxygen."

Arthur Means put the tortured pipe into his mouth, chewed on it. "I think it's possible that we have the wedge we're looking for. We can put down this new shadow company the president has created to replace us. With his interest in saving money before saving lives, if we can get there first, we'll have exposed the president's secret baby as stupid."

"What the hell are you talking about?"

"Ryal forecast the death of the man who had his head blown off in Stamford, Connecticut. You've heard about that?"

The admiral nodded.

"Greer took over the interrogation at this point," Means said, pointing his pipe at the man nearest him. "He can take it from here."

Former Harvard psychology professor Jason Greer got out of his chair with difficulty. Short, overweight, his shrill voice belied his bulk, but his lean, hammered-featured face and protuberant eyes carried a hard, menacing authority of their own. He gave the impression that he was entirely without emotion. The impression was accurate.

"From this interrogation we also learned that there has been some kind of astounding breakthrough in the marine world. By one of our own scientists. Even with my best efforts, I couldn't learn what it is. I don't believe Ryal knew. But I did discover that the experiments are completed. In a file. Both the file and the scientist have vanished. He disappeared the day after the scientist in Stamford was killed."

"Is there a connection?" The admiral was intent now.

"Lundberg, the man who was killed, had been working with the missing scientist, Allan Vaughn. Ryal told us that he also had been in communication with the Japanese."

"What do you learned fellows make of all this?" The admiral's tone was sarcastic, but his eyes were ablaze.

"Whoever is after that sea file is not kidding. I think that's why Vaughn vanished. Violence and murder are rare in industrial espionage. So this must be very big. Ryal didn't know what that file contained, but he did say whoever had it could virtually control the sea —"

"You believe this, Greer? It sounds like

something right off the tube."

"I believe it. A man who thinks he may die does not concoct 'stories'."

"What if this astounding secret is a way to turn out benevolent jellyfish? You know what scientists are. Spend their lives to find out why a flea screws upside down."

"I've had an anectine test run on myself," Greer said quietly. "You're drowning. Going down for the third time. You even make desperate swimming motions. It was the most frightening experience I've ever had."

"Fright often does produce truth," the admiral said. "But can we have another go at Ryal?"

"No, sir," Greer said, his voice devoid of emotion. "We miscalculated. Ryal died."

"That's why I ran part of that tape on Spargo," Pryor said. "To give you a quick idea of the man. All of us think that he's right to turn loose on this. He knows this kind of game. If he succeeds in getting the scientist and his file, we have a feather. If he fails, we aren't touched. No criticism. He isn't with us. Hasn't been for a long time. He was swept out when the Senate was after our black operation. He's a loner. And, sir, he's expendable —"

"Do we have a leash on him?"

"No, sir, but Josef, that foreign voice you heard on tape, is still a close friend of his. We'll get him to approach Spargo. Then I'll talk to him myself."

"What if Josef doesn't cooperate? We aren't exactly in a masterful position these days."

"Sir," Pyror said, "Josef is on a Company pension. He'll cooperate."

CHAPTER FOUR

Harold James Noble, the President of the United States, sat on the Exercycle trying to pump off a pound or two and harden his leg muscles for occasional golfing at Burning Tree, but not working very hard at it, for this was the way he often conducted interviews and made presidential pronouncements.

It wasn't deviating from White House protocol: LBJ had conducted some interviews from a toilet seat, and Jerry Ford sometimes sat before a television screen cheering a football team while deciding the fate of the nation.

Five-feet-seven in his special high-heeled shoes, the President found it gave him stature to sit on the high cycle seat and look down at his seated visitors. Also, it put him in motion, giving him a certain authority and drama that was missing when he sank, diminished, behind his huge desk.

He looked like a fleshy Harry Truman with hair. He wore the same metal-frame eyeglasses, had the give-em-hell President's spunk and push, but not the nasal voice. Harold Noble's voice was deep, clear, and positive, as was his personality.

One columnist claimed that Noble was one of the few really brainy men to sit in the White House, and most certainly the only one who listened closely to his own counsel and had the courage of his convictions. He wasn't pure; no successful politician is. But he was not a buck-passer and he did not delegate authority and responsibility to staff and advisors. All secretaries, State, Defense, Agriculture, Health, Education and Welfare, checked decisions and pronouncements with him before they were made. It was rare that he didn't countermand or amend them.

It was uncontested that the President had the charm of the small-town banker that he once had been, and was able to stir up faith and even fervor in people. Always using simple words, with absolutely no platform style or politician's phony polish, he had the additional talent of perfect timing.

After the financial mess that the fumbling former President had left the country in, the commonsense manner of the man who talked dollars rather than party loyalty or solving the Middle East's eternal crisis, caught the attention of the small segment of the population that hadn't been so disillusioned by all politicians that they refused to vote.

He declared an all-out attack on deficit spending, and announced his attention to make certain that America's goods and services were exported in an abundance previously unheard of. He would bring hard banking sense to the White House and to the country. There would be no more of this nonsense of America's spending more on foreign imports than it received from its exports. One step he took to ensure this was revolutionary and completely without the support of Congress. Any American who bought a foreign car would have a sticker on the windshield as part of its registration that declared, "I prefer to buy Foreign, not American"; his or her insurance fees would be tripled, registration fees quadrupled.

He declared that oil countries could not

operate without U.S. technical know-how and equipment. We would provide no more until reason returned, and America, who made all the other countries' oil gush, received preferential treatment.

He also started a movement to slow down the investment of foreign capital in the United States, saying that "America is not for sale." With this gambit he enlisted a new and enthusiastic portion of the public.

"A tidal wave of foreign investment from Europe, Latin America and the Middle East is sweeping across the United States," he proclaimed in one televised speech. "In the Sunbelt states it has engulfed citrus groves, condominiums, factories. It has swept over ranches, hotels, insurance companies and chemical plants in the Midwest. On both coasts it has swallowed up resort islands, stock exchange memberships, art galleries, banks, and even New York City's last great townhouse, the Sonnenberg mansion in Gramercy Park, purchased by an Austrian baron."

Staring directly into the camera, the President enunciated slowly. "Foreign investors have spent forty billion dollars to buy controlling interest in hundreds of American companies and corporations. There is a secret investment of thirty-eight billion in Arab petro-dollars in America, ranging from farmland and vineyards to construction, engineering, and development firms. Everyone is in on the big grab. We'll wake up one day soon and discover that we don't own our own country!"

It appeared that, finally, America had a leader.

But the stroke of genius that firmly entrenched Harold James Noble in the White House and in the hearts of his countrymen was his openly declared war on industrial espionage. His skill and fire in bringing this message to the people was close to wizardry.

Today, he had summoned four key men to stir them up again. He made it a practice to confer on his pet project weekly, pronouncing that "repetition is renewal." This time, however, he had new ammunition.

The four men sat straight in black Hitchcock chairs, all with closed, patient expressions. Sitting closest to the President was Vice President Philip Modell, young, brilliant, looking more like a hawk-nosed Bedouin than the Jew that he was; the new breed of politician, he had taught law at Yale and had a mesmeric Billy Graham speaking style. His weakness was that he was smug, a smugness born of the security of his family's millions in two department stores and a clothing store chain.

The self-made President, who had started his successful banking career as an assistant cashier in a Midwestern bank, despised Modell. He had accepted Modell as his running mate, mainly because his political advisors pointed out that it not only would ensure the large Jewish vote, but also the black and the liberal. It had.

On Modell's right was Kevin Ogden, a Boston Irish politician, a former ward-heeler that the Kennedy family had elevated to the big time. He had a purplish nose, a mane of white hair that gave him the look of an angry lion, watery blue eyes and an annoying, blustery manner of speaking. The President liked him because he had learned how to take orders. As Speaker of the House he ruled with an iron hand, and was astute enough to convey the idea that it was smart to take care of Number One. In order to do that, he listened closely to the President. But having risen through the ranks of street politicians and the smoky back rooms of Boston, he was treacherous and wily. The President didn't trust him.

Henry Bay, the senior senator from Massachusetts, had the lean features of a Boston Brahmin, accented with an expression that bordered on contempt. He looked sharp and extremely intelligent. He was neither. But he had distinction and power among his colleagues, mainly because he had held his position for twenty years, and seemed to possess the secret to eternal senatorial security. The President thought he was a dolt. But he was the best messenger in Congress.

Next to Bay sat the director of the CIA, Admiral Chester Morgan, looking almost nautical in a well-cut double-breasted navy-blue blazer. The President had some hope for him and his organization, knowing that loyalty was high among the admiral's good points, which included astuteness, ruthlessness, and a fine sense of organization. But the President, believing his opinion was unknown to the admiral, also thought that the CIA's time had about run out, that it had outlived its usefulness because of poor publicity and internal mismanagement. He was closely watching how the admiral ran his outfit. He had a backup plan if his hunch about the CIA was true.

The President set the timer on the Exercycle for ten minutes. He was not a time-waster; he always pre-assembled his thoughts and the points he had to make, leaving nothing to his secretary or press people. He made longhand notes on a ruled yellow legal pad and kept to his time schedule as rigidly as a television newscaster.

As he pumped, the pedals clicking, he said, "Gentlemen, I announce this morning that the very move I have been urging that we make has been accomplished . . ." He stopped pumping. "But not by us."

"What's happened, sir?" the admiral said quietly.

"Britain has made its move. Right now it is the only nation with an export intelligence service for industry and commerce."

He resumed pumping. "Do any of you know who Sir Martin Furnical-Jones is?"

They all shook their heads except the admiral.

"Yes," he said. "He's the former chief of M15."

"Well," the President said, "he's just been appointed head of security for Britain's ICI, the largest chemical company in Europe. It looks like Britain realizes that it is time to make war against industrial espionage while we sit around like a bunch of dummies and let foreigners rob us of our industrial future."

The President glanced from man to man. "I received a report yesterday from the Institute for the Study of Conflict which clearly spelled out the facts. Fifty percent of all Russian diplomats and trade officials in this country are instructed by Moscow to concentrate on spying on our science and technology."

"Can't our intelligence services keep an eye on these people?" Modell.

The President, "Admiral?"

"All foreign officials who are suspected of spying of any kind are under surveillance."

"Do we have reports of any being apprehended?" Modell.

The admiral shifted in his chair. "These reports are for the eyes of the President and whoever he wants to share them with. American industry is too enormous for us to cover minutely. They should police themselves more efficiently than they do."

"Take a leaf from Britain's book." Kevin Ogden.

The admiral nodded. "Exactly. Perhaps you people in Congress can offer suggestions to your constituents in industry about the tightening of security."

"There are no warnings," the President interrupted, "even now, such as that by the Study of Conflict directed against non-Communist nations' industrial spies. We're an open grab-bag. I won't bore you, gentlemen, by reading the details. But I have on my desk a list of over two hundred U.S. industrial secrets and plans that have been stolen and sold in just the past ten months."

He stopped, sweeping the faces of the assembly with a hard stare.

"Did any of you alert gentlemen read the *New York Times* this morning? Or should I say did you have any of your people read it for you and report in?"

Silence.

The President took a sheet of paper from his inside breast pocket and unfolded it.

"Before I read some of this report, I must honestly say that you are acting like a gang of dolts. If you poor bastards can't read, tell me, please, and I'll attempt to get replacements."

Pumping the cycle and holding the paper in his hands, he read: " 'Bonn Fights Industrial Spying.' " He looked up. "Gentlemen, that is what is referred to as a headline. Let's go on, shall we.

" 'In West Germany spies are exchanging their cloaks and daggers for business suits and briefcases. In the first eight months of this year alone, West German counterintelligence agents have uncovered more than forty Soviet-bloc spies, about three-quarters of them engaged in industrial espionage and nearly all working for East Germany —"

He stopped pumping. "Admiral, exactly how many industrial spies have you 'uncovered,' let's say in the last three months?

The Director of the CIA said, "Three."

The President sighed. "I won't go on with this. I expect you can see quite clearly now what is going on in the world and how we are dragging our feet. I tell you now. All of you. I won't put up with this thievery, or our incompetence, much longer."

The timer sounded on the Exercycle. The President climbed down, went and stood beside his desk. That was the signal the meeting had ended. They filed out grimly, like Indian chiefs who had been told that their warriors were lacking in valor.

The President stopped his CIA chief. "Admiral." Morgan came back into the room, eyebrows lifted.

"I've read your 'Top Secret' report. Is it really that serious? Or the usual mixed-up scientific bullshit?"

"I'm handling this personally," the admiral said, looking old, and feeling even older. "It's real. Been coming for years."

The blood drained from the President's face. "This is a first!" he whispered. "Famine! No other President has ever faced it . . ."

"No, sir," the admiral said grimly.

"We'll keep the lid on," the President said. "And we'll lick it. Like you said, we've got the sea as our breadbasket." He shook hands with the admiral and closed his door, standing silently for a minute.

Again, the President set the timer on the Exercycle, this time at five minutes. His next visitors were five young men, all lawyers, four disbarred, all bright, as alert-looking as Doberman pinschers.

On the cycle again, the President nodded, "Chet. Ray. Hank. LeRoy. Mort. Let's keep it short this morning. I just read the riot act to some of my key people. I need your reports as soon as possible on your surveillance of the CIA and your suggestions how our secret team can take over successfully and still remain anonymous. That anonymity is our armor. Our security."

He stopped pumping and said slowly. "I have one of you in the CIA. I will not reveal who he is. He will remain there as one of them until the takeover. He has given me and will continue to give me a timely overview of activities. Your job, as always, is to secretly line up good men for our new team. As you know I also want to know instantly of any fumbling by the Agency on the stealing of any industrial secrets. No matter how small. Be they women's panties or a new way to boil an egg. Of course it would please me if any of you discover CIA stupidities regarding any major theft or even attempt."

When the timer sounded on the cycle, the five men wheeled, almost as one, and left the Oval Office.

CHAPTER FIVE

He could still see Lundberg's head being blown from his body, plopping into the tank with such force that water flew to the desk where the headless body slumped.

He shuddered. Walking to the window, he thought, I knew he was a dud, a sell-out, felt it in my bones. But he was the best in his field. I had to know if it could be done.

Located on the heel of Cape Cod, Allan Vaughn's laboratory was sponsored by Jacob's Landing Oceanographic Institute, as well as the state of Massachusetts, which was highly interested in his project of studying the possibility of commercial lobster farming.

Vaughn had insisted that his lab be apart

from the sprawl of the rest of the Institute, closer to the ocean, where he could obtain a continuous flow of sea water, which was imperative for lobster survival.

Never tiring of standing at the window staring at the Atlantic and curl after curl of breaking waves, he marveled at the timelessness and unpredictability of the ocean. He could understand the pull it had, could feel it himself, its beckoning fascination, an instinctive and chemical recalling of humans to their birthplace.

On the beach before him, shiny from the tide, a large flock of sanderlings moved in such concert that it looked like the strip of sand was a conveyor belt carrying them along. A young herring gull in smoky-brown plumage was in a strange dance, feeling in the wet sand for clams; overhead a great blackbacked gull, looking exactly like a bald eagle, lazily flapped over the sanderlings as if directing their animated-toy rush along the beach.

Purple buoys of the Jacob's Landing Oceanographic Institute floated on the water, marking special lobster traps.

But today Vaughn could not lose himself in this contemplation of the marine scene. He was a frightened man. It was a cold, deadly fright that sat on him like a curse. Not even looking at some of his accomplishments, most visible from the window even through the thin veil of fog that was drifting in from the sea, could turn his mind from the terrible thing that had happened.

Out there were the cubical rearing tanks that he had invented, the nurseries measuring sixteen inches on a side, designed this way because lobster fry, looking more like mosquitoes than baby lobsters, would eat one another. It had taken almost a month for him to dream up the idea of using circulators to move the water throughout the tanks evenly, preventing clusters of cannibalistic larvae gathering in corners. He also thought it a victory that he changed the tanks from wood to fiberglass to prevent destruction by the wood-chewing shipworm.

He broke previous pattern by permitting the eggs to hatch naturally on the females, feeding the egg-bearing lobsters alewives, a fish that he was also studying and able to reproduce in tanks. The hatched lobster fry were captured in the circulating water of the ten-by-four, one-foot-deep hatching tank on a fly-screen box he built, as many as five thousand tiny lobsters trapped at a time.

His studies included lobster courtship; mating; growth and development from hatch, through larval stage to maturity; the regeneration of new legs; migration; habitat; aggressive behavior; sexual responses; effects of warm water on growth.

He had discovered early that the basic processes of life, especially marine life, are a complicated mass of interdependent chemical reactions, not only the development of chromosomes responsible for the division and growth of cells, but also the digestion of food into nutrients.

Vaughn also early in his research had decided that the principles that had made the poultry industry so successful began with genetics, with selective breeding. Working on this theory, he carefully screened over a quarter of a million lobster larvae to find a hundred that, for some reason still unknown, grew 50 percent faster than the others.

Using these fast-growing lobsters for breeding, he also decided that warm water would speed growth, and raised the offspring in circulating sea water held constantly at 74 degrees. Even in midsummer the waters of the ocean never exceeded 55 degrees.

His projections were correct. He was able to

raise lobsters to one-pound marketable size in eighteen months. In the wild it took eight years. It was a major victory. But his secret study of the complexities of chemicals in the lives of his lobsters was even more exciting.

Vaughn was a loner, introspective, not part of the herd, and never had been. His father, a druggist in a small midwestern town, hadn't had the resources to send him to college. He helped, even though he did not share his son's enthusiasm for marine biology, but Allan Vaughn had to work his way through school — first the University of Ohio, then graduate work at Cornell. He worked part-time in hotels as a waiter, then as an assistant desk clerk, and also as a driving instructor at a school in Ithaca. He had thought of another idea to bring in income. Making a list of students' birthdays, he wrote their parents and said that he would supply a birthday cake for their boy or girl, with the correct number of candles, even a special candied inscription and a personally sung Happy Birthday. It worked, and brought in enough income to buy books, food, with even a bit for tuition.

Allan Vaughn had become interested in fish and marine creatures at age ten when his father bought him a small aquarium and he had learned that he could reproduce the brightly colored, interesting creatures. Besides, watching them, thinking about the sea that they came from as they gently finned about in the water, brought him tranquility. He spent hours staring into the tank; every fish had a name.

At forty, with large, intelligent hazel eyes, heavy dark brows, a slow, soft, distinct way of speaking, six feet four inches tall, walking a bit hunched as if his height made him inferior, he had lost quite a bit of his thatch of sandy hair, giving him almost a fringed friar pate. The domed forehead was very high; one could almost sense that fine scientific brain at work. He impressed some, but struck others as a lost scientist.

He liked women, but mainly those who had his interests, those he could talk to, the ones who became animated when he discoursed at length on his favorite subject, lobsters.

Harla had listened and had become more alive than most, her dark eyes flashing as if he were telling of the amours and adventures of Richard the Lion-Hearted rather than the growth rate of a lobster that carried its skeleton on the outside of its body. Harla was with him now in the laboratory. It hadn't been impulse, for that was unlike him, and she had proved a helpful, even creative, assistant.

She was appealing, with her limpid, so very dark eyes, ebony hair molding her beautifully shaped head, sleek as wet sealskin. But they had never been to bed together. He had discovered, almost aghast, that she liked lobsters better than men, was almost as devoted to their project as he was. The realization of what he had done with his life had flooded over him then. Although he was disappointed and often felt that hardening sexual urge when they worked together and she stood close to him, even a few brief sessions with his lobsters made him forget all else. He was a committed man.

Now, he knew that if he didn't disappear, he would also be a condemned man. They would come for him, as they had Lundberg. There was no doubt now that Lundberg had been selling them the tidbits that he had and when they discovered that he didn't have all they wanted, they eliminated him. Who were they? Who should he be wary of? Everybody.

Because Vaughn had the answers. It had taken fifteen years, but he had crossed a new, exciting threshold that no other man had. He had finally isolated the chemicals, identified them. Lundberg could reproduce them synthetically, but he didn't know the secret, didn't know what he was chemically creating. Vaughn wasn't ready yet to release the story of his breakthrough. And when he was he would do it piecemeal, making certain that his research could continue in other directions. The sea was a vast laboratory, its unsolved secrets many. It was the last scientific frontier as far as he was concerned and he intended to blaze his own Lewis and Clark trail through its largely unexplored vastness. The taming and taking of the West was insignificant compared to what he had done. Oil and gold. Limitless protein. It all was there, buried beneath the oceans, waiting to be gathered.

His associates in the disciplines of science concluded that they were successful if they proved out their experiment twice; three times was even more positive. But he had done it *seven* times. Seven lobsters had responded, responded even more perfectly than he could have hoped. So he had it. They had come from the sea virtually upon his command. He was their master. But because of the Lundberg blunder he now was ominously boxed in.

He knew that his accomplishments would not only shake the scientific community, but the world. Results could be more startling and much more profitable and practical than landing on the moon. The astronauts were heroes; but outer space was child's play compared to the complexity of the oceans, a complexity that he could quickly reduce to simplicity itself. He would be a hero. But a dead hero hears no plaudits, receives no accolades, makes no hallmark in history. What could he do?

He felt uneasy about going to Jacob's Landing Oceanographic Institute officials for help, or even to the government. First, no one knew what he really was doing. The smokescreen of working with lobsters to make the commercial farming of them possible was an effective cover. To reveal what he had actually done with both fish and lobsters would place him in an extremely vulnerable position, especially when he wasn't certain how he was going to protect the rights to his secret. Industrial spies were everywhere. Witness what had happened to poor, greedy Lundberg. Also, the professional jealousy of fellow scientists could back him into a corner.

As he stood at his window an offshore lobster otter-trawl chugged into view, and suddenly he had the answer, the way to escape, for a while at least, until he could figure out how to protect what he had created.

But as he stood there plotting to save himself, he forgot about Harla. As his assistant, she also was vulnerable, though of course she was not aware of the true nature of his experiments. Should he tell her what he was planning? They had worked closely together; she deserved to be aware of the fact that his disappearance did not mean the end of the project, but its security until he could surface again when he had worked out a means to protect himself and his life's work.

CHAPTER SIX

As Pryor drove ten miles above the limit, the sixty-five miles an hour seemed like thirty, and the five-cylinder Mercedes diesel engine purred like a pleased cat. Rising high beyond, in a blaze of sunlight, the dome of the Capitol building reminded Pryor of snow gleaming on a distant Himalayan mountain peak, although he had never seen such a sight.

He was projecting on the physical, an old habit he used to wipe annoyance away, now trying to forget the feeling of being a lackey brought on by erasing the evidence of the meeting in the house in Maryland, using rubber gloves, wiping fingerprints off the obvious places, washing and drying glasses, taking the empty ale bottles with him and all of the ashtrays. It had been, supposedly, a meeting of regional sales executives who needed the privacy of an impersonal rented house. Pryor had swept the place for bugs four times. It was clean, he was certain, except for his own secret placements.

The interestate was awash with the seasurf sound of steadily flowing traffic. On this sunny day with a high flight of crows adrift in a blue sky ahead of him, the serene afternoon made Pryor feel that he had been miscast. Placed on a losing team. Why hadn't he stayed with that art class at Yale, or majored in architecture as his instincts had instructed? But he wasn't creative enough. He knew it, and regretted it. The creative were as free as those smart crows lazily flapping across the sky, with no admiral birds to push them around. He remembered then reading about the Great Horned Owl coming in the dead of night to pluck adult crows off their roosts high in pine trees, and sighed aloud, thinking, There is no such thing as the perfect situation; make the best of what you have and be thankful that you are alive.

Suddenly from Pryor's radio two harsh words exploded, wiping away any phony philosophical peace he had conjured.

"Weasel! Communicate!"

"Shit!" Pryor said.

Codes had come in full force during the Kennedy administration, with everyone but the janitor having special names: "Warrior," "Tintype," "Bronco," "Atlas," "Mercury." None had the sting of those assigned by the admiral. One of the surviving streetmen, an accomplished underground professional, was "Rodent."

Pryor tried to ignore the implications of his own code name, but it rankled and gave him a fierce dislike for the arrogant director who had been brought in to shape up the Agency. The admiral was militarily severe, showing no regard for length of service or accomplishments. He had cut the Agency's operation division down to 4,730 from a peak of 8,000, reached during the Vietnam war. He also summarily fired over a thousand officers, most at headquarters. He changed the six-year timetable, making it impossible to accomplish the reductions he wanted by attrition, giving many the ax in the form of a brutal two-sentence pink slip.

Pryor had to admit the admiral had guts. The reports he gave to the Senate Select Committee on Intelligence were in closely guarded rooms, with twenty-four-hour guards, alarm systems, all rooms with double locks and dead-locks. He even had the senators searched for recording devices. For an ambitious man, this took political courage. The senators did not like the admiral, but the Capitol Hill consensus was that they respected him. So that was one leg up on the climb he was making to secure the Agency and regain its old prestige and power.

Pryor knew his Weasel code name came from one of his first assignments: Making DDO (Directorate of Operations) manageable by investigating the booze, sex, and foul play used by Agency stations in the field.

He knew also that he was disliked for his prying, and that his job had been a deliberately difficult one. For the Agency, having lived through a rough process of external criticism, even a report to the President by the Commission on CIA Activities, now found itself under scrutiny again, by its own chief.

Pryor, however, had made some friends during his investigative tour. The clandestine department, HUMINT, was to feel the full sweep of the new broom during the admiral's housecleaning, leaving the intelligence gathering to spy satellites and reconnaissance planes, that department coded SIGINT. After careful survey, Pryor had reported directly to the admiral: "The role of the clandestine operative in cultivating sources and collecting human intelligence is indispensable."

His point was proved and his own job secured when a HUMINT field man beat the satellites and spy planes with the information that China was about to explode an atom bomb. The spy planes had been overflying China's test range at Lop Nor for two years. SIGINT had been found inept, its cameras ineffectual.

Pryor discovered that the agent got the information from the foreign minister of an African nation who had heard it in Moscow. It was received with near-derision in Langley, but the Secretary of State used it in a speech the day before the Chinese A-bomb blew.

Pryor, although he did not control HUMINT, did the hiring and firing at its covert section, North American Division, and posted some world assignments, after clearing them with the admiral. Now, he also had the "plausible deniability" responsibility of creating cover stories to hide connections between the President and illegal operations.

He had convinced the admiral that covert's role still must be to accomplish important missions that weren't legal, but were necessary to protect the United States. Other intelligence agencies had become chary at sharing information with covert ever since a bumbling Congress had rushed in shouting foul. It was, argued Pryor, crucial for our own safety that we be aware of happenings in the intelligence world of other countries. In one month he discovered that the French, Greeks, Dutch, Italians, Iranians, and most African nations did not trust the Agency and would not cooperate. At Pryor's urging, the admiral had made high marks with some of the intelligence community by refusing to hand over to SAVAK, Iran's secret police, Agency information on Iranian dissidents in the United States. But Egypt's intelligence crew, Mukhabarat, was openly worried that its best-kept secrets would be revealed by an inept Agency in Washington, and the effective BOSS, South Africa's superb intelligence unit that knew the pulsebeat of Africa better than anyone else, had flatly refused to feed the Agency any more inside information, mainly because of its country's shoddy treatment by Washington politicians.

Pryor found a phone booth on Wisconsin Avenue, thinking, as he dialed the secret number, of the admiral's lecture on using the telephone. "Telephone messages," he had said, "can be beamed by microwave and intercepted, then fed into computers. Those computers are capable of recording conversations on selected numbers." The admiral cautioned that all calls be made from phone booths, that no revelatory messages be given over any telephone. Pryor knew that the admiral's phone was equipped with a Hagoth, a voice-stress analyzer that measured voice changes in inaudible microtremors in order to detect when someone was lying.

The phone rang just once. "Yes." The word was not questioning, almost inhuman in its coldness.

Pryor gave his code name and location.

"Park your car. Walk one hundred yards. I'll pick you up. Eighteen minutes."

Curious, Pryor timed it. In exactly seventeen minutes the bronze 98 came slowly up Wisconsin Avenue. Armored, with bulletproof, tinted glass, the Olds was more of an office for the admiral than his spacious paneled headquarters at Langley. It was equipped with a bar in the back, a recording system, a hidden special weapons rack, and a direct communications system to Langley, the White House, and key assistants and associates. Seats were covered with brown glove leather that wear had given the slight, almost pungent "men's club" odor of fine leather silkily burnished by distinguished backsides. There also was a klaxon that could be heard for at least one full mile in case of emergency or distress, plus a gas cylinder installed inside each door that could instantly discharge a paralyzing spray through special keyholes.

Super Chief, Pryor thought wryly, you're a cliché.

The Olds stopped barely long enough for him to get in, then the admiral drove on without giving Pryor a glance.

"We fucked up again." The admiral, who rarely used obscene words unless anger limited his vocabulary, spoke softly. "Correction. You fucked up again. Or your people did."

Today he didn't park, but drove slowly, carefully, never taking his eyes from the road as he encouraged traffic to flow around him. It was an annoying technique, never looking at the person to whom you were talking, especially as the admiral's conversation usually was caustic.

Pryor remained silent.

"At the last meeting they said, I forget which one, that this man Ryal was Dublin Irish, working for the Japanese. Right?"

"Right."

"Wrong!" the admiral snapped. "And they used amateurish techniques. We learned to properly use the drug that killed Ryal in the Phoenix program in Vietnam. As I remember, initially, we lost only two hundred out of two thousand Vietnamese interrogated. There is no excuse for so-called misjudgment. Whoever is responsible will have to be disciplined."

Pryor didn't respond.

The admiral snorted as a Datsun veered around him, horn blaring.

"Give whoever pulled this fatal boner a six-month leave of absence without salary. Or better still send him to Iran on a peace mission —"

"Sir, what is the problem?" Pryor said quietly.

"Ryal wasn't Ryal. He was Mead, undercover for the British. One of their aces."

Without signaling, he suddenly pulled into a parking space and turned off the motor.

"Hop out and put a dime in that meter. We won't need more than ten cents' worth of time to finish this."

As Pryor got back in and closed the door, the admiral looked squarely at him for the first time. "We have the name of the scientist who supposedly invented or discovered, or whatever the hell he did, this, I quote, 'astounding' secret of the sea. If those idiots could have kept 'Ryal' alive, someone with interrogative knowhow and a few brains probably could have discovered what this is all about. As it is, it's a mess. The source dead, the scientist vanished —"

"A man in fear of death doesn't 'concoct,' " Pryor reminded gently. "Ryal, or Mead, was convinced that this was a big one."

"I know, I know," the admiral said impatiently. "I suppose it's worth taking a shot at. Give our best effort and hope that we come up with something that will impress on the President that we can always get there first."

He went on to tell Pryor about the meeting with the President, Sir Martin Furnical-Jones, and the findings of the Institute for the Study of Conflict. He conceded that he thought we had an able President who was devoted to saving the country, at least on a dollars-and-cents basis. But that he was slightly paranoid on his pet subject.

"Pryor, he's convinced himself and the

public that industrial espionage is responsible for everything from inflation to unemployment."

Then, surprising Pryor with his sense of humor, he said what a vast improvement this banker-president was over his predecessor: "I never did believe that man could have had hemorrhoids as reported. He had to be the perfect asshole."

Somewhat bitterly he said that with Ryal-Mead dead there now was a new problem. "I suspect Mead was one of Furnical-Jones' men. I hope not. Right now Britain is about the only country of any note that cooperates with the Agency. We still share intelligence. It's saved us three times in the last two years. If Jones learns of what we've done, we've lost another one. If it surfaces in political Washington it could finish us. We only needed one more blunder like this one."

The silence in the car was oppressive.

"This Spargo," the admiral said suddenly. "I've checked him out at COMINT. If he completes your assignment successfully, or if he fails, he isn't the type we want around to prove that we are involved."

He sat staring into the street. "If we deliver, find that scientist before the Japanese do and save his experiment, I go directly to the President. And I don't want to say that a freelance, in fact, a renegade Agency man, was responsible. And if we fail, or Spargo fails, we must not be associated with the action in any way."

"Yes sir," Pryor said softly.

"Can you handle this?"

Pryor nodded.

The admiral's mood changed with the speed of an eyeblink.

"I'm aware that you think I'm a son of a bitch," he said quietly. "But I love my country. I'm doing all I can to give the Agency strength. It's been badly mishandled. Without an efficiently functioning Agency we may not make it. It's the only protection we have. Those smug bastards in the Pentagon spend all of their time thinking about budget. Their intelligence department is so bad that Washington could be wiped out before they could even get their inter-office memos circulated."

He was silent for a moment, watching the traffic flow by. "I know what I'm talking about. I'm a Pentagon alumnus."

He smiled, his hard blue eyes softening. "Yes, Pryor, the rumors are wrong. I can actually smile. But briefly. Before you put your plan into action, go to the new COMINT and check Spargo out. I've cleared you." He fished in his breast pocket, brought out a bright red plastic card and held it toward Pryor.

Pryor didn't take it. "Sir," he said, "I know this new talking terminal of yours is a computer whiz kid. But I'd like to first try the information 'live' from one of my contacts. I think we're overcomputerized. Computer output is only as good as its input."

The admiral was startled. "Are you saying that even our information gathering is faulty?"

"No. I'm saying that I have sources I trust more than I do machines."

Frowning, the admiral slipped the red card back into his breast pocket. "The Voiceout is impressively complete. I checked it out myself."

Pryor shrugged. He had taken his stand. He would really deserve his Weasel code name if he didn't stay with it.

The admiral grinned. "You tracked down that Chinese A-bomb when our technological set-up failed. I guess we can ride with a loose rein on this one."

This was a day of surprises. A confession of patriotism, a smile. No one would believe it.

As Pryor started to get out of the car, the admiral said, "I dispatched a man to Warren,

Michigan, to run a back-trail on Ryal, or Mead."

Hand on the door lever, Pryor waited.

"A British agent is in the area trying to locate him. There is now no doubt that Ryal was doubling, penetrating the Japanese. I am just about convinced that he was onto something big."

"Does this mean that Spargo, if I can get him, should not try to pick up on Ryal?"

"Let's see how he handles it. It could be sort of a blood-test for your man."

CHAPTER SEVEN

Pryor phoned his contact for a luncheon meeting at Charlie's. Charlie was Chinese, but with typical Oriental cunning and flexibility, since Washington has a large black population Charlie also served soul food. His chitlings were famous and his barbecued ribs were not the usual bony, soy-drenched Cantonese offerings, but subtly seasoned, crisp, thick meaty country ribs, a meal in themselves washed down with a bottle of cold Coors beer – one of the few places in town where the mountain-spring brew was available.

As he drove to the restaurant, Pryor thought about the Ferret satellites two hundred miles out in space recording electromagnetic signals from ground stations, ships, and aircraft. Fifty miles beneath the Ferrets photo satellites circled, sending messages to Langley, making prearranged film pack drops; twenty miles straight up, SR 71 photo reconnaissance planes swooped, the SR capable of encompassing an area the size of Florida in one detailed photograph. On mountaintops radio receivers scanned the world airwaves, and a few miles outside Washington, D.C., a giant electronic ear eavesdropped on Europe.

I'm betting that fat little Harry Abel is better, Pryor told himself, pulling into the parking space behind Charlie's. As he locked the door of the Mercedes, a garlicky-soy-peanut oil aroma floated from the kitchen ventilators, making him hungry.

Charlie's was not impressive. It had the usual spacious booths Chinese restaurateurs seem to prefer, which offered the privacy Pryor liked. Faded murals of Canton that looked as if they were painted by not particularly talented children covered every inch of wall space, and a long oak bar in back with high stools was serviced by a fat, bald Chinese bartender whose constant, meaningless smile seemed tattooed on.

Charlie's also had a large fish tank, the

aquarium centered a few feet from the entrance, filled with small piranha, the savage South American flesh-eaters. A medium-size school could reduce a man to a skeleton in minutes. A note on the bottom of the menu encouraged customers to feed the fish, especially leftover shrimp, which they loved. On the side of the tank clever Charlie had lettered in blood-red CAPITOL HILL. More often than not people neglected to feed the fish, and by design Charlie refrained. The show in the tank was in session as Pryor walked by. Two piranha were attacking a third. In a moment all that remained of the attacked fish was a head that seemed to be swimming away by itself, the other two fish, mouths full of living flesh, not pursuing. Pryor suddenly lost his appetite, thinking that Charlie's weird sense of humor could be limiting his income. But maybe not. A look at the aquarium made some quick drinks mandatory.

Charlie, tall, thin, always dressed in a dark suit and a blue chambray shirt open at the neck, wore half-glasses low on his nose, his black, slanted eyes roving above them like birds seeking a place to perch.

Bowing, he said, "Mr. Pryor, gentleman for you is at the bar."

"Thanks, Charlie," Pryor said, waving at Abel, who raised his hand in a Hitler salute. "How're the ribs?"

"Succulent, sir, as usual from my peanut-fed North Carolina pork. Shall I save two orders? I've got a tableful of hungry senators in the private room."

"Right, Charlie. Hold two."

Harry Abel looked like a somewhat seedy supermarket manager who oversampled his own wares in the dessert department, short, wearing his belt cinched below his belly so that it hung out as if he were pregnant. His gray-blond hair was sparse, combed back over the baldness, making his skull look like a baby's. His faded blue eyes held an amused twinkle, as if he regarded life as a humorous episode.

William Pryor found it difficult to believe that this was one of the best of the Agency's streetmen, superb at gathering information, pumping it from unsuspecting people so expertly that they were eager rather than evasive. It's the way he looks, Pryor thought, a rumpled Mister Nobody, one of the great unwashed mass.

Pryor had saved Abel's job when the admiral was pink-slipping everyone in sight. As a result, Abel not only was grateful but one of Pryor's most reliable sources of information, not only on the Washington scene, but on past and present Agency activities. His last assignment had been Iran, where he reported that he thought a revolution was imminent, that the United States could help avert it, that the fanatical bearded religious leader who would spearhead the holy war would make the Shah look like a saint. On that same trip, a few weeks in Thailand convinced Abel that the Thais were our devoted enemies, and not to be trusted, despite our continued financial aid and the outright gift of eleven million dollars in stockpiled arms and ammunition originally destined for Vietnam. Pryor had duly reported this and it had been sent through the Washington bureaucratic assessment-mill that ground so slowly that rarely did it produce anything. But Pryor had a hunch that Abel was right. He usually was.

Abel grinned as Pryor approached the bar. "I held my ravening thirst until your arrival. Ever tried a Sakini?"

"No, what the hell is it? Sounds like a Japanese food processor."

"It is. Two." Abel said to the bartender. "Beefeater. One straight up, one on the rocks."

He turned back to Pryor. "Simple. It's a martini with sake instead of vermouth."

"Isn't sake supposed to be drunk warm?"

"It will be by the time it gets to the bloodstream. What brings us to Charlie's?"

"Let's talk after lunch. Ribs okay?"

"Charlie would ban us from the premises if we didn't keep the faith." They took their drinks to an empty booth and slid in, Abel sampling before they sat down. "Ahh, delish."

Pryor sipped his, stirring the ice with his finger. "Good. Takes the bite off the gin."

"Listen to me, my friend. It pays dividends."

"That's what I'm here for. Especially the dividends."

"What can I do for you?"

"Spargo. Ever heard of him?"

Abel finished his drink with one gulp as a young Chinese waiter arrived with a steaming plate of ribs, two bottles of Coors, and two stemmed glasses. He also gave them each two huge linen napkins. The ribs were eaten with the fingers.

"You can't say Charlie hasn't got style," Abel said, ignoring Pryor's question. "Linen napkins in a Chinese restaurant. It's a wonder the chop suey joints haven't run him out of town."

"Spargo?" Pryor said softly.

"Thought you said after lunch. I talk better on a full stomach."

He bit into a rib, stripping the moist lean meat off with his teeth, chewing meditatively, then sighing with contentment. "They tell me that half the blacks in town are mad at Charlie because he does ribs better than they do. The other half treat him like Father Divine. Wonder what his secret is? These are the best things I ever tasted."

"The real Chinese secret they tell me is to cook fast and eat slowly."

Abel reluctantly placed his third rib on his plate. "All right. I get the message. Spargo, you said. Yes, I've heard of him. A better idea than talking to me about him I'd think would be to get a tape on his performance."

"Yes, I've already heard the tape on Spargo. A short one. Most laudatory."

"Laudatory, shit. From what I hear it ought to be raves. This guy is good."

"I need someone for a very special assignment. He can't be Agency, and he has to be damn good."

"At what?"

"Well, everything, I suppose."

"I wouldn't put Spargo into any of the

stupid slots the media shoves most of us into. Not a spy, a spook, an agent." He poured the rest of the Coors into his glass. "For me, he's a specialist."

"At what?"

Abel shrugged. "Staying alive. Look. Let's figure the world is one big black hole. Something is in the hole that you have to flush out, snake, whatever. Spargo is the ferret. He goes down and routs it out."

"Kills it?"

"Perhaps."

"Not a spook, a spy, or an agent. Would you say that he's an assassin?"

"Me, I'm not saying anything. Let me tell you one of the last items I heard about him."

Abel said that on his way back from a stint as a bodyguard for an Arab oil magnate, Spargo stopped over in Rome for some rest and relaxation. While he was there a former prime minister of Italy was desperately trying to get someone skilled to help him. His ten-year-old son had been kidnapped by terrorists. They were demanding a huge sum, plus the release of other terrorists, the usual ransom demands. The Italian police had located the house on the outskirts of Rome where the ter-rorists were hidden, but they were stalemated because the main purpose was to save the boy. The ransom money had been paid, but the government, always a divided one, had not reached a decision on releasing the other terrorists. The brother of the Arab Spargo had been working for, a friend of the Italian politician, heard Spargo was in Rome and approached him, asking for his help.

"It's a lot more involved," Abel said, "so I'll shorten it. Spargo discovered one of the terrorists' weaknesses. They had holed up without enough groceries. He persuaded the officials to stop the supply of food for a while. They did, until the terrorists threatened to kill the boy immediately. So Spargo had himself packed in the long wooden box that was supposed to hold a large supply of wine and food. He was delivered."

Abel refilled his glass. "The rest of the story is confused. But he killed all six of the terrorists and carried the boy out. Gets free pasta in Italy for the rest of his life."

"Ingenious. But dangerous."

"You know," Abel said, "you just described Spargo."

"Do you know him personally?"

"Not really. Met him three times. The guy's different. Also has a crazy habit. Chews betel."

"What the hell's betel?"

"You know, that stuff from India, from the bark of a tree, I think. Gives a little high, I'm told. I hear he picked up the habit on an assignment in India."

"Any other weaknesses?"

"Who says that's a weakness? Maybe it's a strength. He likes women too. No chaser. Restrained. But no hermit. I also hear that he had the real thing going. An Arab girl. Or a Jew, some say. A beauty. Killed by the PLO. Spargo disappeared for six months after that one."

He drained the beer from the glass with a long swallow and placed it on the table. "I'm sorry for the guy, you know. Few of us ever find the real thing. Then to lose it, and the job you've devoted your life to, is hard luck. Spargo's like a fine surgeon who wakes up one morning and finds that he has ten arthritic fingers and his career is over. Here he is, one of the best we've ever turned out, and because of those slobs in Congress he's now an odd-jobs man, picking up whatever comes his way."

Pryor looked at him curiously. "You surprise me. It appears that heart of yours is as big as your belly. You also seem to know quite a bit about him."

Their waiter arrived with finger bowls, rice china filled with warm water. They dipped into them and dried their fingers on the large linen napkins. Abel picked up the conversation. "Don't think anyone knows much about Spargo. Maybe he's the Reggie Jackson of the team. You know, the standoff super star. Maybe not. But he was the talk of the place awhile back when he outsmarted an ex-Agency director who tried to use him, set him up. Before your time, I guess."

Abel loosened his belt a notch, sighing in relief. "Who says this Chinese food doesn't stay with you?"

"Especially when flooded with Coors."

"Incidentally, you didn't tell me what the job was."

Pryor had devised the trick when he was with the State Department in the Middle East, headquartered in Beirut. He had many dealings with Arabs on several levels; the higher the social strata the more withdrawn and aloof the Arab. It was simple trick, really. You extracted a pair of horn-rimmed glasses from the breast pocket of your jacket, took out a pocket handkerchief, and began polishing the clear glass lens. This produced time to think about an answer or prepare a question. Pryor also had a backup gimmick once the glasses were on; by pressing the side of the eyepiece in a certain place the right lens fell out of the frame. He went through both routines as a matter of habit and to observe results. The lens fell on the table with a clatter; the specially constructed glass never shattered but it was noisy.

Abel chuckled. "Cute. I've seen you do that one before, Bill. It's okay by me if I don't know what you're up to. I get the message. I'd say that this guy could be the very best you could get. If you can get him. I have no idea where he is."

"Good enough."

Abel continued, "But let's keep in mind he wasn't good enough to avoid getting the ax at the Agency. So let's assume he's not perfect. Maybe he's got chinks."

Pryor grimaced. "Who hasn't? I'm betting the chinks are tiny ones that let very little light into his armor."

After Pryor paid the check and Charlie bowed them out, Abel said, "But he's a real pisser, Bill. When he takes a bite at an assignment he doesn't let go. And I'm warning you. He won't take any pushing around."

As he got into his Mercedes, Pryor

wondered how the admiral's talking computer would have summed it up. He wouldn't take the time to find out. He'd try to find Spargo through his old instructor and friend, Kodály.

CHAPTER EIGHT

When he saw the cluster of buildings and a Ford dealer sign ahead, Pryor slowed and pulled in, parked the Mercedes, and walked into the showroom where a bulging man with no hair and a false smile said, "Sir, what can I do to help?"

His smile faded when Pryor said he wanted to rent a car. "Hey, Billy," he shouted, "someone in here wants to see you."

Billy wasn't much better, but he wasn't pig-fat and he didn't even pretend to smile. Pryor followed him out to the area behind the building and selected a dark blue Ford two-door, an unobtrusive Pinto with thirty thousand miles on it. He sat in it, started the motor, listened for a couple of minutes, shut it off, checked the tires, said, "Okay, it looks all right. I'll pay for it now and come by a little later today and leave my Mercedes. That all right?"

Billy was startled. "Leave your Mercedes?"

Pryor nodded. "Just for a few hours. That a problem?"

"No, but —"

"See you later," Pryor said curtly.

Josef Kodály had retired to a farm in northern Virginia, a small clapboard of no particular period or design, except snug and secure, on fifteen acres that he had bought after he had been in the Agency five years, when most land in northern Virginia wasn't considered part of Washington, D.C., and could be picked up for as little as five hundred an acre. It was now worth more than twenty times that.

Josef had also created a new profession to keep him in motion and bring in enough of a return that it wasn't wasted effort. He raised squabs for the D.C. market, mainly for the few fine French restaurants now proliferating. Travel at taxpayers' expense had educated many from Congress, mostly small-time politicians who had once considered sirloin and baked potatoes the epitome of fine dining. Dinners at places like Horcher's in Madrid,

Taillevent in Paris, Four Seasons in Munich, and George's in Rome had created a new race of Washington politicians that demanded the spectacular but would settle for the unusual. They had graduated from Cornish game hens to chukkar partridge and quail, from fried chicken to flambéed duck, from grilled steak to Beef Wellington. Despite their new-found epicurean expertise, few knew what squab were until a political proletarian made the discovery and started its gustatory reputation. As a result, Josef sold every squab he could raise.

Pryor had read the printout on Josef Kodály that was prepared in voluminous detail on every retired Agency employee. It included a geodetic survey of Josef's farm, the price he paid for it, whom he bought it from, what it was valued at now, how much money he had in the bank, what now occupied him, his sex life, drinking habits, and his present political philosophies and affiliations. His phone was tapped, all foreign mail read. Although Kodály was no longer Agency, he was still on a leash, and the strongest part of that leash was the monthly retirement check.

Slightly more than one hour from Washington, the farm sat on a green knoll overlooking a secondary road. There were other small farms on either side, spaced about a quarter mile apart, giving Josef some privacy. Corn fields in late spring green stretched all around the farm. Inheriting Middle European frugality, Josef had quickly discovered that raising his own corn not only netter higher return from his birds, but gave them better flavor and sales appeal. Natural foods were popular and Josef let it be known that his birds were raised on only the purest, "all organic," ingredients, as he put it.

The road up the knoll was unpaved and Pryor raised flags of dust as he drove to the farm, signaling Josef, who came walking around from the rear of the house as Pryor cut the motor. It growled a couple of times after the ignition was turned off.

"Needs an oil change," Josef said. "A Mercedes shouldn't grunt like that."

The photograph in the file didn't do Josef justice. Small, fragile looking, his thick hair slightly salted with gray was tightly combed, unparted; his Stalinish moustache, also gray-speckled, accented a square, stubborn chin. Light brown eyes, sharp, active, moved over Pryor like a finger, probing his strengths and weaknesses. Pryor noted that he was still wearing his ankle-high, laced, polished black shoes, standard equipment when he taught *savate*, boxing with the feet. He wore a spotless blue-denim long shirt over denim pants.

"I got a call that you were coming," he said, voice harsh, accent slight. "What can I do for you?"

"In due time," Pryor said, deciding to exert authority right away.

Josef squinted at him. "Let's remember that it's my time."

The hostility was as tangible as his hard stare.

Although he towered over Josef, Pryor could almost feel the strength and competence flow from him, a human electricity that he had felt spark off other dangerous men he had encountered. He decided to ease off slightly, looking around.

Two outbuildings, newer than the farmhouse, were also white clapboard, one-story, a screened enclosure completely encircling them. Large white birds sat on vertical perches preening in the sunlight. To Pryor, they resembled herring gulls without the black and gray markings. He asked what they were.

"Specially bred," Josef said. "White King pigeons. Raise large squabs, some over a pound-and-a-half at twenty-six days —"

A large, gray Norway rat came crawling around the corner of one building. In a movement so swift that Pryor never saw its start or completion, Josef raised his arm and flashed it forward. Sparkling in the sun, the knife flew like a homed-in nuclear weapon, striking the rat in the neck. It leaped, then fell, twitching.

"That rascal," Josef said calmly, "has been peeling off young pigeons for two weeks. I've had my eye on him but he's always been too fast for me."

"Not now," Pryor said softly.

"Lucked out."

The hard brown eyes held Pryor's. "But you didn't come down here to talk squabs."

"I'm trying to locate Spargo."

Josef walked over and retrieved his knife, wiped it on his pants, and slid it into the sheath on his left arm, covering it with the shirt sleeve again. "I've been out of touch too long. He hasn't been with the Agency for a few years. But you know that."

Pryor nodded. "I understand that you are friends. Teacher and student. Keep in touch."

"That was one student who could teach the teacher. Sorry to see the organization lose him. His knife, I hear, did him in."

He picked up the rat by the tail and swung it high into the air, looping it into a cornfield.

Pryor stood waiting.

"Congress!" Josef said bitterly. "You can use a sawed-off shotgun to blow a man in half, or kill a hostile with a magnum at four feet, but use a knife and you are a creep that doesn't belong in the ranks of the beloved Agency."

"Spargo," Pryor said sharply. "We need him for a special assignment. I need an address. And you there to introduce me."

"Sorry."

"I'm sorry, too," Pryor said. "I understand that you get a certain pension check every month."

Josef had turned his back on Pryor. Like some incredible machine, his right heel flew backward, striking Pryor's right kneecap with such power that it hurled him onto his back.

Josef walked over and calmly placed his foot on Pryor's chest, the pressure keeping him supine, a stone gouging into his back.

"I assume that was a threat."

Pryor tried to sit up, but the foot pushed him back down.

"Now," Josef said quietly, "what do you want with Spargo?"

"You know the rules," Pryor said fiercely.

"This is 'Eyes Only.' I can't tell anyone but Spargo."

"Yeah," Josef said. "I know the rules. And I suspect that you maybe broke a couple barging in here whipping that pension-club over my head."

"Mistake," Pryor said as Josef removed his foot.

"You are right. I take it that you are an Agency messenger boy. I'll give Spargo your message next time I see him."

CHAPTER NINE

Josef Kodály did not trust telephones. It was part of his training. But with luck, he could make it in five hours, driving hard. The farm pickup, a GMC Sierra Grande 15, was well-sprung, comfortable, large enough so he wouldn't be bullied by the trailer trucks on the throughways.

Rain was falling hard when he reached Manhattan. The World Trade Center loomed in the dark day tall as a brooding mountain, the lights coming on in its upper level glittering like mica on a cliffside. Josef slowed on 56th Street, between Tenth and Ninth avenues; the street, slick and black with rain, ran like an open sewer. Wadded newspapers, milk cartons, paper bags, and garbage moved sluggishly along the curb. Neglected slum-lord tenements steamed in the rain like smoldering burned-out wrecks. He pulled in beside a gray building that looked as if it had been built as a survival shelter, an ugly square block, a one-story building without windows, two air-conditioning units set into the wall high out of reach, a sign just under them, black letters on a faded gray background: *Karate: Professional Instruction.* The whole structure was impervious to vandalism.

As Josef stepped inside, a husky, squat Japanese with crewcut gray hair, wearing a white cotton Tokaido karategi uniform, came toward him. Josef noted that he had on a pair of L.L. Bean's ankle-high laced moccasins, sewn from a single piece of thick brown bull leather. Josef also had a pair, which he often used when limbering up during *savate* practice.

Remembering the old etiquette, Josef bowed and said, "Good afternoon, sensei," and took off his shoes. When one entered a dojo, "place of the way," one left shoes at the door and problems with the shoes. In the place of the way there should be no preoccupation, no thoughts other than karate.

Norikura bowed in return. "Welcome to my

dojo." He waited for Josef to explain the purpose of his visit. They were friends, but it was not the Japanese way to show emotion or press the conversation.

Josef examined the dojo before continuing the conversation. It was polite to be restrained.

A large room resembling a gymnasium, it had no furniture; dojo mats were stacked along a far wall. The walls were mostly mirrored so karate action could be observed and criticized. On one wall that was not mirrored a two-tiered rack held a large samurai sword and a tanto, a short, broad-bladed sword. On a rear wall metal sockets held the Rising Sun flag and the Stars and Stripes. Below was the polished bamboo-framed portrait of an elderly Japanese in a black costume, obviously the master who had been Norikura's teacher. There were no trophies; the true karate master is not an exhibitionist. But there was one framed certificate in Japanese, with a black-and-white photograph of Norikura.

Finally Josef said, "May I see Spargo?"

Norikura eyed him keenly, then nodded. Josef had also taught Spargo and merited respect. Norikura nodded toward the rear of the room.

Four young black men in white costumes were grappling with one another, stopping occasionally to compare handholds. Beyond them a man lay on a mat, a young Chinese boy in a black Tiger karate suit on top of him.

As Norikura led him there Josef saw surprise flare in the man's oddly gold-flecked gray eyes, then instantly fade.

Without moving Spargo said, "Welcome to the Big Rotten Apple."

The Chinese boy climbed off and Spargo rose in one lithe movement, not using hands to lever himself up, just a quick push of his body.

He was dressed in a white Lion karate suit of short jacket and long trousers, black edged around the collar and along the piping of the jacket and sleeves, a black Dan belt embroidered in red Japanese characters cinched around his trim waist.

Josef thought he hadn't aged in the two years since he had last seen him, but there was a touch of gray in the sideburns of the dark hair and a tiny net of wrinkles beginning on the temple side of each eye.

They shook hands without smiling. They chatted easily for a while and Josef learned that Spargo was working at the karate school as a favor to his old instructor, who was also conducting another school somewhere in New England.

"Bunch of rich kids," Spargo said. "Norikura may end up with a chain and his own bank."

Norikura smiled. He turned to leave, motioning the Chinese boy to follow him.

"A type came to the farm," Josef said quietly. "Tried to use my pension as a whip. Wanted to recruit you. I wouldn't play."

"Is that him?" Spargo interrupted, tilting his head slightly toward a man who had just entered the dojo.

Josef wheeled, jaw dropping. "The son of a bitch! I don't see how he managed it! He drives a big Mercedes. I would've spotted him a dozen times."

Spargo laughed. "He probably switched cars. No problem. Why don't you drive back to your farm. No need for you to get any more involved in this."

"Guess it's a good thing they retired me. Maybe I should've used the telephone, but figured a smartass like that would probably have it tapped." He clutched Spargo's shoulder, his large horny fingers hard. "I don't have to tell you to take care with these bastards."

"Josef." Spargo touched the hard hand on his shoulder. "Sorry the good days went so swiftly."

Without another word Josef left by a back door that Spargo indicated with a wave of his hand.

Norikura came walking to Spargo with the grace of a ballet master.

"That man. By the door. Wishes you to meet him in his car. A Ford Pinto, dark blue."

Spargo nodded. "Thank you, sensei."

Pryor watched him come through the rain, walking in a loose-limbed way as if he had just jumped off a trapeze net. With the white trousers showing beneath the raincoat he looked like an off-duty hospital attendant or an intern. Until he got close.

He walked around the Ford and got in. There was no greeting. He turned and looked squarely at Pryor.

There was a slight film of blood on his upper teeth. What the hell! Pryor thought, then remembered his talk with Abel and the fact that Sparo sometimes chewed betel, which left a red stain. Rain speckled his dark hair like little jewels; he was slightly over six feet tall and looked lean and hard. Complexion was dark, a little leathery, as if he spent lots of time in the sun, and Pryor recalled that he had been in the Middle East for extended periods. Wonder why we never met, he speculated idly now, but recalled too that he, himself, was never in one place very long while he was there, handling dual roles as usual, being two people at the same time. As a result of his constant political performances, like an actor, Pryor was aware that he did not know himself, did not know who or what he really was. He did know that he liked the excitement and the deviousness of it, but wasn't sure what that added up to in character. Right now he was somewhat unsure of himself.

Small flecks floated in Spargo's eyes like green gold. They were disconcerting eyes, aimed like a pair of derringers. Pryor had the dismaying thought that his ruse to get close to this man wouldn't work.

"I'm Dick Carson," he said. As he started to take a billfold from his inside suit pocket, he felt his hand gripped, so fast he hadn't seen the action.

"ID," he said. "Just wanted to identify myself before we talked."

Spargo held his hand out for the ID. His mind was aflight: Just such a Company-motivated type had probably discovered that

Leah was a Jew doubling and informed the Arabs. Chess, oil, favors exchanged, the United States making that small monstrous move on the board simply to gain a point with the Arabs. That small move had almost destroyed Spargo.

He heard Pryor asking a question but his mind couldn't handle it. He was with Leah. Her Arab name was Salwa Habib, but she had told him honestly what she was, what she was doing. They agreed to call her Salwa. She was a Palestinian Jew, so classically Arabic in appearance and manner that she had no trouble passing. The Mossad had conscripted her when she was sixteen, had trained her well, not only in armed and unarmed combat, but in the intelligence skills. She was twenty-eight when Spargo met her.

Out of the Agency, he was acting as bodyguard to Arab politician Ibraim Al-Sowayel and had been in Beirut on a short holiday. When he saw her, at a going-home gathering for a U.S. cultural attaché, he was stunned. Her hair was long and straight, so black and glossy that it shone even in that smoke-filled, softly lit room. She had been talking to the attaché, an overweight Midwesterner with a chestnut hairpiece and buck teeth that made him look like a monstrous beaver.

She crossed the room, stepping lightly with a natural grace, as if walking barefooted in sand. The host waddled over to Spargo and said, "Go ahead. Stare. That's Salwa Habib. An Arab, from Palestine we understand. But I think she's a Bedouin. She rides like one and does other things too, we hear, like those savages of the sand. Come, I'll introduce you."

Close up Salwa looked unreal, like she had been put together by a sardonic God to torment men. Her eyes were absolutely black. Slightly slanted, they were warm, lively eyes that danced at you, moving from feet to midsection, where they stopped briefly, then on up, stopping at your eyes. It was an effective technique. Spargo felt a warmth in his groin that moved upward as Salwa's eyes did.

She had bold Semitic features, and everything was in perfect proportion. Her skin was a creamy-tan; a narrow scar on the left cheek, not jagged or raw-looking, appeared like a beauty mark. Her long dress was filmy silk, peach-colored, spotted with tiny gold medallions; it fit her loosely, Arab-style. As she walked her body moved sinuously and suggestively beneath the silk.

Her sexuality was as tangible as the scar. He had been in Saudi Arabia too long, as ascetic as an Arab. He was vulnerable.

"Spargo," she had said in a low voice that was oddly coarse, "what an interesting name. What comes before, or is it after?"

Bentley, the attaché, said, "That's it, Salwa. No more, no less. Spargo it is. Spargo you accept."

"I accept." She laughed, and the sound made him feel foolishly romantic. He had the sudden impulse to turn away and leave. He was to remember that impulse later and regret not acting upon it.

Like all natural associations theirs flowered quickly. They danced in the restaurants to the beat of Middle Eastern orchestras, swam in the sea, walked the old city of Beirut in pale moonlight, came to be known as a pair.

Best of all had been the riding. Salwa loved horses, telling Spargo that he had never seen a real horse until he met an Arabian. Two weeks after meeting her she introduced him to her horse, Jibhah, a velvety sorrel. "The Arabs have won me with their horses," she said. "Especially this one. I've had Jibhah since she was a filly. She's the only real friend I have."

She went on to tell him that the Bedouin

tribesmen of the desert said that God had created their horses out of the wind and given it to them as their most prized possession, and it was not to be disposed of lightly. The desert men could not have survived in the vast sandy reaches of the desert without the Arabian horse's stamina and ability to survive on an occasional handful of dates, and in combat, its grace and speed, running circles around cavalry horses.

Narrowing her eyes, she said, "I regret the horse was bred by Arabs. It is the one thing I like about them."

She got him a mare, Marah, and they rode everywhere, along the wide beaches by the sea, through villages, among the Lebanese hills, side by side through olive groves. It had been in an abandoned olive grove, the old trees silver in the sunlight, where they had first made love. Salwa made love as she did everything, honestly, fiercely, pulling him down upon her in the center of the ancient grove of trees, the shadows cast by the twisted, gnarled branches like a surrealistic painting splotched upon the ground.

"I want you, Mister Spargo," she said simply. "Take my clothes off."

Her slim body was nut-brown, long smooth

muscles in her arms and legs, her breasts small, but full and firm with tiny brown nipples that stood up as he touched one, then the other. Without a word, she touched the head of his penis and he hardened instantly. Then she undressed him, quickly, skillfully.

Surprisingly strong, she flipped him over on his back and mounted him, laughing softly, saying, "I'm the better rider."

Later she would say "Love is the only honest emotion. It is a mutual competition in tenderness in which neither can be the loser."

But love had made her the loser. They found her one day in that olive grove where they had first made love. She was smashed, broken, under the body of Jibhah whom she also loved. Jibhah's head had been severed.

The horror of it was the deliberate barbaric brutality. It was a clear Arab message: Kill the enemy. Kill also what the enemy loves. Spargo hoped fiercely that whoever had committed the butchery would come for him too. But apparently he wasn't on the list. He made himself conspicuous. But no one came.

Coldly, he roamed first Beirut, then most of the Middle East, trying to discover who had killed Salwa. But there were too many Arabs, too many deceptions, too many frightened men. It was too complicated. In the end, just before he left the Middle East, he had discovered that it had been his own countrymen who had motivated the murder. Another disassociated Agency man had told him.

"She was picking the PLO off, top man by top man. Knew when and where they would attack next. They were afraid that she would get Arafat. We handed her over as a favor, to kind of balance off our heavy friendship for Israel. Put us in solid with some big Arabs."

"Who?" Spargo had said, softly. "Who?"

Hart, the ex-spy, said, "Not who. They. It was policy. Washington. You can't levy vengeance against an entire city. It's just the whole rotten mess. Forget it."

But he would not forget it. He wanted the man who informed, the man who told the Arabs that Salwa was a Jew, a double.

The voice said, "Have I said something that bothers you? Do I have your interest?"

"Just thinking," Spargo said. "Just thinking about what you are saying. Let's go over some points again, shall we?"

"All right," Pryor said. "It's all pretty simple."

"Nothing is simple," Spargo said. "Except dying."

"That President's special group you mentioned," Spargo said, recapturing the conversation. "Politicians are not my favorite people."

"Nor are they mine," Pryor said.

"What's it all about?" Spargo said. "Why the cute switched car act? Lay it out. I'll give you exactly three minutes." He looked at his wristwatch.

"We didn't have an address for you. Knew Josef was a friend. Hoped he'd cooperate. He didn't."

Pryor told him of the information that had been obtained from Ryal, who was not Ryal but a British agent, that he had died just after revealing the information about a startling discovery in the sea by an American scientist, and had also forecast the death of the scientist in Stamford, Connecticut, who had his head blown off.

"Who is the other scientist? What's his discovery?" Spargo said. "Was the man killed in Stamford associated with him?"

"Allan Vaughn. Association, negative. Negative on the discovery. Vaughn has vanished. We want you to find him before the Agency does. If it's as astounding a discovery as Ryal claimed, and the Agency fumbles by not knowing about it and letting us get it first, with this President in power, we believe it could finish the Agency."

"That's it," Spargo said softly. "Just a routine power play?"

"No," Pryor said seriously. "It's all in a report that I'll get to you. Ryal was working for the Japanese in a double-cover situation. We believe they are after the file too. Before us. The sea is the last frontier. Whoever controls it will be Number One. We can't let anyone else outmaneuver us. We must get there first. I'll even wave the flag. America first."

"Why me?"

Pryor looked straight into the odd eyes. "Whoever is after it is playing rough. We know that you are accomplished in that kind of game. Good men with your talent are hard to find."

"How do you see it?"

"Maybe Ryal should be back-tracked. Without annoying the British. Also there could be a trail in Stamford, showing a connection, or some kind of tie-in. It's nebulous. But it must be there. Two men do not die for a formula that details how to make soap out of seaweed."

"I'm expensive."

"We're prepared. How expensive?"

"Two thousand a week. Plus expenses. Complete flexibility. No case officer."

Pryor hesitated. "Agreed. But I'd like to give you a special number to call. A phone booth. In Washington. I'll be in it every Monday at four p.m. And Friday at ten a.m. I'll need to know what you are doing. At least how you are assessing the thing . . ."

He stared at Spargo. "I'm afraid that as a secret force we can't offer you any protection at all, no official umbrella. You're on your own."

Spargo laughed. "I always have been. I will make progress reports when I can. I promise nothing."

"Fair enough. How much money do you need?"

"Ten thousand. When we talk I'll tell you where to send more as I need it."

"Loose," Pryor said slowly. "But I accept it. I'll have the money, the special phone number, and our report at this karate parlor by tomorrow morning. We want that file. Despite the price in money or lives. We think you can get it. It's that simple."

"I repeat. Nothing is simple," Spargo said, getting out of the car.

Pryor said quickly, "Oh, one more thing. We would not be against your teaming up with Josef Kodály if you need him. Pay him the going rate."

Hand on the door, Spargo turned. "An interesting thought."

Pryor watched him walk through the rain.

CHAPTER TEN

The black Chevette waited in the shadows. There was a full moon. The man in the car thought about the slogan Virginia was using to attract tourists, "Virginia is for Lovers." Too bad he didn't have a date instead of an assignment.

In the clear night he had a good view of Josef Kodály's Virginia farm. It was the only landmark he had. He was gambling that the Ford would pass this way to the place where the Mercedes was parked. He lucked out. The Ford came out of the night suddenly at moderate speed. He followed it until it stopped at the Ford Agency, then waited cautiously until the Mercedes pulled out and was a mile or so up the road.

He kept at least two cars between him and the Mercedes, but due to the late hour the traffic began to thin and soon he found that he was tracking alone behind the blue German car.

In his preoccupation, Pryor hadn't noticed the car. He was wrestling with a problem. He was aware that it was breaking rules to leave any witness alive in a situation where absolute secrecy was required. Josef Kodály must be removed along with Spargo when the mission was completed. It had been a master stroke to suggest that Spargo use Kodály. The temptation to team up with his former instructor had to be a strong one. There was time to devise the means to eliminate both.

As the red button glowed on the dashboard again, he slowed down and assessed the car in his rearview mirror. Black Chevette. Pryor didn't know exactly how the tail-detector worked, but it electronically scanned a car directly behind, and if the car fell back, then came into view again, and consistently followed, the gadget flashed the red warning on the dashboard. He speeded up and passed six cars, two at a time, then wedged between two slower-moving vehicles nearing the capital. In ten minutes, the red light flashed again. He checked. The Chevette was still back there.

At the next exit Pryor left the interstate fast, taking the secondary road paralleling the main highway. The Chevette passed him and then turned at the first road to the right off the secondary.

Fifteen minutes later, back on the interstate, the red light went on and stayed on. The Chevette was back there. Who could have put a tail on him? He didn't want to accept the conclusion that surfaced.

Who knew that he had gone to New York? Only the admiral. Was the CIA director having him tailed? Why? What false move had he made?

Pryor slowed now, made a signaled turn off the main highway on the outskirts of Washington. When he was sure the Chevette had him in sight, he went directly to the special all-night garage, the automatic, microwave-controlled doors opening to his signal.

The man in the Chevette parked, turned off his lights, and got out to investigate. The side door of the garage was open. He went in carefully, silent in Adidas running shoes. There was no attendant. Fourteen cars were parked in the huge space. But no Mercedes. Puzzled, he walked across to the far wall, saw that the center portion wasn't a wall, but a false-front double-door exit.

He ran to the Chevette, circled the garage, then cruised the streets in the area. The Mercedes had vanished. Shiu-Kai Chin was humiliated. Spargo's best karate student probably wouldn't get another chance to serve the master.

Spargo had wanted him to stay with the man in the Mercedes for forty-eight hours and report on his movements. He did remain in Washington for forty-eight hours, but he never saw the Mercedes again.

CHAPTER ELEVEN

The report sent to the karate school in Manhattan pinpointed the dead Ryal's safehouse area as a suburb of Warren, Michigan, but as usual, it was a sloppy job without an address, or even a street. The Agency had trapped the rat, but failed to locate the hole.

Would there be anything of value in that hole? Had the opposition, whoever it was, gotten there first? Would Spargo be walking into a setup? Who was Ryal? Was he actually a double, working for both the British and the Japanese, or had he, scenting greater gain, been a triple, his own man, out for a personal monetary kill?

Spargo was disgusted. Ryal had been killed

by incompetent men, amateurs. If they had handled the interrogation professionally, perhaps leads would be secure and they would know what they were after.

Now it was like standing, face to the wind, trying to scent what was in the dark forest.

If the file actually contained such a tremendous secret, and others were aware of it, it was certain that the trail would lead directly to where Ryal had operated, stealing little secrets from the Detroit geniuses who were too late with too little on the small cars, and who couldn't even produce a road-safe automobile. But that had been a pretty effective cover, the dipping into Detroit's bag of bumble-ups, disguising Ryal's British mission, whatever that was. And what had he gotten for the Japanese? A strong scent of that sea thing? Passing it on for survival reasons, giving them just enough to keep them convinced that he was indeed their man?

Suddenly Spargo realized that he was almost happy, back at what he enjoyed most. The danger, the puzzle, the deception of the chase. It had kept him sharp and alive before. He hoped that he was still sharp enough. The Agency reminded him of things long past, when the world was young and the game worth playing, when the deception was on the other side, not yours. Or had that ever been true? He thought again of Salwa and other treachery, and his happiness faded.

He remembered Jim Harris, Chinese, given the Christian name by a missionary when he was five years old. Good. Brilliant even. He had been given to the communists by the Agency and never heard of again. Why? No one knew. But it must have been the same kind of trade-off that had killed Salwa.

Enough. He was in this for money. It was better than being a professor of karate, an art in which he didn't even believe.

He had flown to Detroit, used a fake driver's license to rent a miserable little Honda from Avis, and had arrived at an inconspicuous motel on the outskirts of Warren at dusk. Dusk, the indistinct hour, in a strange place always depressed him.

He had a feeling he couldn't shake, a foreboding. The Agency had reached into the past for him. That in itself was suspicious. In this society once you were pushed into the past you were forgotten. He had named his price. No problem. There, again, it was wrong. They were small men, hagglers, bargainers, stingy, as if they were spending their own money. He told himself that the reason for such quick agreement was that this was big. And it was true that most of the good men, all of the black actors, in fact, were gone from the company, cut off by Congress, banished, assassinated, or working for other countries or organizations.

He began ticking them off. Ben, in electronics security; Harry dead; and he knew instantly that he was making a mistake. Never look back. He turned to the problem at hand.

He did not like the tedium of trying to locate a man in an unknown situation, where he had to be certain not to leave a trail from which he himself could be tracked. On this one he decided that he was reclaiming an automobile on which payments hadn't been made in six months. He had credentials if he needed them. Merit Credit Company. Everybody accepted it, most without question. People bought cars, some couldn't pay for them; the finance company, or a collection agency, attempted to reclaim the car. It was a natural part of the American way of life.

He had learned this a long time ago: Be simple. Do nothing elaborate or complicated; it touched off alarm bells. Do what people understand. Don't talk down; don't talk up.

Ryal had been a pro and wouldn't have used either that name or Mead. He probably had tried to steal the drunken-driver gadget to solidify his position with the Japanese. He would have had a flexible pose, perhaps as an automobile accessories salesman, or a fabric specialist, a cover that would enable him to move around Detroit manufacturing circles legitimately. In order to preserve his privacy, he would rent a small apartment or register in a second-class hotel where he could move at will without being closely observed.

Spargo remembered locating one agent by the simple medium of waiting until he asked for his mail and key at a hotel desk, a daily routine. Routines of any kind were dangerous for those who played the faceless game.

Carson, or whoever he was, was probably right. It was a place to start and could be profitable to backtrack Ryal, especially since he was playing a dual role. It could also be dangerous; the British, Japanese, or even the Americans could be waiting for whoever picked up on Ryal.

He had been assured that no one knew that Ryal-Mead was dead. But if Ryal hadn't reported in as was usual in cover operations, a search may have been initiated. Spargo would have to watch his own back.

In the field Spargo often liked to wear soft, natural shirt blazers, but for this chore he wore a cheap brown suit off the rack, a tan shirt, and a brown tie, an uninspired costume that made him one of the people. He also wore a pair of clear lens eyeglasses with bold, flaring aviator's frames.

A small black-and-white snapshot of Ryal had been attached to the report. A lean face, the hair thick, dark, smooth, a small white scar above the right eye, bushy eyebrows, hard dark eyes. He could have been black Irish. It was a face that would not be quickly forgotten; hardly an asset with an underground man who sought anonymity. But they said he was a British ace; so probably he was an expert with disguise; some of the best Britishers were.

There were three bars in the area. One was walled with murals of scantily clad women, all with the same face, many mirrors, and filled with women who sat and stared intently into each other's eyes as they talked. The bartender also was a woman; her face was the one that stared out of the murals. But she had changed since her modeling days. She had enormous breasts, a large Grecian wrestler's head covered with tight copper-tinted curls, large suspicious blue eyes. Everything about her was large, even the hand she shot out to grab the photograph.

"Nope," she said tightly in a husky man's voice. "Not one of mine. Never saw the guy."

How convenient for her, Spargo thought, to own her own hunting ground, where she could have her pick of female prey.

The other two were neighborhood hangouts with long, solid oak stand-up bars, jars of Polish sausage in brine on the bar, smoked beef sticks in plastic containers, a stale smell of food, beer, and bodies infrequently washed; television game shows were on in both bars, a proper din so men would not have to think while they drank. Which, Spargo decided, would have been impossible anyway.

Ryal was not known in either. He was not Dublin Irish as his interrogators claimed. It would have been a physical and spiritual impossibility for anyone from that city to stay away from all the bars in town.

After two hours of footwork Spargo finally drew reaction from the photograph in a Mom and Pop drycleaning shop. Pop was at the counter, a skinny man in his seventies. His faded blue eyes were as hard as the formica of the counter where he rested his wrinkled, liver-spotted hands.

"Hate to bother you," Spargo said, so quietly the old man cocked his head to hear him.

"No bother, brother," he said. "That's why I'm here. To help my fellow man."

A Jehovah's Witness, Spargo assessed. "You dislike dishonesty then? A man stealing?"

"You bet your socks!" The faded blue eyes flashed fire.

Spargo went into the routine, finely polished by this time, of his mission to recover the automobile. "He's used it all this time. Probably destroyed most of its resale value. The kind of man that gives us all a bad name and a hard time. Makes us distrust honest people —"

"How can I help?"

Spargo gave him the photograph.

"Not him! Never would've thought it of Mr. Peters. Real nice fella. Always passed the time of day —"

"Accent?"

The old man nodded. "Slight. Spoke like a gentleman. Know what I mean?"

"Clearly enunciating every word. Like an Englishman?"

"Yep. You got it."

143

"Do you have an address?"

He shook his head. "Nope. He left things. Always picked them up and walked them home. Even though we got a delivery service."

Spargo sighed. "This is turning into a real operation. There has to be an easier way of making a living."

"I'm betting you get him. You got that look."

Spargo smiled gently. "Thanks."

As he reached the door, the old man said, "I nearly forgot —"

As he turned around Spargo saw that the Good Samaritan had suddenly become Shylock; the old eyes squinted and the smile was sly.

"Oh, maybe nothing. Don't want to waste your time."

"What is it?"

"Like I said, we're just probably time wasting."

Spargo pulled a five-dollar bill from his pocket and placed it on the counter.

"No sirree bob, I didn't mean no such thing!" His eyes were glued to the bill.

"You've given me a lot of your valuable time," Spargo said. "What was it you remembered?"

"Man came in here yesterday. Asked about the same questions you did. But he didn't give me no reason like you did. Showed me another picture. Mr. Peters looked a little younger. Funny thing, too —"

Spargo waited. Then, "What was funny?"

"This man talked so much like Peters it could've been his brother."

Spargo thanked him and left.

Yesterday. The English were also back-tracking.

He was taking too much time.

Suddenly he remembered a seek-and-find technique that often worked: the telephone.

More often than not the good ones had unlisted numbers, the phones used mainly to receive calls, the bills rarely exceeding the minimum. There had to be an address for any phone, and a name.

Problem was to get the unlisted number, the name, and the address. Spargo had solved that, carrying an ID of a bona fide telephone inspector.

He went into a drugstore to get change and use a phone booth. He bought a pack of Big Red gum and while he was waiting for change he saw a headline in the local newspaper announcing that the lamprey was back in the

145

Great Lakes destroying lake trout and white fish. He entered a phone booth without a door, but still smelling of cigar smoke, and found the number of the local business office. After three interchanges he was connected to the manager, a woman with a quiet, commanding voice. He told her he was an inspector, checking out the report that a horse parlor was operating here, the gamblers using an unlisted phone.

"I can believe it," the manager said. "But do you have a Bell ID? We have to be careful. People want their privacy protected."

"Of course," Spargo said quietly, giving her the ID.

There weren't many who wanted their privacy protected, just six. He dialed the one listed as Peters; there was no answer.

The house was on an elm-shaded side street, Perkins Place; the apartment house looked like an abandoned warehouse that had been renovated by an ambitious but uninspired landlord. Shingled in gray, the stain rapidly fading into drabness, the six-story building was without landscaping or gutters, the rain scouring trenches around the apartment house. Names were on white plastic-covered cards glued to a plywood panel. There were fourteen apartments. Anthony Peters' name was still listed. The superintendent's name was off to the right. Typically, he lived in the basement.

If the English or anyone else had already located Peters, the place could be booby-trapped, an old but effective technique to take out the competition.

The superintendent didn't answer his ring. Spargo opened the front door quickly with a magnetized tungsten wire and walked down one flight to his apartment. No answer. He opened that door, saw the apartment was empty. It took four minutes to find the house keys on a ring hung under a man's heavy green beret on a coatrack.

Peters' apartment was on the third floor. There was no elevator, but there were two stair wells, one leading to the front door, the other the back, a convenient arrangement for lodgers who did not want to be observed by others.

As he opened Peters' door with the superintendent's key, he bent his ear to the knob and listened. There was a faint rattle which he immediately identified. It had been rigged by a professional. The detonator, about the size of a pea, worked on a flat sensor, which was wired inside the door knob.

Nothing happened if the knob was turned normally, opened with the proper key. But if the door was sprung with any of the professional tools, such as a tungsten wire, when the knob was turned, anything within ten feet would be blown up. Spargo had seen three people killed with such a setup in an apartment house in Paris.

The apartment was dark. Spargo moved cuatiously to double windows over a window seat and pulled back the curtains. Pale late-afternoon light spilled in.

The men lay fully stretched out, side by side. Spargo felt for pulse. Carefully he turned them over and examined them. Not a mark on them. Both necks broken. A clean kill. Both had identification, one English, a plastics salesman, the other American, an automobile dealer. Whoever killed them was so contemptuous of their covers that he had left the identification intact.

The report that he had received had not been candid. They had lied, and sent another American to root around. Was there more than one government group involved? Probably. The bumblers in Washington usually worked against one another, hoping something effective would happen.

Something effective had happened. Examining the dead men again, Spargo saw that their necks had been snapped from behind by a tremendous force, probably stealthily, the men never knowing what hit them. He went over the bodies carefully. One thing bothered him: There was a smudging of blood on the fingers of the Englishman.

He began the search, all of the obvious and not so obvious places, in the water of the toilet closet, even the floating bulb that flushed the toilet. The apartment had already been professionally searched, mattress and pillows ripped, pictures torn off, rugs slit and examined.

About ready to give up, Spargo heard the hum of the refrigerator. There were eggs, a canned ham, plastic-covered, half a carton of milk, a jar of marmalade, butter, cream, and a plastic-wrapped container of hamburger. Taking everything out, Spargo cracked all of the eggs in the sink, poured out the milk, cream, and marmalade, probed the butter and ham with a knife. He found it in the hamburger, buried in the center of the meat. The Englishman had probably heard his assassin coming and hidden whatever Ryal had left behind to clue his superiors in on what he had discovered. Hence, the traces of blood on his fingers after he had hidden it in the meat.

It was a plastic-wrapped container of 16 mm film. Spargo wiped it off, washed and dried his hands, placed the film in his pocket and was ready to leave when he heard the faint sound at the door. His eyes quickly searched the wall until he found what he hoped would be here in a second-class apartment, a chute that dropped trash to the basement. He slid the film into the chute opening as the door opened.

"Mr. Peters?" a sibilant voice inquired. "Superintendent."

Automatically, Spargo fell quickly to the floor, hearing an object strike the wall behind him with such force that it shattered the plaster, spraying it onto him.

The man hurled himself like the object, striking Spargo midsection as he was rising, flinging him back to the floor, Spargo twisted as he fell, avoiding the full force of the blade-edge hand strike that grazed his neck and would have broken it if the blow had landed solidly.

The knife was out of his sleeve as the man struck again. Spargo plunged the knife deeply upward, under the rib cage directly into the heart, a technique Josef had spent weeks making him perfect.

The man lay motionless now, curiously light on top of Spargo. He rolled him off. He was in black pants, black turtleneck sweater and wore a black hood with eyeholes. Spargo tore the hood off, revealing the Asiatic face of a young man, almost still a boy. Vietnamese, Korean, Chinese, Japanese?

He carefully wiped the knife clean on the hood and replaced it in the sheath on the underside of his left arm, the Josef position, far enough above the wrist so that arm action was not impeded. He called the knife Salwa: he wondered how Salwa would have felt if she had known he had named it in her honor.

Curious, Spargo walked to the wall and picked up the object that had been thrown at him. It was heavy metal, star-shaped, blunt on one side so that fingers could grasp it in a throwing position, and it had ten extended razor-sharp points. If it had hit him where intended, it would have neatly slashed his throat. He wiped it carefully with his handkerchief and left it where it had fallen; it would give the police another puzzle.

He went to the basement to retrieve the film, which he hoped would be in a trash basket. The large basket was there in the basement under the chute. In it was a wizened old man, his dry dandruff-flecked hair badly colored blond, white at the roots. His neck was broken. The superintendent? The film lay on his chest.

Spargo put it in his pocket. He was halfway up Perkins Place when the name of the odd object hurled at him popped into his memory. *Shuriken.* Weapon of the ninja, the old Japanese sect of "invisible" assassins.

Had they been reborn? Or was someone using their ancient assassination techniques as cover? He hoped that was the case. The ninja were a force he wouldn't want to face. Or had he already faced them?

CHAPTER TWELVE

As usual, he did the unexpected, not returning to New York, or Washington, but going south.

He flew to Atlanta, Georgia, amazed at the size of the terminal. In the five years since he had been here it had outgrown itself several times, with building still going on, the piled raw lumber looking like the aftermath of a series of air collisions. The airport had the look of a place under siege, people hurrying about with strained expressions, planes arriving and departing from every direction and altitude, the sky scarred with jet trails, the noise overhead like a thunderstorm. It was the usual air terminal robot-land; the people seemed to be under the control of an invisible force that had put them in this place where they did not want to be.

As he went through the outgoing-passenger line at the scanner, it picked up the knife on his arm, as he knew it would. The scanner did not have pinpoint accuracy, only a high metal sensitivity. Spargo held his knife-sheathed arm against his side, then nonchalantly took out a pocket knife from his side pocket and showed it to the uniformed guard, who motioned Spargo through.

He lifted off in the travel-worn Delta DC-9 with a sigh of relief. He was able to buy a martini, not made with the clear, clean Boodles he liked, but poured onto ice from a can, a decent drink. In minutes he was given the economy class herd treatment, a snack in a cardboard box. There was some sweet junk, which he ignored, but the sandwich, ham and cheese on a roll, was surprisingly tasty and he ate it hungrily, remembering that he hadn't eaten in ten hours.

He closed his eyes briefly. Two insurance salesmen, returning to Hartford, in the seat in front of him talking about their sexual conquests in Atlanta, irritated him. They were such bull-type amateurs. Taking the hammered Algerian silver cigarette case that Salwa had given him from his breast pocket, he extracted tightly leaf-rolled betel from it and chewed it for ten minutes. It gave him a needed high, erasing the fatigue that was building. Then he went to the toilet, rinsed the light betel crimson from his mouth, splashed cold water on his face and returned to his seat as the "Fasten Seat Belts" light was flashing and the hostess was announcing tinnily over the public address system that they were approaching Bradley.

This time he rented a Chevette. He was continually amused at the power of the American driver's license. Nearly everywhere else a passport or a formal ID was needed to rent an expensive object like a car, usually even to register into a hotel. But in the good old friendly U.S.A. a driver's license opened all doors, brought almost instant respectability, cashing checks, firmly establishing identification. He thought of the five driver's licenses he had with matching birth certificates. They were cheap, but the three passports he had cost five thousand dollars apiece.

As he drove the Chevette from Bradley terminal he was soon caught in the stream of traffic heading south on 84. He observed the fifty-five-mile-an-hour speed for several reasons, anonymity foremost, but no one else did, and his small car was almost forced off the road twice.

But he made Stamford in less than an hour and a half, selecting another motel on the outskirts. After four tries in photo stores and shopping areas, he rented a projector and a screen.

He spent forty minutes in the South Pacific restaurant eating a bowl of shark fin soup and some deep-fried chicken-and-shrimp balls mounded on fried rice. The food was tepid, service slow, and juke box punk rock music jangled his nerves.

Although he was certain that he was clean, he parked yards from his own entrance at the motel and came in silently from a back window that he had left unlocked. He stood in the dark for three minutes, sensitive as a smoke alarm mechanism, listening, smelling for an intruder. In darkness, he silently moved to the door, feeling to see if the thread he had stretched across the entrance was intact. It was. He turned on the lights, went to the bathroom, upended a box of tissues for the film that had been buried in the center.

Carefully he placed it on the reel, plugged in the projector, checking the light, centering it on the convertible screen that he had propped up at the far side of the room.

There were no titles, no voice. The scene was in color: A large tank of water. Six two-foot-long fish, dark fish with whiskers. Spargo identified them as catfish. Two darted in and attacked one fish, then viciously turned on each other. Three swam together, herding into a corner the two who were trying to tear each other apart. Then they separated and each fish in the tank viciously attacked another.

Scene change: Another tank. A blue shirt-sleeved forearm came into view, a hand holding a net. Camera pan to a large tub of water twenty feet from the tank. The hand dipped the net into the tank and brought it out with a large, thrashing catfish. The fish was dumped into the tub of water. This action continued until the tub was full of catfish. The hand with the net then transferred the fish in the tub to the tank with the six fish that were attempting to kill one another.

The camera focused full on the tank. As the new fish entered the water, the aggressive fish froze. They slowly moved their heads back and forth, flicking their whiskers.

The voice startled Spargo. It was a pedantic, rather high male voice.

"They are moving, spreading their maxillary barbels," the voice said.

Suddenly the six aggressive fishes' whiskers stiffened, and they slowly finned toward the newcomers that had been plopped into their tank.

"They are holding their barbels erect," the professorial voice said. "The tips are forming the oval base of a triangulation cone that has its apex in the taste buds of the caudal peduncle. The message center."

The killer fish abruptly stopped all motion, as if they were suddenly frozen in ice.

"Note," the commentator said, "the fighting fish are quiet. They have taste buds everywhere on their bodies, with a concentration in the barbels. More than three hundred thousand taste buds on a single fish."

The camera slowly panned back and forth on the now tranquil scene.

"Catfish," said the voice, "do not use vision either in feeding, or in social interactions. Mechanical sense receptors, including those of lateral line and electrical perception, and the senses of smell and taste control their behavior. Observe."

Spargo counted forty fish in the enormous tank. It now was impossible to distinguish which were the killers. The fish were almost motionless; some virtually lying on top of one another.

"A catfish love-in," the voice was amused. "At a certain population level catfish begin producing chemicals that halt all aggression in their community. Taste buds send signals to nerves that carry a message to the brain. Taste buds on gill arches have a continuous flow of water over them, making the fish instantly aware of the complete chemical composition of its environment."

Then, dramatically, "Behold."

The camera panned to another much smaller tank containing just two smaller cat-fish.

"This tank is divided into precise territories by these two fish. If one intrudes upon the ter-ritory of the other there is a fierce battle. So they keep to their own areas."

The camera moved to another tank holding a single large black catfish.

Spargo sat fascinated.

"This one has defeated and nearly killed the two smaller fish in the tank we just observed."

The arm and hand came into view again; the hand, holding a cup, dipped it into the tank. Spargo was certain that the man was a professor. But why the faceless secrecy?

The camera swung back to the tank with the two small catfish guarding their territories. The hand poured the cup of water into that tank.

The two catfish immediately darted to the far reaches of their territories. Then, suddenly, they sped to a large conch shell in the center of the tank and lay side by side hiding.

"Their chemical language made them instant friends through fear," the voice spelled out. "In that small cupful of water placed in their tank they tasted and smelled the scent of the fish that had formerly defeated them."

The camera moved to the tank with that large fish.

Spargo was astonished by the speed of the catfish reaction.

"In catfish combats, the loser not only becomes lower in status, but its growth is retarded. A loser can drop half of its weight in a month, even though it eats normally. The two fish in the conch shell were once the size of the big one that defeated them."

"But this one also lost a fight, thus its status."

The camera swung to yet another tank, giving Spargo the impression that the background was a large marine laboratory. This tank held a fish slightly larger than the black one that had defeated the two smaller fish hiding in the conch shell.

The camera went back to the tank of the black fish, the arm and hand netting the fish. The camera then recorded the hand moving to the tank of the larger fish that had defeated this netted black fish. It was somewhat confusing, but the camera moved slowly, and the voice explained each move.

The hand dipped the black fish in the net into the tank of the larger fish that once defeated it, holding it there.

Instantly the fish in the tank flashed in, attacking the fish in the net.

The hand moved the black fish, still in the net, to the tank where the two smaller fish hid in the conch shell. The large black fish was dumped out of the net into the tank. It slowly swam around the tank, ignoring the two small fish that it once had dominated.

Suddenly, the two small fish burst from the shell and viciously attacked the large fish from either side, the fierce concerted attack driving the large fish to the conch shell in a pitiful attempt to hide in a shell much too small for it to enter.

"Change in status," the voice concluded. "By chemical communication these two little fish were almost instantly able to tell that their enemy had been defeated by another, thus now was vulnerable. Consequently they have no fear now and attack. If we don't remove this large fish, it is likely that the two small ones will kill it."

The scene ended with the camera focused on the big catfish attempting to squeeze into the conch shell that was about half its size.

The wide eye of the camera also showed a long shot of a purple buoy leaning against a far wall. It sparked a faint memory for Spargo, but it was too fleeting and far away.

As the screen went blank, with no credits or production identification of any kind, Spargo thought, Were five men killed for this? Then, he corrected, out loud, "No, maybe six, counting Lundberg, with his head blown off here in Stamford."

Spargo remembered an old trick of the hunted red fox. Sometimes that astute animal ran among a herd of cattle, confusing its scent for the pursuing hounds behind it.

The police, too many of them, reversed that technique, rushing in like a herd of cattle,

162

destroying the scent of the quarry they hunted.

From past experience Spargo knew it would be wasted time to check the police on this one. They had a celebrated case, in their jurisdiction, of a scientist who had his head blown off, and they would resent competition. With their limited capabilities, small town cops were especially sensitive.

He must do what an English hunter in Africa had taught him: Learn to see this scene properly, project yourself out there where the eye is roving. Carefully examine the landscape, and look for evidence of something that doesn't normally belong on the scene. Is there a rock in a meadow that normally has no rocks?

This had happened to Spargo in Kenya. The hunter had shown him a meadow and asked him to examine it carefully. Spargo had. They returned to that same meadow the next day. The hunter asked Spargo if he noticed anything different in the meadow. Spargo saw a rock but thought nothing of it, and said he guessed not. As he and the hunter walked toward the meadow the rock leaped up and ran. It was an antelope.

What had Lundberg done that deviated

from the norm? Was he a loner who suddenly became interested in women, a talker who stopped talking, a stay-at-homer who had become a traveler? Why was he killed? Was it tied in with Ryal? How?

The report Carson had sent Spargo at the karate school detailed Lundberg's professional qualifications and his work schedule, the separation from his wife and subsequent divorce. It was all very routine and dull. His wife? She probably had been hacked at so often by the local police that her answers would come out by rote.

The trail was cold. If Lundberg had any connection with Vaughn, the missing scientist, no one had yet been able to put it together. And, as yet, no one knew exactly who Vaughn was or where he had worked.

Spargo was racing against time. He remembered an Italian saying regarding the enemy in such a situation. "*Ha il diavolo dalla sua.*" Whoever the adversary was certainly had the devil on his side all right. Spargo needed luck.

Stamford was a city not only preparing for the siege of overpopulation but welcoming it, large areas looking like they had been bombed out, had been cleared by Urban Renewal and were waiting to be filled up with commerce. Fifty major corporations had moved here from New York City, seeking tax breaks and urban living space and pace. Soon they would have neither.

As he walked the town, Spargo could see the twenty-one-story Landmark Towers, bleak as a cliff. North were some elegant shops, south the General Telephone and Electronics building, a glass pyramid afire in the morning sun.

A block ahead Spargo saw the sign MEN'S SHOP. ONLY THE ELEGANT ENTER. He entered to buy a shirt. The clerk looked like a ballet dancer overburdened in a dove-gray suit, mauve shirt, and dark purple tie. He was a baritone and worked at it.

"Sir. How may I help?"

"A shirt. Dark blue. Chamois, please. Brooks Brothers buttondown. Size sixteen, thirty-four."

"Brooks Brothers do not franchise, sir. But I have exactly what you want, slightly longer points —"

Spargo went along, talking about how the city was growing.

The clerk's face darkened. "*Everything* is growing. Especially crime. We're catching up with New York fast. We've been broken into four times in three months!"

"Progress brings problems," Spargo said. "I also was horrified to hear of that scientist who had his head blown off."

That set the clerk off on a conversational spree. Rape, mugging, arson.

Had he known the murdered man, a Mr. Lundberg, wasn't it?

No, scientists wore burlap, sackcloth or something.

Spargo headed north where a scattering of shops were valiantly fighting to retain their small-town identity. One was an authentic copy of a *salumeria* he had visited in Rome, burnt-skin salami, pepperoni, and two golden provolones as thick as Spargo's thigh hanging in the window. The cheese made him hungry. On a hunch he went into the shop. The proprietor was arranging cheese in a refrigerated case. *"Buon giorno, signore."* Spargo said brightly.

The man, large, with silvery, styled hair, smiled and responded, asking if Spargo spoke Italian.

Only a little, he said, but he liked the sound of the language. Spargo chatted about how much the shop reminded him of those in

Rome, how this town was growing, wondered how the merchant felt about it.

"I like the increase in business, but not the problems it brings." He pointed to iron-lattice frames leaning against a back wall. "I have to put those heavy things on every night when I close, or the animals will break the windows and steal everything I've got. Already the lifting has given me a hernia."

"A pity what a new population brings," Spargo said. "Do you think it caused the murder of that man at Janis? The one who had his head blown off?"

The merchant straightened. "Police?"

"No, no," Spargo said hastily, looking horrified. "Just a visitor. I stopped in to ask about a decent Italian restaurant where I could have lunch. I didn't mean to offend."

"I knew Mr. Lundberg," the man said. "A customer. This is also a coincidence. When he first came here to work for Janis he also stopped in to ask me if I knew a good Italian place. Because I sell cheese and am Italian, I get that question quite often. I will send you where I sent Mr. Lundberg well over a year ago. Fraboni's. The Frabonis buy all of their cheese here. Especially my aged Asiago for their pasta."

He tore off a piece of brown wrapping paper, took a pencil from his apron pocket and drew a diagram of streets for Spargo.

"It's an easy fifteen-minute walk. Tell them that Frigo's House of Cheese sent you."

Fraboni's was on one of the few remaining side streets in Stamford that had trees, leafy maples, and was relatively quiet, away from the main stream of traffic and commerce. It was in a renovated shake-shingled, two-story house with a modest sign, *fraboni's* in lowercase letters. The front door opened directly onto the dining room, just twelve tables with starched white tablecloths, apparently mama and daughter as waitresses, both dark, slender, smiling women. The tables were all occupied; there were three bold hand-lettered NO SMOKING signs in the room and two murals of Naples, one a sidestreet summer scene with pasta on racks and about a dozen women turning it to dry; the other was the cerulean bay without a boat on it. The colors were brilliant. Both were signed in the lower left corner, *d. fraboni.*

Beyond the dining room was a small barroom dominated by a gleaming dark oak bar where five men in vested suits sat having lunch and drinks. Two young male

168

bartenders, also dark and slender, resembling the women in the dining room but without smiles, were busy making the daily profit with drinks, martinis in the majority. Spargo found space at the far end, waiting until one of the bartenders came to him.

"Frigo's House of Cheese recommended you for the best dish of pasta in town," Spargo said easily. "Frigo didn't go into martinis. But I can see that he should have."

The bartender gave his first smile. "I think there'll be room for you at the bar in a little while if you want to have lunch here. Probably a longer wait for the dining room. How d'you like your martini?"

"Are you d. fraboni, who painted those good murals?"

The young man was surprised. "No, that's Dom at the other end of the bar." He turned to his brother. "Hey, Dom, you've got a fan. Likes your murals."

Dom put down a bottle of gin and walked over. "Thanks. Those murals have been there three years. You're the third guy who's noticed them. Congratulations on your good taste."

Spargo grinned. "And yours."

Dom went back to his territory.

His brother said, "Now. That martini. How?"

"Boodles," Spargo said. "Bare touch of Boissiére vermouth. Stirred. Straight up."

"Would you go for Beefeater? People in this town think Boodles is some kind of swindle."

Spargo laughed. "In a way it is. Sure, whatever you have is fine."

It was brought in a thin, stemmed wine glass, crisply cold. Spargo nursed it; the bartenders were busy, the businessmen at the bar were making small talk. When a stool was finally vacated, Spargo moved over, and Dom, the painter, walked down to him.

"Repeat?"

Spargo shook his head. "No, I'd like a little wine with my lunch. Another martini and I wouldn't taste either the vino or the food. I'm told that would be a shame."

Dom laughed. "You're sure not from this town. What's your name?"

Spargo gave him the name he was using, Sam Hall.

Dom gave him a vocal menu. Spargo selected a dish of linguine with white clam sauce, a salad of Boston lettuce with lemon juice and olive oil, no vinegar to spoil the flavor of the wine, which would be a half bottle of Soave Bertani.

Dom approved the selection. "Mama made

the linguine fresh this morning. The clams were brought in this A.M. also, by a fisherman cousin from Norwalk."

It lived up to the billing. Spargo beckoned Dom. "Please give Mama my compliments."

"Thanks, I'll tell her. She'll sure be pleased on account I think you know what you're talking about. Where are you staying in town? Come back for dinner this evening. Osso Bucco!"

Spargo told him what motel, regretting it immediately, but did make a reservation for dinner. "Town's sure bursting at the seams. Good for business though?"

Dom nodded. "But we got our regulars. Factories and such bring in some bad types and then the beasts of prey. See those 'no smoking' signs all over the dining room?"

Spargo nodded.

"We don't like smoking in that room. But we had to plaster them all over and enforce it because of the potters. The town's full of pot smokers. Sit there puffing away and spoil everybody's appetite. Makes you wanna vomit, not order a meal."

"Looks like you've got some other bad types too. Didn't a guy get his head blown off here? What was his name, Sunberg or something?"

"Arthur Lundberg," Dom said soberly. "Yeah, that's a strange one. The cops are hot to break that one down. Can't figure it out. Decent guy, minded his own business."

"You knew him?"

"Yeah. Lundberg came here once in a while. More often after he shed that big blond leech of a wife."

Business was slow now, the diners and drinkers gone from the bar. The other Fraboni brother came over.

"He liked our linguine too," he said. "With *calamari* sauce. Joked about it, said he was a marine biochemist all the way. Even his belly."

"Yeah," Dom broke in, "but a strange kinda guy in a way. Quiet. Always staring into space. Ask him a question, took a couple of minutes for it to register. Loosened up here a while back though. Took himself quite a load on."

He turned to his brother. "Eddie, what was that freak drink he drank like it was water or something?"

"Pisco sour," Eddie said. "These guys who really don't like to drink come up with some beauts. I lucked out on that one though on account of the time I spent behind the bar at the country club here couple years ago among the Brandy Alexander crowd."

Spargo said, "Pisco sour. South American, isn't it? Wonder why he wanted that instead of the other cuties, Adam's Apple, Wallbanger, or something?"

"Oh, he had a reason all right," Dom said. "Lundberg was the kinda guy that had to have a reason for everything he did. Like the squid in his pasta."

Eddie broke in. "Said he was going to the place the drink originated. Wanted to give it a try."

"Going to Pisco?" Spargo said. "When?"

"Not long before he lost his head."

A half hour after Spargo had departed, Dom looked at Eddie as they were washing and drying the bar glasses. "Pretty smooth, don't you think?"

"What?" Eddie said.

"That guy, Sam Hall. Got quite a lot out of us about Lundberg without even seeming to be interested. Everybody else gets all stirred up when they ask about our headless celebrity."

"Oh, I don't know. Natural. Like you said, the murder's got everybody interested. Better than TV. Makes Kojak Sunday school."

"But we got a hundred easy bucks involved here."

Eddie whistled. "Forgot. Yeah, that Asiatic guy, the specialist in letter-bomb crimes."

"Right. Said he'd deliver the century if we could come up with information about anybody except police nosing around. Hall's the first guy who found out, from us anyway, that Lundberg went to Pisco sour country. Get on the phone. Let's collect the hundred."

Spargo stopped at a roadside phone booth on the outskirts of Stamford. He would place one call, perhaps two. The report stated that the president of Janis Chemical Company, where Lundberg had worked, was J. K. Bolk. One of the State Police involved in the investigation was a Lieutenant Matt Johnson.

Spargo had a little difficulty at the switchboard until he stressed that he was State Police, *not* city, then he got through to Bolk immediately.

"Hello, Lieutenant," a thin voice said. "What can I do for you? How is the case coming along?"

"Slow, sir. Slow. But it's a complicated one, as you know. I have one last question, then we'll do our best to leave you alone. We all know how busy you are."

"Yes. What is it?"

"Could you tell me if Lundberg asked for any time off recently?"

"I'll have to ask Personnel. Hold a minute."

In forty seconds Bolk was back on the phone. "Yes. His mother was ill. In Vermont. He took a week and a half. Anything else?"

"No, sir," Spargo said. "Thank you very much."

One more call. Peruvian Embassy in New York. This time Spargo was State Department. His question got immediate results. Arthur Lundberg had indeed had his passport visaed for Peru.

CHAPTER THIRTEEN

From the air the nine Isles of Shoals look like a Spanish flotilla circling for a conference.

With a total of 205 acres, the isles – Appledore, Cedar, Duck, Malaga, and Smuttynose – are part of Kittery, Maine. Londoners, Seavy, Star, and White belong to Rye, New Hampshire.

At the turn of the century, these glacier-scarred, granite-domed little islands were exclusive summer resorts. Now, except for Appledore, which is headquarters for a university's teaching marine laboratory, and Star, with a hotel, they are mainly a natural paradise for gulls and other seabirds that come to them for summer breeding from a winter range extending southward to Bermuda, the West Indies, Texas, and the Yucatan.

Each Friday *The Queen Gull* leaves the harbor at Portsmouth, New Hampshire, promptly at 8 A.M. for Star Island, where the hotel, a rambling relic, is still mostly intact. Today, the weathered-shingled Victorian monstrosity, standing on the barren island like a scaly sea creature risen from the deep, is owned by a religious sect, The Devoted, their religion an admixture of Baptist and Holy Roller. *The Queen Gull* was a huge old ferry that could easily accommodate the two hundred Devoted whose members ranged in age from nine to ninety.

This morning as the old boat pulled out of the harbor sounding its horn, there was a man aboard who was not a member of The Devoted. There was nothing unusual about this, for anyone could board the ferry, spend a couple of hours roaming around Star Island, or sit on the broad veranda and watch the sea or the members of the sect at their croquet or volleyball games, then return to Portsmouth.

This non-member had brought his own tea in a thermos, and a delicate sandwich of wafer-thin Black Forest ham. He stood at the rail watching the herring gulls flow behind *The*

Queen like a long tail, munching his sandwich and drinking his tea. It was well over an hour out to the island, the boat moving slowly, but the time passing swiftly with the captain pointing out the highlights of the trip over the boat's public address system.

Smiling youths were waiting as *The Queen* docked, ready to carry luggage, although most of The Devoted preferred to carry their own, handle their own responsibilities, which was part of their religion.

The non-member waited until they had all disembarked, then left *The Queen* and walked to the far side of the island where a small outboard motorboat was tied up. He hopped in, untied the mooring, and cast off, revving up the motor. About a mile out, he idled the motor, opened an attache case, and took out a black hood that he slid over his head; then he headed out for an island that began to take shape before him.

This was Seavy, owned by an eccentric woman from Boston who refused to sell it, but did lease it on occasion. It was currently leased to a physical-fitness group that was using it for training purposes.

Two men were waiting at the small dock when the motorboat came chugging in, they, too, in black hoods. The hoods were constructed in such a way that they could be worn at all times, even at meals.

As the man leaped from the boat, one of the two on shore tied it up, the other bowed his head in respect to the visitor. "A radio signal has just arrived," he said, as they walked toward four old weathered houses on a rise toward the middle of the island. "Your immediate attention."

At the largest of the gray houses they were met by two more hooded men. One said, "I have written out the message. It is in your room."

His room was the largest, with a double bed, an old scarred oak dresser, two straight, wicker-bottomed chairs, a small desk and chair, and a tiny bathroom with a sink and a toilet. There were no rugs on the random-width hardwood floors. There was an ancient, musty smell in the room. Two paned windows overlooked the sea.

The rain had increased and waves were holding up foaming white heads. He stood and watched for a while, then went and sat at the desk. After he had read the transcribed radio message, he rose from the desk, went to the head of the stairwell, and called to the man below. "Please have Number One come. Thank you."

Number One was not really "number one." He himself was. But he was here only on weekends. Number One was permanent and in charge of the training. He had come direct from the mother land and was of the old family, the twelfth generation of the Brothers.

There were no names here, except on very rare occasions. He himself was called only N. All wore hoods, which was part of the ancient costume. When one in training had protested the hood, he had said, "I do not want personality from you. I want performance."

He himself thought the hoods, the numbers rather melodramatic and perhaps unnecessary. But the plan was Tokura's, and Tokura always knew what he was doing. He had thought of the formal training for industrial spies, a move that had netted their country billions of dollars. This ninja training was just another facet of the same planning. Strength combined with stealth had now become necessary, the ability to strike as well as to steal. N sighed. He did not like industrial espionage, no matter what its benefits. Stealing, kidnapping, other men's brainchildren was not his idea of inspiring work. He was a teacher, taking pride in his handiwork of skilled violence. Let the others plan, he thought.

The gathering of trainees, the instructions, the results, were a master pilot plan. If it worked well here it would be duplicated where needed in other countries. Tokura would soon be here himself, to survey what was being done and to press the search for that American marine scientist who had, according to the small clues they had purchased, apparently attained the unobtainable.

He heard Number One coming up the stairs, softly, gracefully, as usual. He rose from his desk and bowed. Number One bowed in return.

For a moment no word was spoken, then N said, "How is the program going?"

"Well. Our people, as expected, do well. Some of the others try, some do not try very hard."

N walked to the desk. "Has Number Five returned from Michigan?"

"I have heard nothing."

"For one of his skill, it was not a complicated mission. He should have reported. Send Number Seven to investigate. Cover: A car manufacturer from home making cost comparisons. We must know what happened.

This should have been done yesterday."

Abruptly, he changed the subject. "We will go to names. How is Sorg doing?"

"He is so superior. He likes only guns. He considers what we do here child's play."

N nodded. "We have had trouble with him. He does not follow orders. Sorg is able, but arrogant. His last two assignments were successful but messy. It was believed that a little time here would teach him discipline."

"No," Number One said. "No discipline."

"All right. I have just received a radio message. Apparently someone has picked up Lundberg's trail in Stamford, discovered that he went to Pisco. He is tall. Dark hair. Looks fit. Can be easily identified by small yellow flecks in gray eyes. We want Sorg to eliminate him if he reaches Peru. The Russian method. An accident. No guns. This is priority. We do not want that experiment uncovered."

N continued with his instructions. Sorg should be registered into The Club in the Country outside of Lima, which was under their control. Then if Sorg completed his mission, he was to be eliminated. "He does not follow orders," N said. "That is dangerous."

Number One bowed. "Is that all?"

"We have a man in that restaurant in Pisco

named for their famous raw fish dish. He has fugu?"

Number One's smile was in his voice. "If this man is so able that he evades Sorg, we will see that he eats our delectable fugu."

N nodded. "Yes, Ortiz in Pisco is a creature of habit. He will eat at that restaurant and he will order that raw fish dish, as he always does. He is alive because he knows nothing. Did not see our leader and Lundberg together. Doesn't know about the secret of the sea."

N sat at his desk. Turning, he said, "It is possible this other man may have gathered information that will lead him to the area where that scientist who fed Lundberg information worked. He must not leave Peru alive."

"I will put all plans into immediate operation," Number One said. "Will you join us and talk with the men soon?"

"Yes," N said. "I will be with you shortly. Do we have anything interesting for dinner? I discover that a ham sandwich is not food. It is a fabrication."

"I am sorry that we do not have fugu. But our men caught some fine sea bass this morning."

"Excellent! That alone makes the trip worthwhile. I haven't had a fish fresh from the sea since I was here last."

As Number One reached the door, N said, "If this man from Stamford somehow manages to leaves Peru alive —"

"I don't see how that is possible."

"No plan is perfect. Ours is weakened because his death must be an accident. We do not want to draw attention. But if somehow he leaves Peru alive, we may have to go to the direct method. Ninja method. Perhaps even you and I as a team. Our country must find this Vaughn, the scientist, first. From what we have learned from Lundberg it will be a disaster for us if any other country obtains this secret file."

"Try not to worry it so much. You are like a dog with a bone in its throat. Think about the sea bass. Our Peru plan will function well."

After Number One had gone, N went to the window and stood watching the sea. It had calmed, and several gulls were soaring. Beyond, along the horizon, he could see fishing boats, and above, a jet vapor trail, pluming out as if a cloud had just been set afire.

He'd have to move now, go talk to the men, watch some exercises. This was an elite force;

most were his countrymen, but there were some foreigners, too, men who could easily be used and not identified as his people. These were the mercenaries, the Sorgs, used but not completely trusted.

The island was a place of scrubby, stunted bushes, rocks that stood like miniature pyramids, and areas overgrown with poison ivy. But a wide beach curved along the outer edge where it faced the west; the sand, white, smooth, hard-packed, was the ideal place to conduct exercises and assemble the men. They often worked until the sun sank into the sea.

Today, the thirty men were there awaiting N. He walked slowly, hooded head up, watching the sun above the horizon, assessing the amount of time he would have to talk and watch the performances before dusk.

There was a cliff face on the east side of the island, sheer, vertical rock. That would have to be scaled as darkness fell.

The men were already into preparing for the work ahead, convincing themselves they were turning into leopards, their wills forcing them into a different phase, the old ninja way. As their breathing became deeper, they counted aloud, backward, from an imaginary flight of stairs, focusing their "five" minds onto a single point of concentration.

They then performed two hundred knuckle pushups, then fifty wrist pushups, the wrists supporting the entire weight of the body.

While they rested, breathing hard, N talked.

"I will be quoting Andrew Adams from his *Invisible Assassins*, or partially quoting Mr. Adams, for he is incorrect in his assumption that the ninja existed only from the thirteenth to the seventeenth centuries. The ninja lives today. Four of your teachers directly descend from thirteenth-century ninja families and have been trained in the art almost from the day they were born. You know them as Numbers One, Two, Three, and Four."

He went on to explain how the ninja's ancient clans had created the secret, most strange and chilling art in all of Asia, Ninjitsu, incorporating Bushido discipline as well as the skills of all martial arts known at that time. Swordsmanship, bow and arrow, spear, stick, rapid sword draw, chain, and scythe.

"And *kumi-uchi*, unarmed combat," N said. "As you know, I give some instruction in that. In judo. I will not attempt to teach you fifty takedowns, but only three or four of the most effective that relate to body structure and mind."

N walked to a mound covered with glittering objects. "Here, all with their own special names, are ninja weapons. Daggers, dirks, darts, star-shaped spurs, medieval brass knuckles, garrotes, caltrops, lead-weighted bamboo staves, rope ladders, grappling hooks, guns, grenades, smoke bombs, eyeblinding powders, acid-spurting tubes."

N told them that they would be taught to become proficient in many of these ninja weapons, also in modern guns, knives, and acids that kill instantly.

"We are not teaching you to kill," he said. "We would rather you did not. But if you must, then you will be prepared. The ninja way, which, in itself, is enough to put terror in the heart of any opponent."

He said that they also would be taught the art of disguise, another ninja accomplishment. "Ninja do not always wear this black hood and black costume. Only at night, and only when great stealth is required. We want you to be able to appear as a postman, a priest, a carpenter, a member of the opposition. This means if you go on a mission you must be completely schooled in manners, geography, customs, language, personal backgrounds. Here, in the United States, this won't be too difficult. Our own leader will demonstrate that one day soon."

He pointed out that Seiko Fujita, a ninja descendant, claimed that a ninja could jump over seven feet vertically and walk the 350 miles between Tokyo and Osaka in three days.

"So we want you physically fit. You must learn to scale sheer cliffs, stay submerged under water for several minutes, and, through reduced breathing techniques, appear to be dead to deceive enemies.

"You must learn to use the *tonki*, the small throwing weapons, darts, dirks, and the star-shaped pointed *shuriken*. They can be easily hidden and with them you often can best even a man with a drawn gun."

He told them that tonight six of them would be fitted with the *shuko*, a spiked hand. With an instructor leading, they would then scale the cliff-face on the east side of the island.

N beckoned two men. "Numbers Two and Three will now engage in combat. They have been doing this since they were twelve years old. Watch carefully. Number Two, on the left, will be using the bamboo staff, or *shinobi-zue*. Three will carry the *kyoketsu-shogi*."

The two men walked slowly toward one another. Number Two seemed to be unarmed;

Number Three carried a simple staff, which he used as a walking stick.

Suddenly, Number Two whipped a cord from around his waist, threw it at Number Three. It had a round metal ring on the end, which snaked around the staff defensively raised by Number Three. Using it adeptly, Number Two rapidly drew him close, also yanking a double-pointed knife from his waistband. Seemingly pulled off balance, Number Three appeared to stumble. But as he fell forward, he flipped his wrist and a long knife appeared at the end of the staff. Quickly he held it against Number Two's throat.

Both men stopped the action and bowed.

The assembled men applauded.

"Do not underrate the old ninja weapons and methods. They are weapons of surprise," N said sharply. "Using either of the two weapons just demonstrated, a skilled man could dispatch about any armed opponent."

He then told them that they would assemble here tomorrow morning at eight for judo instruction.

As he wheeled around and walked back to his quarters, flanked by the four ninjas, N had only one thing on his mind. He hoped that Sorg would perform his last mission on earth successfully.

CHAPTER FOURTEEN

All the way back to Manhattan that purple buoy Spargo had seen in the film gnawed away at his memory like a tiny creature frantically attempting to dig its way out of an earthen cave-in, but never quite making it. The elusiveness bothered Spargo. His memory had saved his life on several occasions. Was he losing some of the mental attributes that had given him secret strengths?

The film was strange. How did the fact of fish that tried to kill one another, and communicated chemically, add up to the scramble to get the film? Ryal first, the three dead men in Warren? What was its message?

Spargo was aware that it wasn't exactly news

that fish, and other creatures too, had their own methods of communications.

He remembered reading about the remarkable crow that had special calls for assembly, alarm, for locating food, summoning one another. One psychologist had even proved that each crow in a flock gives itself a sound-name, a caw-name, which can come in long or short caws, with long or brief pauses between the caws. He found that one crow would declare that its name was *caw-caw*, another *caw-caw-caw*, and they consistently used these names to identify one another.

So humans weren't the exclusive communicators. Thus the message in the film was a subtle one that he hadn't been able to read.

Again, he rented a projector and screen and took them to his apartment that he still managed to keep in Gramercy Park, an elegant little third-floor walkup in a rose-brick Mansard-roof building that he had had for years. Quickly he set up the screen and projector and ran the film.

Nothing.

He ran it again. Still nothing. Again. Then again. Zero. He decided to rest a bit, make a needed Boodles on the rocks. Then he sat trying to concentrate.

Why would a buoy mean anything to him? Was the color important? Or was it the buoy itself?

Then he thought with distaste of tests the Agency had made of the human brain a few years ago, hoping to be able to penetrate and command the brain's functions, and thus the thinking of the opposition.

They had conclusively proved that inside the human skull two brains work together side by side, each with a different perspective and function. The brain had two hemispheres, with a bridge, the corpus callosum, between each hemisphere with its own duties. The left hemisphere controls the right side, the right, the left side. Each eye communicates with both hemispheres, but the visual fields are divided. Signals travel quickly from one hemisphere to the other through the corpus callosum, but a direct signal to either hemisphere from the outside is faster and more accurately perceived than a message relayed from one side to the other.

He remembered the young male "volunteer" who had had his brain bridge, the corpus callosum, surgically severed. The right hemisphere then could not relay information to the left brain hemisphere. They put an apple in the man's hand. The left hemisphere could not identify the apple because that information was trapped on the other side.

The volunteer sat with the apple in his hand, saying over and over, "Shit! Shit! Shit!" Three hours later when he still could not identify the apple, he began to get hysterical and threw the apple in the face of an interrogator.

Spargo sat trying to bring his memory fully alive by recalling those brain experiments, sorry that he remembered the man with the apple. Let's see, he thought, the right hemisphere has the artistic and musical ability, spatial perception. The left handles language and has the analytic ability. Thus the left, the language specialist, would see the word *fish* spelled out on a fish face drawing, while the right would recognize the face without identifying the letters.

Letters. Did the buoy have any letter, or even figure identification?

He went to his desk, got a magnifying glass, started the film, stopped it at the buoy and bent and studied it with the magnifying glass.

There, faintly, on the bottom left were the lower-case black letters *j. l. o. i.*

J.L.O.I. J.L.O.I. Meaningless.

He left the film on and went back and sat

staring at the buoy, trying to make associations. Buoy. Water. Boat. Did he own a boat? No. Did he ever rent one? No. Wrong. Yes — three years ago. He had leased a motor-sailor for two weeks to get away from the world. Where did he go? Martha's Vineyard. Nantucket. Where else? He sat back with a sigh of relief. Jacob's Landing Oceanographic Institute at Jacob's Landing. He had come through a forest of little bobbing purple buoys, all marked j.l.o.i. He had touched port there at historic Jacob's Landing to spend some time on the Cape.

He got up and switched off the projector, rewound the film, placed it on his desk for packaging, rolled up the screen, and put the projector back into its case.

He sat, thinking, wanting to rush up there immediately and forget about Peru and Arthur Lundberg. But he had trained himself to take a situation in steps. It was chess. Forget that and you fumbled. He would go ahead, trying to discover why the murdered Lundberg had made a secret journey to Peru, then tackle the Cape. He had a hunch it all began with Lundberg.

But what about some sort of action at the Cape now? How? Simple. Josef! He was authorized to hire him. Josef's phone rang for a long time. Spargo let it ring. He probably was with his pigeons, but there was a bell outside, so if he was there he'd answer eventually.

He did, a gruff "Hello."

All Spargo had to say was hello. He could almost see Josef's sudden alertness.

"You clean?"

"Sweep it for bugs twice a day, Spargo. Trouble?"

"No."

"I'm glad. I thought maybe I brought you some hassle with that creep who trailed me to the karate school."

"No, I'm employed. Wages good. Been authorized to bring you in. If you want."

"Let me hear."

Spargo gave him a terse rundown. "I'll save most of it until I see you. These are the bits and pieces."

He told him briefly about the strange film. "I'll mail it to you there, special handling. Bury it. Well. We may need it later. But I don't want it here in my place, and I don't want either of us to carry it. I figure six men have been killed because of the message I can't read in that film."

"Six? You got some fun and games going on

this one. Think I'm up to it?"

Spargo laughed. "If you aren't I'm in trouble. You taught me everything I know."

Josef grunted. "Hardly. Okay. I'll get my neighbor to feed the pigeons. He'll steal a few squabs and say the rats got 'em. He won't be wrong. How long will we be on this one? What's my paycheck?"

"What do you want?"

"This cutting into yours?"

"No."

"Five hundred a week. Remember, I still have to get up pigeon feed and I won't be here to peddle my squabs to the great gourmets."

"You're a bargain. I don't know how long we'll be at it. Does it matter?"

"Not really. I'll be there. Where?"

"Cape Cod. Falmouth. Fancy motel there. Beachcomber. Decent food. I stayed there once. The tourist season's on the build, so get going after you receive the film. Book us each a double room. Not close to one another. We're not penny-pinching on this one. So take the rooms on both sides too. Build a protective vacuum around us. You know the routine. In the back. Overlooking the pond. Make it loose. We're not sure of length of stay. Or when our friends will arrive for those other rooms. If you just happen to let them know we're IRS that won't be bad either. Also, if you can do it without ostentation, see if you can find out anything about a scientist, could be with the Jacob's Landing Oceanographic Institute. Name, Allan Vaughn.

"Before you leave, go to Nicky and have a couple of IRS ID's run through. Tell him I said keep it quiet. Use one of your names that you have a driver's license to back up. I'll be Tom Judson on this one."

"Why IRS?" Josef grunted. "I hate those shits. I don't even want to *pretend* to be one of those miserable, sneaky mice."

"I'm assuming that where we're going foundations are pretty big. Scientists are out of touch with reality. Their experiments need foundation money. I heard of one guy who spent a million in ten years trying to prove that sea worms living at a certain depth actually came through a crack in the ocean floor, from another world. Never proved it, but I guess he had fun. I've a hunch that it will be natural for the IRS to mosey around and see if everything is legitimate. And, face it, in our great democracy most people are forced to treat the IRS with respect. They've got a gun at everyone's head."

"Okay," Josef said grudgingly. "But are you sure Nicky's still in business?"

"He did a job for me a month ago. He's at the same old place. See you on the Cape. Watch your back. Don't make waves. Wait until I get there."

"Where you going to be?"

"Nowhere," Spargo said.

"Sorry. Been out of touch. One team member should never tell the other where he is. The opposition could nail one and get the information from the other."

"Something like that. I'll see you in about a week, or less. I hope."

"So do I."

Nicky Victor. Spargo thought about him for a moment. In his early seventies now. Used to work for the Government Printing Office. Genius with a printing press. Do anything. He did it once too often. Printed some fake airline tickets for some friends. The Agency got wind of it, backed him into a corner. Got him to resign from the government job, set up his own business in a small town in Virginia, backed by the Company. He turned out passports, ID's, could duplicate exactly anything that had ever been printed, yen, rubles, government bonds. Basically honest, he had never been tempted to turn out currency. But he would have been the master of it. Nicky was so good that his business became successful legitimately. Spargo had done him a couple of favors, including getting him his largest legitimate customer. Consequently, all of their transactions remained secret.

CHAPTER FIFTEEN

The tray was lined with turquoise velvet, the knives glittering like jewels. They were all of fine Solingen steel, made in that German region where men had been masters of knife-making for two hundred years. These were chef's knives, ranging in size from a three-inch parer to the foot-and-a-half chef's broad chopping knife.

Salwa was in the center, inconspicuous between a long, slender boning knife and the chopper. Spargo had used this cutlery salesman routine before. He was going to Peru to sell his wares to the chefs in restaurants and hotels. He had credentials to match. It had two advantages: It was the perfect way to get

Salwa into any country, past any scanner or customs. She was now legitimate. It also gave him a fair cover enabling him to move rather freely.

No airport or customs man had ever looked at the case of knives, lifted Salwa out and said, "This isn't a chef's knife. This is a concealed weapon." Beautiful as she was, her talent was lost there among all the shiny Solingen steel.

Spargo lifted her out now to put her through her morning paces. He slid her into her sheath and practiced holding his right arm down, Salwa sliding into his hand, smooth rosewood handle always falling exactly right. It had taken many months of practice to perfect this. A fumble could mean Spargo's life. Salwa had been handmade by a Solingen master out of a solid bar of the finest carbon steel. Like all true masters, he had breathed life into her. For Spargo, she was truly alive.

He thought of Josef now, his instructor, and, more important, his friend. A Hungarian who hated the Soviets, and tried to pass that hate on to all of his students ("Hitler was a kind and thoughtful man compared with those in the Kremlin today. Remember, always, they are your deadly enemy, out to take your freedom. They are the enemy of God and of

Man, respecting neither"), Josef was a master with a knife, unbelievably sure and swift.

He could sidespin a knife to cut a dangling rope, throw its balanced weight to halve an apple, hurl it with enough force to split a thick pine board, or have it suddenly appear in his hand and with a delicate, lightning thrust send it through the belly of a practice dummy.

Shortly after they had met at The Playhouse in rural Virginia they had been walking on the grounds taking a break from instruction, when thirty feet away a rattlesnake glided out of a stone wall on the backside of the property and lifted its flat radar head to have a look at them.

Josef had his knife out faster than Spargo could snap a finger and sent it in a sidespin, nearly decapitating the snake. He shoved the knife into the soil to clean it, then spent ten minutes polishing it with a pocket handkerchief while he talked and they watched the snake's wiggles grow weaker. The serpent hadn't even had time to muster a rattle.

A poet, Josef. That day he went on to say that ancient grimoires or magic texts recorded that the knife not only had the power of Mars but also the strength of Justice.

"A knife," he said, holding the blade up to see if he had removed all trace of rattlesnake, "stands for full physical power, for charisma, the ultimate in the art of persuasion."

Josef despised the gun as loud, coarse, a bully that required small skills and no talent. He also believed that the knife had psychological advantage, arousing terror in most men.

His knife was lightly weighted for accurate throwing, had a needle point and razored edges, and with his skill and power behind a throw his students believed he could kill an Angus bull with one flip. He kept his knife in an ingenious triple-lined glove-leather sheath strapped above his right wrist, handle end down so he could, by stretching his hand straight out, summon it instantly from his sleeve as if it were alive.

Josef had a peculiar way of walking: He usually wore laced, highly polished black shoes and stepped gingerly, as if testing his footing, fearful of breaking through the earth's crust. But he was fearful of nothing. It was merely that he was as careful of his feet as he was his hands. Spargo discovered why Josef had this abnormal regard for those elegant feet.

"They always expect you to throw a punch, make a karate chop or pull a gun," Josef had said during one instruction period. By then Spargo was imitating the master and had a sleeve sheath exactly like Josef's. It would take him years to have as talented a blade but he was working on it.

This day, Josef had said, "Draw your knife swiftly."

He did as directed. Fast as a flick of light, he had the knife kicked out of his hand with the point of Josef's right shoe. Spargo never expected it, and was shocked.

"Not Jap nonsense," Josef said. "Not jujitsu or karate. French. *Tirer la savate.*" He recalled the bawdy World War I remark about how the French women so imaginatively make love with their mouths and the men fight with their feet.

He told Spargo that he had learned *savate* in Paris twenty years ago and that with the technique he had defeated armed men twice his size.

"I prefer it to karate. With practice you can see any karate move coming, get set for it. Not so with *savate*. And when you are adept you can kick backward as well as forward."

He said that a real karate master, however, probably could give him some trouble. "If so, then I use the knife and always win." ·

Seeing Spargo's expression, he said, "Dirty pool? We should fight to the finish, each using his own unarmed technique?"

He shook his head. "No. In any kind of a fight, success is all that counts. Even if you have to saw the guy's balls off. Never forget that. There are no Marquis of Queensbury rules of fair play in this business. You win. Or you lose. It's that simple."

Savate gave Spargo more trouble than the knife. Josef had him begin with difficult deep-bend exercises to limber him up for high kicks that began with Spargo kicking as high as his own head, then painfully progressing to the point where he could reach two feet over his head. This was difficult and took several weeks for him to do it easily without feeling that he was tearing ligaments in his legs.

Josef then had him kick a bag of sand with his bare feet until he thought that his toes were merging into one great blister. With shoes on he assaulted the heavy bag, kicking it at exact points outlined in chalk, learning to spear his driving foot straight out at varying elevations.

For three months, a demanding male ballet dancer taught Spargo how to properly exercise leg muscles, whirl gracefully and remain balanced, and high-kick with precision. Spargo practiced for hours at a stretch, kicking golf balls from Josef's hand without touching Josef's fingers. It took six months to win grudging approval from Josef, this granted only when Spargo was equally adept with both feet in keeping a soccer ball in the air for one hour. Soaked with sweat, exhausted nearly to the point of hating that thin, sardonic face, he finally heard Josef say, "All right, Spargo. Tomorrow we box with the feet."

Substituting moccasins for leather shoes, Josef kicked Spargo in the head six times, groined him, weakened his thighs with speared-foot jabs, pummeled his leg muscles until they were sore to the touch.

Spargo barely touched Josef seven times. But Josef was happy about it. He advised Spargo to target his kicks to the knee, stomach, or throat. "Use the testicles only as a last desperate resort," he said, eyes atwinkle. "Remember, you too are a man."

A walking case of murder unsuspected, Josef. He conquered by surprise and skill. It was believed that he could take any man at the CIA Playhouse, except possibly Norikura; he would not even practice-fight with the Japanese who was also giving Spargo lessons in karate.

Once, though, when a visiting *jujitsu* specialist challenged him to a fight, Josef shrugged, turned away as if refusing, then winged around in a blur of motion and kicked him under the chin. For good measure he had his knife at his throat before the wonderfully agile Japanese expert could get off his back.

Spargo respected him. He also had high regard for Norikura and his skill, and liked him as a man, the reason he had been helping his old Japanese instructor at his karate school.

But Spargo considered karate mainly exercise, his version of jogging to keep himself in shape.

He daily practiced the skills Josef had honed. Today in his apartment in Gramercy Park, he danced around, spearing his right foot in various heights and positions, front, then kicking straight out behind, continuing until he was breathing hard.

Then he spent ten minutes with Salwa, sliding her into his hand. Finally a round hard green watermelon was placed on a stool at the far end of the living room. He brought Salwa from her sheath twenty times and flipped her with accuracy into the same slit in the melon until it split and fell apart.

He cleaned up that mess and went into his bedroom and packed for Peru.

The Lufthansa 747 came in hawk-high. Sighting Peru dimly through the cloud cover, Spargo could see the stewardess' words assuming geographic shape beneath them.

"Ladies and gentlemen, *señores, señoras, y señoritas*, below is Peru, the third-largest country in South America, bounded on the north by Ecuador and Colombia, east by Brazil and Colombia, south by Chile, west by the Pacific Ocean."

Three times the size of California, some of the half-million square miles of Peru could be seen in their diversity as the plane made its descent; the long, narrow ribbon of rainless desert along the coast, the fifty fingers of rivers pointing down from the mountains, girdling their route to the sea in green, the high plateaus, the sun converting the snow-peaked Andes into mountains of silver, the interior of the country unfurling its great dark carpet of tropical rain forests and jungles, the fourteen-hundred-mile coast a long unbroken streak of seablue, reflecting like a jagged mirror, throwing the sun back.

The two stewardesses who spoke English

like Berlitz and Spanish like poetry came along the aisle chanting "Fazen your seabelts," as the jet changed the pitch from that steady great heartbeat to a series of disturbing roars.

Four taxis had brought Spargo to New York's Kennedy Terminal, expensive but an effective put-off for even the most patient of tails. When he left each taxi Spargo spent time shopping for a book, some handkerchiefs, going out side exits.

There may have been no need for the wild animal act, but the training was so ingrained that it became habit-pattern. He could see no one at the airport, and boarded the plane quickly, at the last minute, through the boarding ramp. No one would have had time to buy a ticket and follow him. He seriously doubted that anyone on the plane had any interest in him, including the stewardesses who were paid to have an interest.

They were losing altitude rapidly now, the 747 dropping into a heavy tunnel of cloud, vision mostly gone, but Spargo could see the right wing bend and flex, absorbing and cushioning the wind-current shock.

Suddenly, through a rip in the cloud mass, there was Lima spreading before him, modern buildings standing tall in sun haze; beyond, the gleam of the sea.

The unknown assassin has the odds in his favor. He is the man who isn't there. Even if the intended victim is a professional, he cannot be on guard constantly. There are always moments of letdown.

Sorg thought of this as he stood leafing through folders at the Government Information booth at Lima's Jorge Chavez International Airport, fifty feet from where the man he was to terminate was arranging for a Rambler, the only U.S. model available from the rental agency.

This was the man all right: Over six feet, dark hair, looked lean and hard, complexion dark, a little leathery as if he spent lots of time in the sun. But the clincher was the eyes; light gray with gold flecks floating in them. With those eyes, he was a marked man. Why doesn't he wear colored contact lenses? Sorg wondered.

Sorg stayed within earshot until he had what he wanted, hotel and name. Not Sam Hill this time, the name the man used in Stamford. Now he was Tom Judson. Sorg had also been several passengers behind this Judson when he went through Customs and opened his box of kitchen knives. Perhaps he really was the salesman he claimed back in Stamford.

Sorg's instructions were to get to this man's hotel first and arrange an accident. Whoever he is working for will know something is wrong, but they will not be able to prove it. Make it simple, he was told. Use the Russian weapon. Then put him into the bathtub, run some water, prop him so he doesn't slide into the water. Heart attack. Happens all the time.

The "Russian" weapon probably hadn't been invented by the Soviets, but they used it more than anyone else. It was noiseless, simple, terribly effective. A cylinder of compressed hydrocyanic gas, it was fired from a unit that looked like a flat, plastic, easily concealed water pistol. The cylinder was pierced by a metal pin when the trigger was pulled, releasing the gas and spraying it five feet.

It wasn't a weapon that pleased Sorg; he preferred a silenced .38 at close quarters, a brain shot, or, for distance, a scoped .308 rifle with soft-nosed bullets. Both certain weapons. This gas gun had two faults: No range. You had to be close to the target. And it could backfire. A mask has to be worn so if the spray squirted back you were protected. But Sorg had mastered the technique. He had used it successfully five times.

He had no trouble with a taxi. He'd be at the hotel in plenty of time before Judson, or whoever he was, got there. Arranging a car rental as Judson was doing in this banana country would be a big deal.

Sorg's driver, a thin old man who looked like an Indian with tuberculosis, opened the door of the old beat-up Fiat like it was a Rolls, and tried to talk in broken English on the way in to Lima. Sorg looked at him coldly, and the old man gave up. Sorg didn't like to chatter. He wanted to think about the job ahead. It was half of the pleasure. The Fiat wasn't much better than a bicycle, but the old Indian was pretty good in traffic and they made time.

Lima reminded Sorg of Mexico City. But there were more Indian peasants here with those shawl-like things over their shoulders, wearing what looked like discarded old derby hats or a combination of a derby and a high-crowned uncreased weathered fedora. Like birds, the men wore brightly-colored clothing, the women dull green or brown. But, as in Mexico, there were many smartly dressed men and women. It was a large city, which surprised Sorg.

They came spinning along Paseo Colon, a

hundred-and-fifty-foot-wide boulevard with a green tree-fringed park at its end. Buildings they passed were Spanish colonial style, two-storied with pale pink roofs, the tiles over-lapping like fish scales. Almost every building had an ornate balcony overlooking the boulevard.

The Bolivar Hotel also was big, its facade covered with ornately worked stone that made the Hiltons look like hunting lodges.

Sorg sauntered to the desk. The clerk, a young man with no hair and a pencil moustache, raised his eyes from the register.

"Judson," Sorg said breezily. "Does he have his usual suite?"

"No," the clerk said, almost by reflex. "Room 490. Shall I – Señor. Señor –"

Sorg ignored him, throwing a quick thanks over his shoulder as he went back out the front door. He had located the bank of elevators and a stairwell.

He waited outside until a car pulled up with five people. He was close behind as they went into the hotel, and he had no trouble entering the stairwell without being observed by the clerk, now busy with registrations.

A thick moss-green rug ran along the cor-ridor. Sorg went across it softly as a cheetah.

No one around. Good. Judson was probably clogged up in traffic outside the city. It would have taken him at least a half hour to rent the car, check it out, and get on his way. Sorg probably had at least fifteen minutes on him.

Sorg took the little flat gas gun out of his inside jacket pocket. He checked it. The gas mask was strapped around his waist under his loose vest. He'd have time to put the mask on after he got inside and selected the kill position.

Studying the door, he saw that it had an ordinary lock, which he could easily spring. He took a plastic credit card out of his hip wallet and ran it quickly through the crack. He sprung it on the second try.

Sorg turned around and quietly closed the door.

As he faced into the room Spargo threw a *tameshiwari*, a fingertip thrust that could smash through a board.

It struck Sorg's nose, crushing it.

The pain was so surprising and intense that Sorg screamed. But he also pulled the trigger of the gas gun.

Spargo's next finger thrust nearly tore out Sorg's right eye. The power of the thrust whirled Sorg around.

The gas gun fell to the floor, throwing its spray directly into Sorg's face.

Spargo ran to the far side of the room and threw open the balcony doors. He went outside and stood, retching and coughing.

His instant reaction saved his life.

He stood on the balcony, gasping for air, watching Sorg writhing on the floor. When the body was inert, Spargo waited another fifteen minutes.

Then he came into the room, still wobbly, and opened all the other windows. He went back onto the balcony and stayed there for another half hour, not sure of what kind of gas it had been, but fully aware of its deadly swiftness.

Sorg was the passport name. Spargo knew it. A Dane, it was thought, headquartering in Asia. Freelance. One of the good ones. He went through all of Sorg's pockets, carefully examining everything.

Spargo was puzzled at how they had reached him. He would try to work that out later. One fact was clear: He was on the right track. Someone didn't want him here. Why?

The unknown factor had saved his life. Just as it had brought him to Peru. The girl at the car rental agency at the airport had been unusually efficient and helpful, suggesting that she take care of all of the time-consuming paperwork, send him to the hotel by taxi and have the rented Rambler delivered to the hotel. He had probably beat Sorg to his hotel room by minutes.

Spargo drove with the dawn along the winding road by the sea, the coming light shimmering on the water. Pastel-colored fishing boats, sails unfurled, were heeling toward the open sea pushed by an offshore breeze.

As the light came he could see people begin to move, walking along the side of the road, some driving llamas before them. The dark, hard-faced men and women in ponchos and straw hats probably were *Quechua,* numerically largest of the Sierra Indians. The peculiar long-necked animals made the scene unreal, like a scenario written for a travelogue.

He was counting heavily on luck. He always did, contrary to the rules of his training that went, "Luck is a fickle factor; count on your physical and mental assets, not the intangible."

But he had always been lucky; perhaps it was something one was born with, like a good memory, or a talent for painting or making money.

He was lucky now as he entered the outskirts of Pisco, but he did not know it then. Prodding his memory alive on the purple buoy had made him especially sensitive to anything marine. Thus when he saw the building by the sea, the name *Instituto Marino* over its main entrance, he slowed and drove into the parking area to the left of the building.

He sat looking at the sea, searching for an approach that would be logical. He could hardly use his knife-salesman routine with these specialists of the sea. He would have to use the name Tom Judson; it was on his passport, and a visaed passport was necessary to enter or depart from this country.

Would the news of Lundberg's death have reached Peru? Would it matter? Could he be investigating the death? Or would that close doors? Probably.

What about the same approach they would be using on the Cape: IRS? Tax man, give him the opportunity to perfect the technique. But how would that go? He was in Peru on another matter and had been instructed to come here to substantiate that Lundberg was actually here on business. Suspicion, questions would be natural. What business? Lundberg was making a tax deduction for the entire trip, and this was just a check. We are certain that Mr. Lundberg would not attempt to cheat his government. But inasmuch as he, Judson, was already here, it should be a simple matter to clear up.

He ran through it twice. Sounded feasible. Unless they asked for more identification than his passport. If he played it well, perhaps they wouldn't ask for any identification.

He apparently played it well, for he had no difficulty. He also had the impression that the woman, a fat lady of much scientific self-importance and a moustache, sort of liked the idea of the North American wiggling under a tax scrutiny.

"That would be Carlos Ortiz you want, Señor. He handle most of the visiting dignitaries. He has perfect English. I remember that he been with your Mr. Lundberg while he stay here."

There was Pizarro in Carlos Ortiz. He was the physical embodiment of the fact that Peru had once been Spain's most important vice-royalty in South America.

Slender, with dark hair and eyes, he had a languidly graceful way of moving. But the Indian was there too, in the coarseness of the hair and the patient placidity of the eyes. The Inca also showed in the regal manner that he carried his fine-boned head, and in the long, straight nose.

Ortiz went with Spargo as he registered at the Hotel Paracas, a small white-washed place with a shiny green-tiled roof, a plant-filled terrace, and a long, lofty view of the sea. They had decided that they would talk over lunch. Ortiz had a favorite place.

Spargo drove and Ortiz talked, after saying how much he liked automobiles from the United States. "Their names," he said. "I like their names. Take this one. Rambler. Catchy, no. Apropos, yes? This is what I mean. I do not understand Buick, Oldsmobile, Cadillac, but Pinto, another beauty, eh?"

He liked to talk and soon was into Peru, saying that it was fortunate that his country was ruled by a military junta, that other than Cuba, it was the only leftist government in Latin America.

"Most of us believe," he said, "that to be ruled by generals is an excellent idea, especially now that Chile and Ecuador are beginning a strange arms buildup."

They drove to a small restaurant, Ceviche,

in the harbor. As they sat at a table covered with a blue fabric matting with intricate designs of fish cleverly woven into it, Ortiz said seriously, "We have just accomplished a miracle of which the world should be proud. We have actually begun the difficult task of taking oil from the jungles of the Amazon Basin and are bringing it out on the Amazon River to Brazil. In another year we should be self-sufficient in oil. In one more year we will become an exporting nation."

Spargo didn't interrupt; the fact that Ortiz liked to talk was an asset. If he talked as freely about Lundberg.

"You know about our Incas?" Ortiz asked.

Spargo patiently shook his head. He could listen well. And wait.

"Fourteen Incas ruled Peru. For over three hundred years. Taught the people how to farm on steep mountainsides, worked out involved systems of irrigation, used guano for fertilizer, controlled soil erosion, used stone in construction —"

"Lundberg," Spargo said softly. "Was he interested in the Incas?"

"He was impressed with the fact that though they had no form of writing, or even any knowledge of the wheel, our Incas built fantastic highways linking the four parts of their empire. They even invented a decimal counting system and solar and moon calendars."

He laughed, a dry, embarrassed sound. "I am sorry, Mr. Judson. This is not getting your job done. But few people have much to be proud of anymore. Scratch a Peruvian and he bleeds Inca blood."

He forced himself to stop the dialogue. "You must be hungry. Let us order lunch. But first, let us have a drink. Shall we try our national drink. Pisco sour?"

Spargo said that he had never had one and would like it. Ortiz went on to tell him that the name of the restaurant, Ceviche, was also the name of a popular fish dish, raw fish, corvina, marinated in lime and lemon juice, garlic, chilies, red onion. He recommended that as first course, and then *Arroz con Pato*, duck with coriander leaves, and beer.

When the drinks arrived and they were sipping, Ortiz said, "Pisco is our brandy. Egg white, lemon juice, and sugar give it its name. That and the fact that it originated right here. Mr. Lundberg was very fond of the drink."

"As he has claimed in his tax return," Spargo said, "he was here concerning his specialty, the sea. Is that correct?"

"Oh, yes," Ortiz said. "He was here to make a study of our famous anchovy. *E. ringens.*"

The waiter arrived with the ceviche. It was not the same waiter who had served the drinks. This one was pure Indian, coarse coal-black hair covering his head like a bathing cap, features blunt as molded clay. Ortiz looked at him with interest as the waiter picked up the empty glasses and left.

As Spargo was about to taste the raw fish, Ortiz said, "Just a moment, please." He reached over and took Spargo's dish, exchanging it for his.

"Your fish looks a little on the sparse side. For your first taste of our dish I'd like you to have choice portions."

Ortiz lifted a piece of the fish on the plate that had been Spargo's. "See how transparent this is? Actually it doesn't look like the flesh of the corvina at all. But I imagine it was just cut too thinly." He tasted it. "Excellent flavor though."

Spargo ate slowly. The fish had finely grained white flesh. The juice of the lime and the lemon had chemically cooked it without the benefit of heat, making it tart and tender. The chilies gave it fire without destroying flavor.

Ortiz sat smiling at him. "You obviously approve. I am happy."

Suddenly he winced, running a finger along his upper lip. He held up his right hand and studied his fingers. "I'm getting a strange tingling in my lips and fingers." He shook his head, closed his eyes, then opened them. "Perhaps I can't take those hot chilies anymore. That would be a pity."

Later, as they left the restaurant, Ortiz said, "Perhaps we should go immediately to the beach and talk about what Lundberg did there? I'm not feeling like myself at all. So let's go directly there."

"Later," Spargo said, "when you feel better. This is only a tax matter. It can wait."

"No, I'll be fine. A walk by the sea probably will help."

Spargo drove along the sharply curving highway that followed the contour of the seashore, turning off when Ortiz indicated, onto a secondary road surfaced with crushed white shells, the road angling directly to the harbor.

After they parked and were walking across the sand toward the shore, Ortiz explained the inactivity of the fishing boats in the harbor. The anchovies, one of Peru's leading assets, billions upon billions of them, had mysteriously disappeared. No one knew why. "Many marine scientists had come to investigate. Lundberg was one."

He explained that Lundberg took many samples of sea water, asked questions about Peru's currents, about the northern and southern populations of the anchovies, where in the Coastal Current that they were mostly found.

"He was aware," Ortiz said, now speaking with obvious difficulty, "that . . . our female anchovy lays twenty thousand eggs . . . in two years. He knew that the anchovy schools . . . do not move at random, that they prefer . . . the cold water of the Coastal Current."

Ortiz had arranged for Lundberg to rent a boat, in which he went out several times. "He and the other man."

"What other man?" Spargo said gently.

Ortiz seemed to be recovering. "Oh, they weren't aware that I knew, so I said nothing. I was naturally interested in what they were doing. In fact, I was surprised and disappointed that Lundberg didn't ask me to go along with him. I watched from shore with binoculars. The other man was short, slender, an Asian. I had never seen him before, or since."

224

Ortiz was suddenly in pain now, his eyes rolling. Spargo knew that he should stop him, get him in the car and take him home. He probably had a massive case of indigestion. Maybe the hot chilies had finally gotten to him. But Spargo was into it now and he wanted more answers.

"What else did they do? Did they fish? Go underwater? What?"

"They brought glass containers with them. Or rather Lundberg did. He poured the contents into the sea in different locations."

Ortiz coughed, then, with effort, straightened. He stood looking at the sea. "Then a strange thing happened. Must be just a simple coincidence. The day after Lundberg went out in the boat, some anchovies began coming back. Not many. But they hadn't been here in many months, so it was enough to get the fishermen excited. Then the next day. And the next. More fish . . . returned –"

He was having extreme speech difficulty now. "Then . . . after Lundberg left . . . again no anchovies . . . Still they have not come . . . back."

He grimaced. His face contorted in a rictus of pain. He held both hands tightly across his stomach. He opened his mouth. Green bile poured out. He turned beseechingly to Spargo. Then he fell, slowly, face down in the sand.

Stunned, Spargo turned him over, wiping the sand from his nose and mouth.

There was no pulse. Spargo lifted an eyelid. A brown eye stared back, dully as that of a dead fish. There was no heartbeat. The stomach was hard, rigid. Spargo felt his lips. Cold as ice.

The lines suddenly burst in Spargo's head. "These be three silent things. The falling snow . . . the hours before dawn . . . the mouth of one just dead."

Ortiz, who loved to talk, would talk no more.

He had substituted his dish of raw fish for Spargo's. It had killed him.

Fish: Aggressive catfish. Vanished anchovies lured back, perhaps by Lundberg. Fish that poisoned.

How did it all add up?

Spargo had one certain answer: Someone was anxious enough that he not discover what Lundberg had done in Peru to try to kill him.

He took the hammered silver cigarette case out of his breast pocket, extracted a tightly rolled betel leaf, then, chewing it, thought that he had liked Ortiz. There was a naive, eager quality about him that was appealing.

They would find the wrong man on the beach. Seeing an upturned, abandoned, rotting rowboat up the beach gave him an idea to win some time for himself.

Reluctantly, he dragged Ortiz to the boat, a strange stench already arising from the body. He carefully turned the rowboat up and over the body, completely covering it.

Then he walked back across the beach to the Rambler; holding down a desire to drive as fast as he could, he drove through the night to the air terminal at Lima.

CHAPTER SIXTEEN

They did not meet at the White House. It was a secret room in Blair House. The Secret Service of course knew that he went there on certain occasions. They did not know what the occasions were. They knew his movements, but no one knew his motivations. It was part of his strength.

It was one of those rainy days in Washington that gave the city a dismal gray, dripping aspect. As it did many people, rainy weather affected Harold James Noble, the President of the United States. It put him in a dour mood.

The meeting room was austere; a desk, two chairs. The President's chair, behind the desk, was higher to compensate for the fact that he would not be talking down from his Exercycle as usual. The chair in front of the desk was squat, hard-seated, uncomfortable. There were three steel engravings of sailing ships on the walls, a rose-and-green rug, a small beige sofa; behind it a bank of paned windows. There was no warmth, no decorator's cheer. It had the cold, unfriendly look that he wanted, a sealed room for sealed reports, not camaraderie.

He stood watching the rain streak the windows, then walked over and looked into the street, waiting for his visitor to arrive.

He did not try to convince himself that this was a secure hideaway. He had the Service sweep it carefully for bugs before and after he arrived. He could not be certain that the man he was waiting for was not activated, able to record their conversation. But he was almost certain. He could destroy the man's career with one telephone call.

It was difficult for him to think of the largest problem of all: the oncoming famine. It seemed unreal, a dream, happening at another time and another place. All Presidents had problems, but none had faced this.

He thought then of the time when he was a boy and had asked a farmer why he planted four kernels of corn for every plant he hoped to harvest. The farmer had replied, "One for the maggot/One for the crow/One for the cutworm/And one to grow."

It wasn't enough that the insect horde was wiping out our food supply, but another report had arrived late yesterday stressing that the goddamned bugs were also destroying our forests. The gypsy moth, the tussock moth, the spruce budworm, and the southern pine beetle were wreaking devastation on huge areas of woodland, defoliating and killing millions of valuable trees, last year alone destroying enough board feet of lumber to build over one million houses.

One of his first steps had been to call in a horticultural futurist from the University of Arizona's Environmental Research Laboratory, a bald, bespectacled scientist who was so cheerful it was disgusting. This was the man who had produced food for the space program at five hundred dollars a pound.

As was to be expected, he lectured: "We'll be up to a world population of six billion by the year 2000, so we've got to change our old concepts or starve. Instead of farming by the square foot, we'll do it on a cubic volume basis by controlled environment."

He explained that he was already growing lettuce on a styrofoam sheet that floated on a stagnant but nutrient-rich pond; that plants, tomatoes, eggplant, were being grown inside in chemical soup, that he also was readying an air-inflated greenhouse to grow vegetables with desalinated sea water in Abu Dhabi on the Arabian Peninsula.

"Right now, sir," he said proudly, "we are experimenting with nitrogen-rich sea water to grow saltwater plants that we call 'halophytes' that can be used as protein-rich forage or seed crops to feed animals and people. With these halophytes we can green up twenty thousand miles of the world's desert coastlines."

Problem was that scientists lived too far in the future, had no realization of cost, speed, urgency.

And he couldn't tell this man or anyone else about what was projected. But carefully, he felt him out on the possibility of a famine. A famine brought about by insects, rodents, change in weather pattern.

The horticultural futurist had laughed. "Nonsense. We'd outsmart 'em every time. In less than twenty years we'll all be fat cats regardless of those insects, even the weather."

"Twenty years?" the President said carefully.

"Yep, maybe give or take a couple of years."

But as President, he had problems other than bugs and scientists ignorant of time. He had, he felt, finally awakened the key people to the very real danger of industrial espionage. He had a choice new fact that had arrived at his desk this morning. This would be used to stir them up again.

The Japanese were actively training ten thousand new industrial spies every year.

A goddamned army of spies! All aimed at America!

He had almost two more full years in office, perhaps time to straighten out some of the rest of the mess his predecessor had created. It was that administration that had sent a U.S. general to Iran to talk the ruling junta out of forcing that madman, the Ayatollah, out of power, and thereby caused not only the junta's assassinations, but placing the United States in an untenable position with Iran and much of the Middle East.

Knowing that the CIA had to be partially responsible because of its bad advice and intelligence, hc was ready to discuss that Agency with calculated coldness and no compunction.

Through the rain-pocked window he saw his man crossing the street now, belted coat sparkling with raindrops, thick gray-white hair protecting him like a helmet. But it was a young man's springy step.

Noble was behind the desk as the visitor entered without knocking, as instructed. The President nodded. "Thanks for coming."

The man took off his coat, placed it over the back of the sofa, and sat in the chair in front of the desk. As yet he hadn't uttered a word.

The President stared at him. "Anything yet?"

He shook his head.

"When?"

"I don't know."

The President sighed. "Let's go over it. Spell it out again. What's my purpose in putting you in the Agency as my man?"

"Do we have to do it this way, sir? I'm prepared to give you a report."

"There are no solid developments, is that right?"

"Not completely. But —"

"Then let's proceed as I suggested. Clarify it, so to speak. I've found refocusing sometimes gives renewed impetus."

He looked down on the man. "Shall I repeat my first question?"

"I am secretly in the Agency to report to you

on activity from the very top. Also to immediately pick up on any blunders on the part of the Agency connected with important U.S. industrial secrets."

"Correct. In this regard, you have reported that an industrial spy perhaps working for both Japan and Britain was interrogated by us and died as the direct result of that Agency interrogation. At the point of death, he had revealed that he was on the trail of a tremendous breakthrough in the world of the sea. A breakthrough, I understand, that is so important that the actual control of the sea is at stake. Is that correct?"

"Yes."

"The Agency has hired a so-called freelance to try to discover what this secret is and to locate a vanished American scientist who is supposed to have discovered it. Is that all right so far?"

The man nodded.

"Why a freelance? You haven't told me."

"If Agency men take on this mission and fail, they are in a more vulnerable position than ever. If an outsider is secretly assigned and either wins or fails, the Agency takes credit on the one hand, and will have nothing to do with the failure on the other. But I don't think there will be failure."

"Why?" the President asked. "Is this man some kind of intelligence genius?"

"I understand he is one of the best men the Agency ever had. Cut off when Congress started snipping off the black operations. Obviously a mistake. Some of the missions this man has accomplished were almost as difficult as the one we have him on now."

"This — What is his name?"

"Spargo."

"This Spargo is in action now, I take it. What is he doing?"

"I understand that he is backtracking Ryal, who gave the initial information on the breakthrough before he died. When he reports to the Agency, I will try to bring you up to date."

"Let's package this a bit. When this Spargo gets his hands on that scientist and his file, the CIA expects to confiscate it. Instead you secure it and bring it to me. I expose the CIA for the bumblers they are. You take over as head of my new secret force that will supersede the Agency."

The President tapped a long forefinger on the desk. "I suppose we could say, to use D.C. language, that we are dealing with our cover impediments by creating a truly clandestine but elite corps of operations officers. This is an extremely delicate undertaking that will require adroit handling by our most experienced people. We will not dissolve the present Agency but keep it in a puppet position, discharging all potentially dangerous operators. This, if we get that file. Then I can tell the people what has happened. If that doesn't work then we have to mark time. As you know, I do not like to mark time. We've had too much indecision in the White House. It has caused most of our problems."

"I believe it will work," the man said. "Spargo is not a superman, a James Bond, or any of that incredible junk. He is just a highly trained professional who usually succeeds instead of failing."

"Another black mark against the Agency. If Spargo succeeds, we point up that he never should have been severed from the Agency. The good men were pushed out, the poor ones stayed in power. I hope if Spargo does pull this off that he will be properly compensated?"

"I haven't been told."

"I respect Admiral Morgan," the President said. "I am certain he is a patriot. And he has done a good job in trimming the fat from the Agency. But he doesn't have your background in intelligence. He's tough. But he's in over his head. That is one of the principal faults of the Agency. They continue to place politicians at the top, or others who are unskilled in the trade."

The President placed his hands flat on the desk. "Let's be positive. Chet Morgan just gave me a report on China. China watchers have only been able to guess at the agricultural and industrial output of that country. Now, for the first time since 1959, Peking has published detailed data. In 1978 with a crop totaling 304.75 million tons, it was the world's leading producer of grain. It also ranks among the top three coal producers of the world, fifth in steel, among the top ten in oil. Chet Morgan has closely matched all of this information before it was published. Peking's steel figure was 31.78 million tons in 1978. Morgan came up with 31.7 million. Close. Commendable intelligence. China will be our next real threat. But that kind of CIA efficiency is a rarity. Before you arrived I was thinking of the mess the Agency and the last President made in Iran and the Middle East —"

The President arose from his special chair, walked over and stared out of the rain-streaked window. He looked small and fragile.

"I haven't told you this before," he said slowly. "But Nixon was framed on that Watergate mess. By the CIA. The President was compiling a damning file on the Agency. It had gotten too large, was actually controlling not only other countries, but some of our major political figures. It was in a masterful position, becoming stronger than the President and the Executive Branch. It also used terror tactics, would not account for vast sums of money. So when they learned that the President was after them they sent that so-called 'White House burglar' to Watergate to destroy Nixon."

He slowly walked back to his desk. "I am not out to get Admiral Chester Morgan. I am out to help my country by reorganizing an inept Agency that should no longer have the enormous power it still has. Misused, misdirected power. But I will do this properly. I want you to get together a file on all of the good men, the loyal men. We must keep our intelligence apparatus intact. Improve it. You and the others in your group will be the intelligence watchdogs not only for your own organization, but of what is left of the CIA."

Sensing that was the closing remark, the man arose from his chair.

"Counter Intelligence Agency," the President mused aloud. "If only it would 'counter.' They did not even know of the existence of this sea secret we are trying to obtain. A foreign agent unearthed it. And one of our own scientists developed it!"

He hammered the desk with his fist.

"The sea!" he said harshly. "The last frontier! It is a thousand times more important than our wasteful adventure to the moon. Whatever has been compiled in that scientist's file must be secured as quickly as possible."

He stared coldly at the man in front of him. "I am relying on you. If you fail, not only do we all fail, but Chet Morgan may discover who and what you are."

Unmoved by the threat, the man stared back, his light eyes steady. "We won't fail."

The President smiled. "Watch your back. Chet Morgan may be an old sea dog but the salt water hasn't softened his brain."

CHAPTER SEVENTEEN

The rain had stopped; the sun was making a final appearance before dusk, sparkling on the rainsoaked privet hedge outside Admiral Chester Morgan's office behind the high walls of the Agency compound in Langley, Virginia.

The Admiral walked to the window, clasped his hands behind his back, and thought of the early days when he had stood on the bridge of a destroyer, captain of all he surveyed. From far away he heard a church bell ringing, too preoccupied to count the strikes.

He thought sourly of the fact that Congress was even permitting public tours of this facility that used to be secret, that one by one they were pulling all of the teeth from the Agency.

Even the action of the guards and guard

dogs that used to patrol the compound had been canceled.

He knew that KGB had not loosened control. In fact the Soviets had given that agency more importance and authority, more secrecy, stepped up its covert, was actively training more assassins.

The sun dying on the hedge in front of him saddened him, its last glow reminding him of his age and the seemingly insurmountable struggle ahead with the bureaucracy and shortsighted men.

The sailor in him resented this assignment, all this deviousness, this weird gadgetry, this experimentation with minds and lives, this wearing six masks. But when he was offered the job, his pride forced him to accept. Now that he had it his sense of order and efficiency required that he stay in and make this ship seaworthy.

He thought now of the parody someone had pinned on the staff bulletin board. "Of intelligence I have so little grip/that they offered me the Directorship/with my brassbound head of oak so stout/I don't have to know what it's all about/I may run the ship aground if I keep on so/but I don't care a fig; I'll be the CNO."

If only it *were* Chief of Naval Operations, he

thought grimly. Then he would be in total control. Today he had received a mind-reeling list of intelligence weapons from the Office of Special Operations, spelling out the cooperation of the companies that had developed them, among them General Electric, IBM, Squibb, Du Pont, and Pfizer.

The most ingenious involved undetectable bacteria and chemicals that could be transmitted in an ordinary letter. Simply opening the letter would result in anything from a severe headache to extreme hallucinations.

There were a dozen microphones, so tiny that they could not be detected except by professionals who knew exactly what they were looking for. Fifteen variations of LSD; four truth drugs, so effective they could quickly lower a person's discretion level, without that person's even being aware of it. Wireless, batteryless sending sets that could emit tones reflecting changes in activities in the places they were hidden.

A chemically treated handkerchief, exposed for less than a minute, picked up factory or other fumes that then could be perfectly analyzed and identified.

One of the cleverest was a stamp-moistening desk sponge that could absorb traces of body chemistry that upon analysis revealed exactly what kind of people, race, sex, had been in the room during that period of exposure.

And yet, he thought, with all of their cleverness, these inventive geniuses can't win the battle against the bugs. We have never managed to exterminate as much as a single species.

As he watched the rain drip from the privet hedge, he thought again of the briefings he had had with the scientists whom he had sworn to secrecy. There was no dodging the stark fact: We were facing certain famine.

Insects were increasing so rapidly that the weight of their world population of five million species exceeded that of humans by a factor of twelve. Boll weevils alone cost the U.S. farmer $260 million a year. From last year's destruction of 10 percent of all crops at an annual $6 billion cost, it now was up to over 30 percent and $18 billion.

The chemists were now attempting to defeat the bugs by tricking the females that mate only once a lifetime into mating with males that had been sterilized by exposure to radiation. But that, like the other non-spray solutions, was complicated, terribly expensive, and time-consuming.

He had a fierce longing then to be on a ship again with a crew of men he knew he could depend upon. Here, he was in a vicious political arena where he was just learning how to fight. He suspected that the crafty President was not exactly an ally, but he wasn't certain. The President himself had appointed him. He seemed to be happy with the fat-trimming, the reorganization. But, even with the new problem of famine that no one could now talk about, the President remained obviously unhappy with the Agency regarding industrial espionage. His priorities were mixed up.

There must be an all-out concentration on the food problem, no political divisiveness until they licked the insect attack.

Nature was acting up, an unbeatable Nature, sending her signals to let us know we don't rule supreme. There would be panic. Black market. The poor would suffer again. The rich would eat.

Suddenly, he thought, what about these experiments of Allan Vaughn? Had he actually developed some scientific system to control the sea, as the dying Ryal had claimed? It seemed preposterous. As he knew, the sea gave up its secrets hard. But now it had become imperative to discover what Vaughn actually had in that file. He was American. When it was pointed out that the United States was facing certain famine, along with the rest of the world, wouldn't he help us turn his findings into an asset for us? Or would greed rule him as it does most men?

As the admiral stood at the window deep in thought, the sudden ring of the phone whirled him around. He was brusque as usual, routinely switching on the Hagoth voice analyzer as he picked up the phone. "Yes. Go ahead." His eyes sought the dial of the analyzer as it recorded. Stress.

The voice on the other end of the line continued at length. Finally the admiral said, "Very good. Well done." He hung up.

Picking up the intercom, he said, "Get me Pryor. On a secure line. Immediately."

It took ten minutes.

When the phone rang the admiral had been about to reissue his order.

"Pryor," he snapped. "Listen. Then we'll talk."

He picked up the telephone that he had previously answered, activating the recorder, holding it close to the mouthpiece of the phone in his hand.

"Sir," the voice said. "Reporting as ordered

on surveillance in Warren, Michigan. Our man there terminated. Also what we believe to be a British agent. Also an Asian. Also the superintendent of the building. Three were killed by what looked like karate death chops. The Asian was knifed. The apartment of Ryal was a mess. Completely torn apart in a search. Obviously whoever committed the murders was looking for something that Ryal had hidden in his apartment.

"When we originally picked Ryal up for questioning we had not yet located that apartment.

"We are not interfering with the police. We will notify the family of our man in the usual way. I am staying in place until I receive further instructions from you."

The admiral's voice. "Very good. Well done."

Now he replaced that phone on its cradle and picked up the one Pryor was on.

Pryor's voice: "Yes, sir."

The admiral: "It looks like Spargo has passed his blood test. Has he contacted you?"

"No."

"I'd assume that the Asian is his work."

"So would I."

"It looks like you may be correct in your

assumptions. Ryal must have been onto something so big that murder is unimportant. He also must have left something revealing behind. Could there have been another of the opposition whom Spargo didn't eliminate? Another who found what Ryal had hidden? Or did Spargo find whatever it was?"

"He is to call me on a secure line tomorrow, sir. I will report to you immediately."

"I hope that your faith in Spargo is justified. We now have six people dead and do not know what the hell this is all about. But one fact is clear —"

"Sir?"

"We absolutely must find Allan Vaughn and discover what Ryal was babbling about."

CHAPTER EIGHTEEN

Spargo awoke before dawn in his apartment in Gramercy Park. He had hoped that the trip back from Peru, the jet lag, would tire him so that he could sleep through the night. But the old insomnia was back.

He staggered out of bed, filled a cup with water, stuck it in the Amana microwave oven for two minutes and dunked a double-strength bag of Japanese green tea in it until the water was green-gold.

Later, after a fried egg and two strips of bacon, he sat planning his day. He would immediately leave for Cape Cod to meet Josef and call his contact from there.

He always rented a car, each time using a

different name and driver's license. He was a bird of passage, a deceptive bird of many colors.

Today the car was a dirty tan two-door Dodge Aspen, comfortable, but not conspicuous.

As he left Manhattan, something gnawed away in his head, making him uneasy. It didn't materialize until he got on Route 95. He had told Josef that he was using the name Tom Judson. That would be the IRS cover name in Cape Cod. Mistake. He had used that name in Peru and his cover could be blown if any of the determined opposition in Peru tracked him to the Cape. He cursed himself for twenty miles, then decided to forget it for a while and enjoy the ride.

He'd stay on 95 until Rhode Island, then switch to Route 1, picking up 138 across the Bay, then Route 6 along the water, and 28 into Jacob's Landing.

When gulls began to appear over the water along the shore, hanging in an upsweep of wind current, motionless as if they were painted there, he thought about a trip he had taken on a Norwegian freighter. One of the crew was using his job as a cover and Spargo was assigned the task of staying with him until he made contact with the opposition. Narcotics, plus espionage.

Spargo had been friendly with the captain, a blunt, sixty-year-old seaman whose bold, wind-leathered face could have been the model for the prow of an ancient Viking ship. The captain had a nephew, an ornithologist, who had written a book on gulls.

"Don't look beyond a gull's beauty, or all you'll get is disgust," the captain had said. But he liked to talk about the birds and some of the facts had stuck in Spargo's mind.

"They are the most widely distributed of all birds, the original survivors," the captain said.

The old captain had been particularly impressed with his nephew's discovery that each adult gull is a member of an exclusive club system that dates back more than a million years.

Each spring, when the gulls return to their summer residences, they re-form the private clubs, by species and by status. Even a small gullery of two hundred birds would have as many as four separate clubs, formed for the social life and the preservation of the species.

The forming of the clubs each spring begins with a huge parade, all of the gulls joining in a walk around the rookery. Next is a concerted flight with all of the birds flying over the area where they had been born. Then one old, aggressive gull glides from the parade in the sky and stands alone, head high. At this signal, all birds land, and what seemed to be a formless collection is converted into a series of close social circles. Each club has a male leader, with several associate males just a step further down in the status-by-age-and-aggression scale. Once the clubs are formed the gulls belong to them for life. Like all clubs, these have newcomers, brought in by other club members – the clowns and the playboys, the swashbucklers that flirt with older females, the unfortunate that other members harass.

"The gull people," the Norwegian captain had called them.

The gull people's population grew rapidly as he neared Jacob's Landing. He hoped that Josef would be all right, feeling a twinge of guilt for recruiting him for this mission that was getting increasingly complicated and rough. He had a deep affection for Josef, all wrong in this trade. They tried to take me out three times now, Spargo thought, and I'm not sure even at this point who "they" are. Strong suspicions, but no proof.

Jacob's Landing wasn't deep into the Cape.

251

Seventy-five miles from Boston, this extreme southwestern tip fisted out from the arm of the Cape into the Atlantic. Actually into Vineyard Sound.

As he drove into the Landing proper, Spargo saw that it wasn't much more than that, a landing. There were two large gray ferry slips where the ships came and went from the island, two real estate offices, a small Cape Cod information center, five motels at varying distances on the rises beyond the harbor, three dingy greasy-spoon seafood places, a stand-up doughnut shop, a Greek restaurant that smelled like it was burning down, and two marinas where several inboards and outboards and two small sloops were tied up.

The sea's salt spray had given building shingles, docks, even roofs, a dull silver sheen. A long dock bisected ferry slips and marina, its pilings encrusted with barnacles and crowned with dusky brown young herring gulls.

At its end an elderly man with a well-worn yachting cap sat on a canvas stool fishing and smoking a pipe. Spargo, remembering the carefree days when he had drifted in here past the purple buoys in the motor-sailor, envied him. Some of the buoys were bobbing out there still.

To the right of the ferry slip on the edge of the water was another dock, an ancient one rotting by the sea. In the distance were the purple smudges of islands drowning in heat haze.

Jacob's Landing Oceanographic Institute was also on the edge of the sea, a complex of buildings of various sizes, mostly brick, one long, low, gray structure was nearest the sea. The overall aspect was neatness and affluence.

Falmouth was just a few miles away, the Beachcomber much as he remembered it, low, one-story buildings, barn-sided, stained dark brown, much of it covered with Baltic ivy to give it false antiquity, in low key good taste.

He drove up to the office to register, asked for the reservation for Tom Judson and was loftily told by a blonde who had just blossomed out of teenage into ERA authority that no Judson was registered. Taken slightly aback, Spargo recovered and asked for Joseph Kulik, a favorite of Josef. He always insisted on using his first name and a foreign last name, always too close to his own.

"A double room," the clerk said, "out back, facing the pond."

Spargo left his bag in the car and sauntered out to the pond, stood watching seven white

Pekin ducks and a whistling swan sail nervously around, all with wings pinioned, all looking as if they'd like to leave the prison of polluted water as soon as possible. Two small boys stood throwing popcorn at them which the birds ignored, paddling to the middle of the pond to avoid the annoyance.

Spargo waited until the boys left, then began whistling "Laura," an old signal of theirs. In three minutes, Josef appeared at the door of the room closest to the pond, saw Spargo, grinned and walked fast to greet him.

"Hello, Mike Larsen," Joseph said. "Glad you could make it."

They sat on a bench and talked.

Josef told him that Nicky Victor had been told that Spargo was using the name Tom Judson on a present assignment, thought it poor strategy to use the same one up here and fixed up the IRS identification in the Larsen name.

"Good old Nicky," Spargo said gratefully. "I made a mistake, glad he picked up on it."

"What's going on, Spargo?" Josef said. "I'm dancing in the dark."

Spargo told him about Ryal; Warren, Michigan; Lundberg in Stamford; Peru; the sea file of Vaughn — as much as he knew.

Josef whistled. "We've got a beaut!

I think I'm underpaid."

His Stalin moustache flared in the old way, and he seemed full of vitality. Spargo suspected that he was as fast and as skilled as ever. Men like Josef did not get rusty.

"Like you thought, Allan Vaughn was here," Josef said. "At the Jacob's Landing Oceanographic Institute. Two weeks ago he walked away and hasn't been heard from since."

Working as the old pro he was, Josef filled Spargo in on the Institute. First, know your background:

Jacob's Landing Oceanographic Institute, starting as a small summer marine laboratory, had by 1942 become a year-round operation and an institution, expanding until its annual expenses of one million dollars during World War II grew to a fourteen-million-dollar expenditure today. It was the largest employer on Cape Cod, with a resident scientist staff of one hundred fifty, plus five hundred other employees.

"So," Josef summed, "I think your idea of us being IRS is okay. These guys spend money like there's no tomorrow."

They went out and got Spargo's bag and parked his car, Spargo chewing a cylinder of betel while they checked him in. As they

255

walked to Spargo's room, Josef continued his fill-in.

"Vaughn has an assistant. Gal. A looker. I rustled about a little, introduced myself, said my boss was showing up soon and that we were going to do a little checking of the books and Vaughn's operation. She's cool, aloof, but like you said, she'll cooperate with the IRS. I had an idea —"

"Yes?" Spargo took the betel out of his mouth, wrapped it in a tissue, and placed it in a waste basket beside an ornate dresser that looked like varnished wood but was pressed plastic.

"Seems a famous fish expert, an ichthyologist, a Korean, is going to lecture today at a place called Mertz Hall. Vaughn's gal will be there, as will a lot of the professional people from the Institution. I thought it would make sense if we went, give you a chance to see the girl, sort of size her up, and at the same time get a feel of the place without exposing yourself."

"Good idea. When?"

Josef checked his watch. "Forty minutes."

It gave Spargo time for a quick shower, a change into chinos, a soft blue chambray shirt, and sneakers, fitting for the Cape. Protective covering. Camouflage. Josef was in his farm denims, also good.

Josef noted Salwa on his arm as he came out buttoning up his shirt, nodding approval. "Looks like she grows there."

As they drove to Jacob's Landing in Spargo's Aspen, Josef filled him in on Mertz Hall where the lecture was being given.

"Big red brick building," he said. "New. They spend a lot of money on everything connected with the Institution. I got a brochure on the area. Interesting. At least to me."

On the site where Mertz Hall now stood had been the Dodd Brothers' odoriferous Guano Factory. Before that, the whaling days had had Jacob's Landing up to its elbows in blood, extracting whale oil. Later, when whales became scarce, the Landing became a deadwater. The Dodd brothers changed that in 1860 with their discovery that the mid-Pacific islands of Howland and Baker, where seabirds had been nesting for generations, were covered with thick deposits of excrement.

The Dodds reasoned that sailing vessels returning to New England from Pacific ports without complete cargoes could bring back seabird guano. The Dodds would convert it into fertilizer, blending it with organic

257

material from scrap fish such as menhaden.

Cotton and tobacco farmers liked the result so much that by 1871 the Dodds were selling forty thousand tons a year. But by mid-1880 cheaper and more effective fertilizers began to appear, guano sales dropped, and by the end of that century the Dodds were out of business.

"Like old Jacob Van Atta was," Josef said, "when the use of whale oil ended with discovery of petroleum. Jacob's Landing was named after Jake. He was the first sea captain to bring a sperm whale to port here."

"You're getting me in the mood," Spargo said. "Too bad we can't just bask in the sun and eat up the atmosphere."

They parked the Aspen and joined about one hundred lined up to hear renowned Professor Kim Dong Jo of Korea lecture on the most valuable fish in the sea, the bluefin tuna.

The auditorium could seat five hundred. Spargo and Josef were moving to bury themselves inconspicuously in the center row, when Josef said, "There she is. Blue jogging suit. Up front."

Spargo stiffened. Smooth shiny black hair, high cheekbones, slightly slanted eyes, lithe even in the running suit, she could have been the younger sister of Salwa. Perhaps slightly more beautiful.

Josef touched him. "I said a looker. But I didn't realize she was that good. Want me to introduce you after the talk?"

Spargo shook his head. "Let's wait until we visit the lab. Straight business approach."

A young scientist from the Institute introduced the speaker, a slender, bald, very old Asian, who coughed politely into the microphone on its stand on a small podium. It worked properly, so he stood silently waiting for the scientists to settle down, his eyes roaming the hall.

Then he began, in perfect English, his sibilant voice so soft that without the public address system he would have been inaudible. His expertise was in the scientific aspects of probing the personality and lifestyle of the tuna. He told of his experiments with acoustic telemetry of temperatures of free-swimming fish, using acoustic transmitters.

"We were amazed," the professor said, "when one bluefin with a stomach transmitter swam from surface water into depths as much as eleven degrees centigrade colder and remained there for four hours before returning to warmer water."

He had proved conclusively that the bluefin can do what a few ichtyologists had suspected for a long time. "It can regulate at will its deep body temperature," the little man said dramatically.

Even though he wasn't familiar with the subject, Spargo found that the lecture held his interest. Everyone else there, including Josef, obviously felt the same. Spargo could see the back of the head of Vaughn's assistant near the front. It shone like rubbed ebony.

The Korean went on to say that a tag returned to him from Japan showed that a bluefin released in the Straits of Florida in May 1977 had been caught again off Recife, Brazil, in March 1979. "Thus," he said, "it has been proved that a giant bluefin of the Bahamas not only crossed the Atlantic and traversed the Arctic Circle, but also crossed the Equator."

There was sustained applause as Kim Dong Jo bowed and sat down.

The little Asian had them in his pocket now. They were crowding around him, shaking his hand, congratulating him. These were all scientists of the sea and the Korean had fascinated them with his experiments. Spargo saw the dark girl, Vaughn's assistant, move toward the Korean, and the two of them stood talking for several minutes. Then, approaching them was a squat figure that looked familiar, even from the rear.

When the man turned around, Spargo saw that it was his friend Norikura, owner of the karate school in Manhattan where he had instructed.

CHAPTER NINETEEN

The old Korean professor and Norikura were among the last to leave Mertz Hall.

Spargo and Josef approached them from the rear. Spargo touched Norikura lightly on the shoulder, and the Japanese whirled around quickly.

"*Sensei*," Spargo bowed. "Who's minding the store?"

Norikura said, "Spargo!" He looked at Josef. "Kodály. What are you two doing here?"

"Taking it easy for a few days on the Cape," Spargo said easily. "Who's running your school in Manhattan?"

"Your best pupil, the Chinese, Shiu-Kai Chin. My other school isn't far from here. The professor here is an old friend of my family. He brings me news from home. He stopped in Japan on his way over from Korea. Come meet him."

The introductions were made with a feudal Japanese flourish, with much bowing, and congratulations on the lecture, the Korean professor then standing back and eyeing Spargo keenly.

"Will you be here long, Spargo?" Norikura asked. "Long enough to come visit my school up here?"

"I doubt it, *sensei,*" Spargo said. "Josef is raising squabs to keep himself busy. There's a big squab operator in Medford, Massachusetts, he wants to buy some new stock from. I just finished a job and am relaxing, tagging along. We both like the Cape and thought we'd shoot over here, get some sea breeze, some fresh fish, then finish up Josef's business and scoot for home."

"Yes," Norikura said. "Will you be able to come back and work with me soon again? Many of the students miss you."

"I don't think it will happen right away. I have a couple of other little jobs upcoming. Sorry, I like being with you. And there never was a day that I didn't learn from you."

Norikura bowed, smiling. "You flatter. At this point I can teach you nothing."

"Modesty, Norikura," Spargo said. "One of the finest of Japanese traits."

They shook hands and said good-bye, Spargo and Josef driving off, the professor and Norikura remaining.

As Spargo's car disappeared, the professor pointed at a bench beyond Mertz Hall overlooking the sea. "Let's go sit and chat."

As they sat the professor said, "He's the man. Note the gold flecks in his eyes."

"Strange, you can know a man for years and yet miss little details like that. Even when he was my student at The Playhouse I never noted that. Too busy with the training, I suppose."

"Detail can destroy," the professor said. "It must be remembered."

Norikura smiled. "I congratulate you on your attention to detail, Tokura. You played Korean Professor Kim Dong Jo to perfection. In the best ninja tradition."

"We have a film of him lecturing. A week with that helped. The professor is helpless in a hospital in Seoul. He will never know. It will make no difference if he does. The lecture was all fact. His fact that I obtained from one of his files."

They sat silently staring at the sea. Tokura pointed at it. "That water covers two-thirds of our planet. Yet we take less than two percent of our food requirements from the oceans. Japan takes more than anyone else. We must or we would starve."

Norikura nodded.

"You know that your friend Spargo was the man we did not eliminate in Peru. We must now correct that. Our Number One man must do it. You."

Norikura turned and faced Tokura. "No. Someone else must do it."

"I command you to follow my instructions. We cannot risk any more inefficiency."

"No, Tokura. A Japanese does not kill a friend. You know that. Spargo has been helpful in assisting me perfect my cover of the karate school. I have known him for years. I admire him."

"So do I," Tokura said dryly. "But he is an obstacle. I will now tell you a fact that I have been ordered by the Motherland not to reveal. In a very few short years there is going to be world famine."

Norikura stood up. "Is it certain?"

"Yes."

"There are others more effective than I. I

still cannot do it. He trusts me. I was his teacher. It would be like putting a knife in the heart of a child."

"That experiment in Peru conducted by Lundberg proved to me that Allan Vaughn has made an astonishing discovery. The anchovies there had mysteriously vanished. Lundberg brought some of them back by sprinkling a solution into the waters."

"How was it done? What was it?"

"We don't know. And Lundberg didn't know. Enough. Three countries are aware of Vaughn's discovery. Japan. Britain. The United States. No one knows what it is. Only Vaughn. We must obtain his file. If we do not, Japan will be in terrible danger. When it comes to survival, there is little charity. Or chivalry. We would hate to beg Britain or America for food. Our old hatred for them still burns."

"The Soviets aren't in this?" Norikura said.

Tokura smiled. "No, in that huge complex in Dzerzhinsky Square in Moscow the KGB teaches murder mainly. They are adept at the brutal situations such as marching in and killing helpless serfs as they did in Afghanistan. But they have entrusted their industrial espionage mainly to untrained diplomats. We are superior. Of course much superior to the United States, and the British are running out of trained operatives. Most of their good ones are retired or approaching an age when their effectiveness is questionable."

"How did the British get onto this?"

"Ryal doubled on us. He was a good man. Trained by me. Very effective. But loyal to his own country. We have picked up on one of their men in Michigan where Ryal last was seen. He is here. A Stephen Copeland. Older. Experienced. Very good. He must be taken out. I'll handle that. But your friend Spargo will be the main obstacle."

"I will do anything else to help the Motherland," Norikura said sadly. "I have proven that. But I could not live with myself if I destroyed Spargo."

Tokura stood up. "I respect you as a man. But I must report your disobedience. I am convinced everything is right here where we are. We will find it. Can you handle Spargo's friend, this Josef Kodály? Is he formidable? He doesn't appear so."

Norikura smiled. "You, more than most, know looks deceive. Yes, Josef is formidable. Yes, I think I can handle him. I know his art. I have watched him instruct −"

"And doesn't he know yours?" Tokura said.

Norikura nodded. "It will not be easy. But it can be done."

"Good. We must clear away all obstacles. Then we concentrate on locating what we came for."

"You have done a masterful job of putting our people in place here," Norikura said. "If you remove Spargo and Copeland, the whole chessboard is yours. You are in control."

"Only time itself will prove or disprove that." Tokura stood, a fragile old man. But Norikura knew his strength, his brain, his ruthlessness.

"Send me two ninja," Tokura said suddenly. "They will second me and we will handle Spargo. And Vaughn."

"Vaughn?"

"Yes," Tokura said. "As soon as we discover where Vaughn's file is, I want him eliminated."

"I do not have two ninja," Norikura said. "We lost one in Michigan and another broke a leg in a cliff-scaling exercise rescuing a clumsy student. We have only one ninja available. But we have a very good advanced student I have much faith in."

"Who? Do I know him?"

"Yes. Hideyoshi Oda."

"Oda." Tokura was thoughtful. "Descendant of warlords. I know his father. I knew he would develop."

"He has. He is the best we have produced so far."

"Perhaps," Tokura. "But still not a ninja."

"Do not worry about Oda. I can have him and the ninja here within six hours, eight at the very latest."

Tokura nodded. "Excellent. I have a legitimate cover to be here for several days. Americans lump all Orientals together. Thus the ninja and Oda will be associates come to assist me on the remainder of my lecture tour. But we must accelerate. Spargo and the Britisher Copeland's being here means that they are also getting close. I believe I know where Copeland is, what his cover is. I'm not certain. But in the interest of speed I hope that I am correct."

"Patience," Norikura said.

"The cat waits for the mouse," Tokura said. "The mouse does not wait for the cat. Someone always makes a wrong move."

CHAPTER TWENTY

"Coincidence?" Josef asked Spargo.

Spargo was thoughtful. "We've learned to suspect coincidence, I know. But *Norikura?*"

Josef was blunt. "To be honest, I never was high on Norikura. All Japanese leave me cold. I'm a simple soul. I can't forget Pearl Harbor and some of the unforgivable things they did."

Spargo shrugged. "You know, Josef, we're in a terrible trade. The only thing we trust is our appetite. Norikura has another school up in this territory. I knew that. It's natural that he would drive a few miles to visit a family friend here lecturing. We're making a federal case out of an innocent happenstance."

"Sure, sure," Josef said.

They were eating breakfast in Josef's sunny double room overlooking the pond, the ducks and the regal swan still out there seeking sanctuary in the middle, still avoiding children with popcorn. Breakfast was two pair of small fresh-caught flounder sautéed in sweet butter and shirred eggs baked with cream and fresh chives.

Spargo finished, wiping his mouth with a napkin, and stood, stretching. "We've got to get going and talk to that girl of Vaughn's." He looked at his watch. "And I have to phone my contact —"

"The type I knocked on his ass?"

Spargo laughed. "You didn't tell me about that. How did it go?"

"He's an arrogant bastard. There's also something about him I don't trust. He's one of these butter-won't-melt-in-their-mouths types the Agency turns out like they come off an assembly line. Get going. Make your phone call. I'll send for another pot of coffee and watch the ducks and swan outwit those brats."

Spargo was to make the call to Carson either on Monday at 4 P.M. or Friday at 10 A.M. This was Friday, and it was exactly ten minutes to ten.

Although he was certain that his motel room was clean, he wouldn't make the call from there. There was the matter of a switchboard, or a motel clerk who would record the call and bill him. He'd make it from the phone booth he saw near the pond.

The telephone booth was open, with no door. Spargo gave the operator the memorized number, inserted the change that was requested, listened to three short rings, then the voice.

"This is Carson," Pryor said carefully.

Without giving him a name, Spargo told him about the experience in Warren, Michigan, but omitted any mention of his trip to Peru. He did not believe in disclosing more than necessary in any single report.

"Any pickup?" Pryor said. "A trail?"

"No trail. But I did find a film. Bunch of large catfish trying to kill one another. Senseless, so far, but I'm studying it to see if it may have some answers, at least a location —"

"Anything yet?"

"No —"

Two women in pantsuits were passing the booth now, one braying, "This Beachcomber here at Falmouth doesn't compare with the one in Maine —"

Quickly, Spargo clapped his hand over the mouthpiece, hoping the voices hadn't been loud enough to reach the ear on the other end of the line.

"Where are you?" Pryor asked. "How can I get in touch?"

"I'll contact you when I have anything more," Spargo said curtly. "The film may be the contact point when I get the thing figured out."

"Meanwhile, I wait. Is that it? I expected more from you. Time is important. We must —"

Spargo quietly placed the phone on its cradle.

As Spargo and Josef drove to Jacob's Landing Oceanographic Institute, fog was drifting in off the sea, feather-wisps that floated high, then vanished. They could see ships in the distance looking as if they were sailing across the horizon of skyline and cloud.

Replicas of Cape Cods were rising all along the narrow road from Falmouth to Jacob's Landing, the neat structures looking authentic, shingled, stained a convincing gray that looked like the patina colored by sea-weather and salt-spray.

Josef was driving, Spargo thinking about Allan Vaughn, wondering why he had disappeared. Voluntarily? Taken? Was he alive? Part of the task now would be to put together his lifestyle, find out what made him tick, what he had discovered. Would his assistant know? Would the people who killed Lundberg, and inadvertently, Ortiz, also try to eliminate her?

Stephen Copeland had selected his position, on the edge of the long dock that bisected ferry slips and marina, with the skill of a military leader, which he once had been. It commanded an overall view of the entire area of Jacob's Landing, yet it was so removed, so latticed with pilings that it was natural camouflage. It was sheer luck that he found the old yachting cap, that, with the wrinkled chinos and denim shirt, made him look like one of the natives. Actually, he was rather enjoying sitting here in the sun fishing. Hadn't as much as a nibble yet, but he could watch the comings and goings of Jacob's Landing carefree and unnoticed as a stray cat.

Formerly with MI6 and SIS, Copeland now was a member of an elite task force of industrial counter-espionage. He was a meticulous operator, especially good at rescue and mopping-up missions. He had been trying to locate his team player, Ryal, for over a week. At the last address they had for him in Warren, Michigan, Copeland had discovered that Morland, sent before him on the same errand, had been killed.

Musing about that now, Copeland thought, this is getting bloody. Industrial espionage had always intrigued him, the outwitting of the opposition, the getting there first, the chess moves, using men. He had never encountered murder in this field before. SIS and MI6, yes. But Ryal had been playing a dangerous game, doubling.

Ryal's signals had placed the marine scientist Vaughn here at Jacob's Landing Oceanographic Institute. Last signal had been almost hysterical. "I think he's got it," Ryal had signaled in code. "Vaughn has completed his research, has a file of all his experiments. He can control the sea. How, I don't know yet. But I have 16 mm film that may clue us in."

Then nothing. Ryal had vanished. So had Vaughn. Copeland suspected that Ryal was dead. He remembered then the words of a talented German military tactician, who was it? Probably Von Moltke. No plan, the German had said, survived contact with the enemy. That certainly seemed to be true where Ryal was concerned. But what enemy had he contacted? Japan? U.S.? Was Russia involved?

Hearing footsteps behind him, Copeland casually turned his head. For the first time he had competition. Another fisherman.

Young, in faded denim, wearing sunglasses, big mirrored lenses, the hair glossy black, the complexion dark, not a black, but with those masking glasses it was difficult to tell.

He had a large metal chest, a long wooden pole, and a fishing rod. What was the pole for? Copeland wondered idly. He said brightly, "Good morning. Hope you change the luck. Guess the fish are all out to lunch."

The young man laughed. "I'll try to tempt them with dessert."

The newcomer rigged up his fishing rod, opened the chest, and baited the hook. Looked like some kind of red artificial worm.

Then he moved the chest closer to the edge of the dock, cast out his line, sat on the chest and began to slowly reel in the line, giving the lure on the hook motion.

The visitor wasn't chatty, Copeland discovered to his relief. But he was disappointed that his solitude was broken.

The sound of a motor. An American car, looked like a Dodge Aspen, was coming along the seaway, turning into the drive for the Oceanographic Institute, two men in the front, the driver with an old-fashioned, flaring moustache.

They sat fishing for ten minutes. Copeland, lighting his pipe, was deep in thought as the smoke curled above his head, his eyes on the tip of his fishing rod.

Carefully the newcomer picked up the long pole, and laid his fishing rod down. In one beautifully coordinated movement, he stood, stepped closer to Copeland, touched the bottom of the pole releasing a long, needle-thin knife that sprung out of the other end of the pole. Without stopping his forward movement, the fisherman pushed the knife deep into Copeland's right eye, twisting it upward into the brain.

Copeland said "Ah!" then toppled backward, flat on the dock.

Quickly, the other man withdrew the knife, which vanished into the pole tip, opened the chest, removed two heavy metal weights, tied one around each of Copeland's legs, then gently pushed him off the dock into the deep water. The Englishman sank without a trace, the water sending up circular swirls.

The fisherman closed the chest, picked up his fishing rod and the long pole. Then, having second thoughts, he set them down, folded Copeland's canvas chair, gathered up his fishing equipment, walked away from the dock.

Allan Vaughn hadn't worked in the Institute proper. His headquarters was the long gray one-story building closest to the water. It did not have the institutional look of the rest of the red brick buildings and it was far enough from them to give it an exclusive air. It even had its own private drive, and its area was completely encircled by six-foot chain-link fencing.

As they opened the fence gate, Spargo could see a complex of what looked like swimming pools behind the main buildings, pools with cement arteries that fed water to them directly from the sea.

Entering the building, Spargo instantly saw that it was the place where the catfish film had been made; the tanks were there, spaced about an area that was almost as large as a football field. Evidently Vaughn had needed much space, for the dozen tanks ran from large to enormous. In the largest were seven huge lobsters, their claws pinioned with broad black rubber bands. The purple buoy that had led him here was still propped against a far wall. From the rear of the laboratory, a mousy woman in a green smock, with frizzy brown hair just short of an Afro, peered at Josef, recognized him and said, "Oh, you again. Is this the day of the inquisition? I'll get Miss Brownlee. She's in the office."

While they waited, Spargo identified on tables along the walls electron microscopes, Petri dishes, test tube retorts, optical microscopes, a freeze-dryer gas-exchange balance and PH meter, ultracentrifuge beakers. The lab was extremely well equipped. Spargo had once used a cover as a chemical engineer on a drug mission and had done his laboratory homework.

Along a near wall, electron micrographs were pinned. On the table at which the girl had been working was a three-thousand-RPM centrifuge and some Koch plates.

She had been smoking; there was the bitter smell of burning tobacco, the pungent odor of too-ripe fish. On a table not far from the tank containing the large lobsters was a metal tray with pieces of fish, food for the lobsters. The overall effect of the room was orderly dishevelment.

The west wall was a bank of windows looking directly on the tanks behind the building, which Spargo now saw were circular.

The girl in the smock came from the room in the back, followed by the dark woman Spargo had seen at Mertz Hall. She had on a white Brooks Brothers shirt, open at the neck but buttoned down, a well-cut blue denim skirt, and what looked to Spargo like India-leather, open-toed sandals. Around her neck was a beggar's chain of green agates that spilled down her white shirt front like running fire.

As she came toward them in a lithe stride, Spargo felt his heart pumping. She looked so much like Salwa it was incredible. The limpid, almost black, slightly slanted eyes, the creamy tan complexion of the Semite, the Arab or Jew, that head held high, hair smooth, black, glossy as the wing of a crow in sunlight. She had fuller breasts than Salwa, but the same long, slender, well-shaped legs, the same assured walk. She was younger and did not have Salwa's sophisticated air. Her cheekbones were higher, more pronounced.

"You must be Mr. Larsen, Mr. Kulik's boss," she said, her voice low, somewhat deeper than Salwa's. She also did not have Salwa's sly, sexy trick of sizing a man up, the dark eyes running from toes to head in a slow, calculating assessment. Her look was direct.

"I'm Harla Brownlee, Dr. Vaughn's assistant."

"My pleasure," Spargo said. "I'm not really Mr. Kulik's boss. Just have a grade on him. We're a team." He took his wallet from his breast pocket, extracted the IRS identification and handed it to her.

She read it carefully, then looked at Josef. "I told Mr. Kulik I'd do anything I can. I'm sorry Dr. Vaughn isn't here. He's really the one with the answers." She was easy, direct, but slightly distant.

"Do you expect him soon, a day or two?" Spargo said. "We could come back."

She hesitated. "Frankly, we're not certain when he is returning to the lab. He's been working terribly hard and I suspect that he's off for a few days' rest. He does that occasionally. Quite abruptly. Comes back refreshed. But I should be able to give you most of what you want."

She was covering for Vaughn; his disappearance obviously was not common knowledge.

"Please forgive what may appear to be picky little questions," Spargo said. "It's just the nature of our work, dot the *i*'s, cross the *t*'s, so to speak."

"Oh, I've been exposed to IRS before," she said. "But neither of you look like what most of us expect from your feared organization. That pinched CPA look."

"Well," Spargo said briskly, "this is an expensive operation. That's obvious." He waved a hand around the room. "Lots of deductibles. Do you have a list?"

She nodded. "Yes, I can get one for you."

Spargo walked close to the tank containing the large lobsters. "Aren't these giants? Freaks? What do the marks on the back signify?"

"Yes, they're hardly dinner lobsters. But not freaks. Sea lobsters. Breeders. The marks were painted on them by Dr. Vaughn. They then were released in the ocean. A lobster fisherman returned them. For a reward. From the hour, date, and position where they were trapped, Dr. Vaughn can read all kinds of important information."

"What kind of reward would a lobsterman

get for these?" Josef said curiously.

"Fifty dollars each. Dr. Vaughn's name is on their backs. The lobsters were returned directly to him."

"Three hundred and fifty dollars," Spargo said.

She nodded. "All to one man."

Spargo raised his eyebrows. "One?"

"Yes, rather odd. But then many odd things happen when you work with the sea."

"Are all these fees deductible?" Josef asked.

She nodded. "It's an important part of our work."

"Just exactly what is your work?" Spargo said.

"Well," she said, "I'm a marine biologist. But Allan Vaughn is a lot more. He has all of the degrees, B.S., M.S., Ph.D. in marine biology, biochemistry, zoology, organic chemistry; he did one thesis on neurophysiology, working on recordings in individual taste receptor cells, another on olfactory reception in catfish."

"Impressive," Josef said. "I'm not sure what it all means. But impressive anyway."

"Didn't Vaughn more or less concentrate on one subject?" Spargo said.

She pointed at the tank. "Lobsters." Motioning them to follow, she walked to the windows on the west wall. "See those circular tanks out there? They are Allan Vaughn's laboratory. He designed all of that himself. Our entire operation is sponsored by Jacob's Landing Oceanographic Institute and the State of Massachusetts. Allan Vaughn is attempting to perfect a system for farm-raising lobsters. Bring them to America's dinner tables in much less time than it takes now."

"How will he do that?" Spargo said.

She smiled. "Do you really want to know?

He nodded.

"By studying lobster courtship, mating, growth and development from hatch, actually through the larval stage to maturity. He also is studying the regeneration of new legs, migration, habitat, aggressive behavior, sexual responses, the effects of warm water on growth. And shell —"

Spargo laughed. "You were right. That is more than I need to know."

"Books," Josef said suddenly. "I suppose that's a substantial deduction."

"Yes," she said, pointing at three shelves bulging with books in the rear. "But Allan Vaughn's favorite reading is an inexpensive paperback on that top shelf. The notes of a biology watcher. Lewis Thomas. His *The Lives of a Cell* won the National Book Award."

Spargo sauntered back to the shelf, pulled out the paperback, perused a few pages, then replaced it.

"But a new system of ours is by far more expensive than books," Harla Brownlee said. "Films."

Spargo said, "Motion picture films? Eight millimeter?"

"No, sixteen. In color. A photographer was here this summer introducing a new system to us. Film Files, Incorporated, he called it. The perfect way to keep the Institute, the State, and foundations up on our progress. Much better than papers being read or lectures."

Spargo took out his wallet and found the photo of Ryal. He walked over and showed it to Harla Brownlee. "Is this the photographer?"

She looked at it carefully. "Yes, that's Henry Leasor. He did a number of films for us. How come you have this photograph?"

"He has done the same sort of thing for other laboratories. Claims he charges a certain fee. We always check that sort of situation out."

Josef picked up. "Any chance of us seeing one of the films?"

"You are thorough." Harla Brownlee was thoughtful, withdrawn.

"Our job," Josef said. "Mundane. But there you are."

"Yes. I suppose I can show you some film. If you think it necessary. We have a screening room back of the building. Small, but adequate, I guess."

She went over and talked with the fuzzy-haired woman working at a table at the rear of the building, then came back to them. "Joan will get things set up, then we can take a look."

They talked while they waited, Spargo and Josef with the expected questions, Spargo breaking pattern by asking if she lived here and included the living quarters as part of her personal deduction.

"Are we off the lab now and onto the personal?" Harla Brownlee said sharply.

"No," Spargo said quietly. "Habit pattern, I guess. This is strictly a laboratory audit. Forgive me."

"It's okay," she said. "I just don't like the oblique. Anyway, right now I live in a motel, The Lighthouse. Nice. But rather expensive. I'm still trying to get a small house. So far no luck."

It was a small screening room. The scenes flashed huge on the white screen. It was the same technique used in the catfish film, no people.

The camera focused on a wide metal frame on the floor of the laboratory, like a trough, but Y-shaped. On one end was a large circular metal trough; on the other two small ones. These two small circles were separated by the branches of the Y, which were half-full of water. Huge glass jars were feeding water into each small circle through rubber hoses.

The same voice that described the catfish activities took over here. Spargo assumed that it was Allan Vaughn.

"This is an experimental Y-maze," the voice said. "We use it for various tests. Today we will introduce a young salmon, placing it in the large circle on the bottom."

A hand holding a small transfer tank with a fish spilled it into the large circle. The camera now focused on another hand, holding a bottle, withdrawing liquid from it with an eye dropper.

"You will note that the salmon is making no effort to leave the large circle and investigate its surroundings. Now observe."

The hand held the eye dropper over one of

the small circles at the other end of the maze, and carefully squeezed out a single drop.

Suddenly, the immobile salmon twisted its body into an S-shape, turned completely around in the large circle, darted up the long water-filled metal arm of the extension into the small circle where the drop of water had been placed.

The voice: "That was one drop of water from that salmon's home stream. The salmon followed the chemical imprint of that water and ignored the other water completely."

Another deep, half-puzzled voice: "This could indicate then that in addition to identifying chemical signals you have also broken down the chemical components of that home stream and isolated the homing chemical."

The original voice, which Spargo now was certain was Vaughn: A chuckle. "Perhaps. But we must not jump to conclusions. This is only an experiment."

The screen went blank.

"We'll show you one more," Harla Brownlee, sitting beside Spargo, said. "Isn't this a more dramatic and interesting way to show our sponsors what we are doing? We think the expense worthwhile."

A telephone shrilled.

Joan, rewinding the film stopped and went to answer.

"A Professor Kim Dong Jo," she said as she came back to the screening room. "Says he met you at Mertz Hall after his lecture."

"Sure," Harla Brownlee said easily. "Interesting man. Show the film of Ali. Don't wait for me. I've seen it fifty times."

Joan fiddled with the projector for a few minutes, switched off the lights and started the film. The scene began with a single lobster in a tank.

The voice: "This is a female. When receptive to sex, she is in the shell-molting stage. Right now she is not receptive. Incidentally, all lobsters are aggressive. They fight one another all of the time. Except at breeding time."

The camera now panned to another tank containing one large lobster.

"This is Mohammed Ali." The voice was amused. "He's licked every lobster in the place."

A hand with a net entered the scene, netting Ali and releasing him into the tank with the single female.

Ali swam directly to her. He shot out his left claw and tried to tear out her eye.

She spurted away. Like boxers, they flicked their claws at each other.

Ali used his weight, throwing her off balance with his heavy right claw.

He opened his left scimitar pincers and snipped one long antenna from her head. Still twitching, it floated to the surface.

"Enough," the voice commanded. The hand with the net scooped Ali from the tank.

"Ali would have immediately cut her in half," the narrator said. "He has killed three females this month."

The hand holding the now familiar bottle and eye dropper reappeared.

The voice of the scientist: "This bottle contains a substance in solution which was extracted from a molted female lobster ready to mate."

The hand held the eye dropper over the tank where the female lobster cowered in a corner. Thumb and forefinger squeezed out two drops of solution.

The hand with the net returned Ali to that tank of the female.

Again Ali spurted for her. Halfway to her, he abruptly halted and stood upright. Then, in a clumsy ballet, he bounced toward the female.

"Those two drops of the solution not only suppressed Ali's aggression, but forced him into the mating dance." The voice then startled them with its abruptness. "Now watch!"

As Ali continued dancing, the female suddenly surged from her corner. While he danced, she cut him with her left claw. At the same time she attempted to crush his head with her large right pincers.

Before the hand with the net rescued Ali, the female had torn off half of his antennae.

"She probably would have torn Ali apart. Then eaten him." There was finality, anti-climax in the voice.

"It wasn't her sex signal that attracted Ali, so she ignored it."

The screen went blank.

Josef said, "Jesus!"

Joan turned the lights on and Harla Brownlee walked in.

"Didn't want to interrupt," she said cheerily. "How did it go?"

"Dramatically!" Spargo said. "We're not sure that we understand any of it. But it certainly is spellbinding. Worth every nickel you spent on it."

"Glad you agree," she said.

Her attitude had changed. She seemed warmer, friendlier.

As they left the screening room she put her arm through Spargo's. "I'm going to offer a bribe. Tempt you to be kind to us."

"Offer away," Spargo said.

"Tomorrow is my jogging day. I spend too much time at a desk, the rest standing looking into fish tanks. So I need the exercise. I've found a beautiful, lonely, peopleless expanse of beach where I can run for miles. You're invited. You can finish your questions on the jog. I'll even bring a little picnic."

She looked at Josef, smiling. "You're invited, too."

Josef chuckled. "I'm not a jogger. I'll sit in the sun and wait you two out."

"I'd be delighted to run with you by the sea and share your picnic," Spargo said.

Harla Brownlee laughed, shaking her hair loose, eyes sparkling. "I wear a swimsuit beneath my jogging suit. If the sea's calm a swim would be fun."

"I'll skip the swim and settle for the jog," Spargo said lightly, thinking of Salwa strapped to his arm. He never was without her.

Harla Brownlee excused herself. "I have

some lab stuff to chat up with Joan."

"Would it be too much trouble?" Spargo said. "We'd like the name and address of the lobsterman who caught those seven giants for Dr. Vaughn."

She was suddenly aloof, businesslike, impersonal again. "Is that necessary? These fisher folk are reclusive. They resent being bothered —"

"It's three hundred and fifty paid-out dollars," Josef picked up on it. "An item we must check out."

"We know it's all legitimate," Spargo said. "But it's routine."

"He lives on the shore," Harla Brownlee said sharply. "I don't know where. His name is Harry Paucek. He's in the phone book. It's the best I can do."

Spargo said it was good enough and that he looked forward to seeing her tomorrow.

As they left, Spargo reached to the top of the lab bookshelf, took Allan Vaughn's favorite paperback reading and slipped it into the pocket of his seersucker jacket.

CHAPTER TWENTY-ONE

The early moon had risen as they drove along the ocean road to Falmouth. The sea glittered, whitecaps rolled toward shore. Late gulls cried in the darkening sky.

"What do you make of all that?" Spargo said.

"I make it that Harla Brownlee has suddenly become interested in Spargo."

"Let's see how that develops."

For some reason that puzzled Josef, Spargo was curt. But he always had been complicated.

They were silent then, caught up in the paradox of the two films they had seen.

"Was that catfish film we stashed more of the same?" Josef broke the silence.

Spargo nodded.

"What do you think it adds up to?"

"To the fact that Allan Vaughn is one very smart marine scientist. He hasn't yet exactly taught his catfish to catch mice but he's getting close!"

"I was thinking of the lobsters. Vaughn seems to be into some kind of crazy chemicals, sex chemicals. Wonder why?"

"These guys spend years learning everything there is about any subject they tackle. Our contact didn't let me in on what Vaughn's file contains. But they want it bad and they're paying us very well to produce. I was also told it is for God and Country. The United States positively must have Vaughn's sea file. Problem: No Vaughn. But I suddenly have a thought on that. Let's discuss it over dinner."

When they returned to the Beachcomber they checked their rooms carefully for any sign of intrusion. Both appeared clean. It was difficult in a motel, for maids came to clean up, often to turn beds down. The old thread-across-doors couldn't be employed and neither could a half-dozen other simple but successful detection gimmicks.

Spargo decided that he was going to try to locate the lobsterman Harry Paucek and invite him to dinner, get him out of his own environment, loosen him up. But when he finally got Paucek on the phone the fisherman was distant, reserved. In his hard New England voice, he said he always had an early dinner with his wife and couldn't make it. He finally agreed to come to the Beachcomber and talk over after-dinner brandy.

Spargo also decided that before dinner he would have a drink and look through the paperback he had taken from Vaughn's laboratory. He made a Boodles martini and sat in a slippery plastic uncomfortable chair, leafing through the book.

Lewis Thomas turned out to be a clever, amusing writer; everything in his *The Lives of a Cell* was interesting. But Spargo finally zeroed in on a chapter that Vaughn had apparently read and reread; there were check marks on pages that also had edges turned down in several places.

That chapter, "A Fear of Pheromones," Spargo read carefully. "What are we going to do if it turns out that we have pheromones?" Lewis Thomas wrote.

What on earth would we be doing with such things? With the richness of speech, and all of our new devices for communication, why would we want to release odors into the air to convey information about anything? We can send notes, telephone, whisper cryptic invitations, announce the giving of parties, even bounce words off the moon and make them carom around the planets. Why a gas, or droplets of moisture made to be deposited on fence posts?

Comfort has recently reviewed the reasons for believing that we are, in fact, in possession of anatomic structures for which there is no rational explanation except as sources of pheromones – tufts of hair, strategically located apocrine glands, unaccountable areas of moisture. We even have folds of skin here and there designed for the controlled nurture of bacteria, and it is known that certain microbes eke out a living, like eighteenth-century musicians, producing chemical signals by ornamenting the products of their hosts.

Most of the known pheromones are small, simple molecules, active in extremely small concentrations. Eight or ten carbon items in a chain are all that are needed to generate precise, unequivocal directions about all kinds of matters – when and where to cluster in crowds, when to disperse, how to behave to the opposite sex, how to ascertain what *is* the opposite sex, how to organize members of a society in the proper ranking orders of dominance, how to mark our exact boundaries of real estate, and how to establish that one is, beyond argument, one's self. Trails can be laid and followed, antagonists frightened and confused, friends attracted and enchanted.

The messages are urgent, but they may arrive, for all we know, in a fragrance of ambiguity. "At home, 4 P.M. today," says one female moth, and releases a brief explosion of bombykol, a single molecule of which will tremble the hairs of any male within miles and send him driving upwind in a confusion of ardor. But it is doubtful if he has an awareness of being caught in an aerosol of chemical attractant. On the contrary, he probably finds suddenly that it has become an excellent day, the weather remarkably bracing, the time appropriate for a bit of exercise of the old wings, a brisk turn upwind. En route, traveling the gradient of bombykol, he notes the presence of other males, heading in the same direction, all in a good mood, inclined to race for the sheer sport of it. Then, when he reaches his destination, it may seem to him the most extraordinary of coincidences, the greatest piece of luck: "Bless my soul, what have we here!"

It has been soberly calculated that if a single female moth were to release all the bombykol in her sac in a single spray, all at once, she could theoretically attract a trillion males in the instant. That is, of course, not done.

Fish make use of chemical signals for the identification of individual members of a species, and also for the announcement of changes in status of certain individuals. A catfish that has had a career as a local leader smells one way, but as soon as he is displaced in an administrative reorganization, he smells differently, and everyone recognizes the loss of standing. A bullhead can immediately identify the water in which a recent adversary has been swimming, and he can distinguish between this fish and all others in the school.

There is some preliminary, still fragmentary evidence for important pheromones in primates. Short-chain aliphatic compounds are elaborated by female monkeys in response to estradiol, and these are of consuming interest to the males. Whether there are other sorts of social communication by pheromones among primates is not known.

The essay continued, commenting upon the possibilities in discovering human pheromones and what could happen, with several amusing conjectures.

Spargo made another martini and sat thinking about what he had read until Josef appeared for dinner. It was obvious: Allan Vaughn was into pheromones. But not once in all three films was the strange word mentioned. Why?

They decided to eat in the Beachcomber dining room, realizing their mistake as soon as they entered. The huge room was full of noisy, relaxing tourists. A harried waitress told them that yes, indeed, there was a bar and that gentlemen often ate there. They lucked out. It was a dark pine-paneled room with bold, local paintings of old sailing ships on the walls, a pleasant, fat, skillful bartender, and a fast perky young waitress who nearly ran as she took and delivered orders.

There were only six other diners in the large dark room. It also would be an excellent place to pour Harry Paucek after-dinner brandy.

They were hungry, enjoying fresh-caught ocean perch that had been lightly dredged in cornmeal and deep-fried just right, the flesh white, sweet, and moist. Not epicurian, but satisfying.

While they were awaiting dessert, fresh raspberries in heavy cream, Spargo said, "If you were Allan Vaughn and had an assistant like Harla Brownlee and you wanted to disappear for a while what would you do?"

Josef stared at him. "Move in?"

"She's attractive as hell. Be hard to resist. Also a smart move. Best way to get lost is in your own terrain, take on protective coloring. I don't think he really vanished. I think Harla Brownlee is probably covering for him with Institute authorities, maybe the same way she did with us."

"It's good thinking," Josef said. "But what's the point?"

"I told you about that biochemist Lundberg, lost his head in Stamford?"

"Yes. I forgot about him."

"I didn't. I think he was in some way working with Vaughn. Selling what little he knew. Didn't know enough. Tried to overextend. Got wiped out. Scared Vaughn into hiding."

They sat silently, finishing their raspberries in cream.

"I'd like to meet Vaughn," Spargo said. "If he has moved in with Harla Brownlee, is hiding, I'd think he would have to appear sometime. It'll probably mean a long wait. But it's a shot I'd like to take. You don't have to come along. Stay here and sleep it off."

"No," Josef said gently. "I'll come along and nursemaid. I see now why you asked where she lived."

"I phoned the Lighthouse. I know her location."

"When do we make this move?"

"Right away. We're short of time. We'll stake out the Lighthouse after we see lobsterman Harry Paucek. That lobster situation of his is, as they say, bizarroid. It interests me."

They met Harry Paucek at the motel office and escorted him to the Beachcomber bar.

Paucek, easy, tall, lank, his wind-bitten face tan, leathery, his eyes a startling blue, his hair grizzly but abundant, said "Nice place. Never been here. Martha don't take to booze in restaurants. Says you can buy a bottle for what a glass costs in places like this."

Spargo laughed. "Martha's right. But

302

sometimes you're trapped."

"Right you are," Paucek said. "Could've had you out to my place. But I figured we could talk freer here. Martha didn't want me to talk at all. She don't cotton to the IRS."

"Can't blame her," Josef said. "But we're just doing a job like everybody else."

"Certain," Paucek said. "I know that. Why I'm here. What can I do for you?"

"You can have a jot of brandy with us," Spargo said. "Ever try it in a cup of nice strong black coffee?"

"Nope. But I'm willin'."

The little waitress who did her duties on the run had hot black coffee and a bottle of Courvoisier on their table in ten minutes.

They silently toasted, holding the cups up, then sipping.

"Spoil you for coffee," Paucek grunted.

They talked about fishing, lobstering, why Paucek came here to avoid the hard winters of his native Maine.

"These fisher folks 'round here," Paucek said. "Just fancy themselves lobstermen. They don't pull their pots enough. Let 'em set out two, three day at a time. Amateurs —"

"Not professionals," Spargo said softly, "who can catch seven giants in a single day."

Paucek looked at him. "I got a hydraulic winch. Means I can go out farther. Keep my pots deeper where the bigger ones are. But those luggers I caught weren't no skill. That was just dumb luck. First time anything like that happened. And I been lobsterin' all my life. And my father before me."

"Did you personally return the lobsters to Dr. Vaughn?" Josef said. "And did he pay you fifty dollars apiece?"

"Yep. Those lobsters bought Martha the color TV she's been hankerin' for."

"How did Dr. Vaughn act?" Spargo said.

"I thought he was a-goin' bust out of his skin, he was that excited."

"Did he say anything?" Josef.

"Just 'I did it! I did it!' "

"What do you think he did?" Spargo.

Paucek scratched his head. "Blamed if I know. But it all was a mixed-up kinda thing."

Paucek went on to say that lobsters, especially the huge ones, were wanderers, moving in a wide radius in the ocean. He also had understood that Dr. Vaughn had released those seven in areas ten miles apart.

"But I got 'em all. In my pots, spread no more than two, three miles apart. Funny thing —"

"Why?" Spargo said. "Don't all kinds of strange things happen in the sea?"

"Sure do. But by all laws of chance I shouldn't have taken *all* of them lobsters. Some should've ended up in another man's pots miles away from mine."

"Do you have any explanation?" Josef said.

Paucek shook his head. "And not for the other things, neither."

He went on to tell them that lobsters were normally attracted to the pots by the bait in them. But that these large lobsters had eaten plenty before they came into his traps; that when he picked them out of the pots and placed them in baskets, pieces of herring and squid fell out of their mouths, a result of their overeating. And it was not the kind of bait that was in the pots. He used no squid or herring. So hunger had not attracted them.

He also said that all lobsters, but especially the big ones, were mean, aggressive, hard to handle. Not these. They were placid, tranquil, let him handle them without any trouble. "Two were even doing a crazy kind of dance. Standing straight up.

"More'n that," Paucek went on. "In every one of my pots the bait wasn't mine. I use perch racks. Someone switched bait bags on me."

The moon had been misty, but now it swam free from the veils of cloud and the night was clear. It was about a ten-mile ride to the Lighthouse Motel, all of it along the water that now lay flat and as reflective as a huge mirror, reproducing perfect replicas of the moon and stars.

The Lighthouse was obviously named for an old abandoned lighthouse that stood behind it, tall, dark, silent as the ruins of a Greek temple.

Flagged walks ran from the motel to the guest bungalows all the way to the beach. Every fifty feet carriage lamps on thigh-thick cedar posts stood like robot doormen. Right now the lights were extinguished.

Harla Brownlee's bungalow was number fifteen, closest to the sea. It was after two A.M. and the motel was dark, as were all of the bungalows.

Spargo had suggested that they park the Aspen off a secondary sandy road that angled toward the sea away from the road that led into the motel. They walked in silently on the sand, the distance about a half-mile.

The motel itself was casting long, deep

shadows. In the darkest of the shadows were two plastic-belted sun chairs. They sat in them, watching Harla Brownlee's bungalow.

It was a long wait, a silent wait; neither man could talk, and after a while even their companion, the moon, entered a cloud trap, struggling briefly but losing the battle, surrendering to the darkness. First signal that dawn might be a possibility was the stirring of the gulls, faint croakings, then wing-flapping as they awoke on the beach and began scolding one another.

The slight sound came first, the door of Harla Brownlee's bungalow opening, a bit at a time, cautiously. Then a tall man emerged, looked back once, waved, then strode toward the parking area.

A shadow detached itself from the longer shadow of a nearby bungalow.

The moon emerged briefly and Spargo saw a long, gleaming metallic object flash from the smaller shadow; the tall man stumbled and fell to the ground.

"*Manriki-kusari!*" Spargo said, getting up from the chair, which tumbled, making a metallic clicking on the flagstone.

The shadow whirled, again something flashed from it, and Spargo felt sharp pain lance in his left arm. He pulled out a many-pointed metal object that had buried itself in his flesh, high on his left arm, missing his throat by inches. "*Shuriken*," Spargo whispered. "Ninja!"

Moving fast, Josef ran forward a few feet, searching for substance in the shadow that had now moved toward the fallen figure that was trying to get up.

Stopping, Josef made a long, careful throw, his knife aglitter in the weak moonshine.

The shadow fell forward, toppled beside the taller man.

Moving quickly, Spargo and Josef reached them simultaneously. The shorter figure struggled to get up. With a quick, graceful movement Josef reached it first, his right foot flicking out, catching the man in the throat.

With his foot, Spargo turned him over, a short man, dressed completely in black, wearing a hood. Spargo removed the hood. He was Japanese, a ninja, Spargo was certain.

Josef was helping the tall man get to his feet, a linked chain wrapped tightly around his neck, like a snake. The man groaned as Josef removed the chain, his neck welted, bleeding.

"Which car is yours?" Spargo asked.

"The blue Volkswagen," the man said weakly.

They walked him to his car, and got in, Spargo beside the man in the front seat, Josef in the rear.

"Close, Dr. Vaughn," Spargo said. "You can thank the man in black for saving your life. The chain that was thrown was a *manriki-kusari*, just an immobilizer. Next he would have broken your neck with a *koppo* chop, or slit your throat. Probably a chop. The ninja use their hands when they can."

"Ninja?" Vaughn croaked.

"Japanese assassin," Spargo said.

"I thought it would be the Japanese," Vaughn said. "I was pretty sure Lundberg was dealing with them, and they finally got him."

"What's this all about?" Josef said softly.

"Who are you?" Vaughn said shakily.

"Government," Spargo said. "U.S. Sent to locate you when it was learned that you had made a spectacular breakthrough in marine science. Why did you 'disappear'? Where did you go?"

"The man back there that you dispatched is the reason I disappeared," Vaughn said. "It was simple. I colored my hair dark, wore dark glasses, joined the crew of a lobster trawler that works far out. I'm good with lobsters, so it was a natural. Harla Brownlee, my assistant, was kind enough to put me up at night. I got back from my work late, left here early, so there was no problem. Until tonight."

"Why are they after you?" Josef said.

Silence.

"Pheromones?" Spargo said.

Vaughn chuckled weakly. "You might be right. '*Pherein*, to carry.' '*Horman*, to excite.' Both from the Greek."

"Excite what?" Josef said.

"My lobsters, of course. Excite them into breeding. I've been working for years to perfect a process to produce so-called farm lobsters. My breakthrough is that I am now able to raise, in captivity, or domesticity, whatever you want to call it, one-pound marketable lobsters in fourteen months. In the wild it takes eight years."

"Is that your breakthrough?" Spargo said quietly. "Your amazing feat of cutting almost seven years from the time necessary to bring lobsters to market?"

Vaughn nodded.

"They may try to get you again," Josef said.

"They won't find me," Vaughn said confidently. He looked at his wristwatch. "In exactly two hours I am leaving on a cruise, a scientific expedition for a foreign nation. I won't tell you which one. They have asked me to go along as chief marine scientist. We are going to cruise some distant islands and study the marine life. Well financed. I'll be gone six or seven months. By the time I have returned everything will be straightened out. I'll get the credit I deserve. That's what I really want. Not government interference, not offering what I've discovered up for grabs for other researchers to steal."

"Good luck," Spargo said. "You feel all right now?"

Vaughn rubbed his neck. 'Sore throat. I'm grateful to you two." He reached a long arm across the seat and shook Josef's hand. "I owe you my life. Maybe some day I can repay you."

"That's all right," Josef said gruffly. "Glad we were here."

"So am I," Allan Vaughn said. "So am I. Sorry, I have to be off. Lot to do in two hours."

They could hold him and question him, but Spargo could sense the determination in Vaughn. He had not run for help, but tried to work out his own protection. Like many other scientists he obviously resented governmental interference. No, let him run. He'd be back, and he'd be valuable.

As they stood and watched him drive away, the Volkswagen's red tail lights fire-flying down the road, Spargo thought, what has he come up with? Has he learned to read marine creatures' signals that could perhaps tell him where there were deposits of oil or natural gas? He remembered the Geological Survey had estimated that between sixty-five and one-hundred thirty billion barrels of undiscovered oil, and seven million trillion cubic feet of untapped gas lay in the U.S. continental shelf out to two hundred meters.

Hadn't scientists learned to communicate with dolphins? Wasn't the Navy using them successfully in underwater experiments, rescuing men, carrying messages?

What Vaughn had said he had accomplished with lobsters was impressive, but not important enough to have the United States and Japan, and who knew what other nations, racing to get his formulas, his file. Vaughn's real secret was known by someone, or they had guessed at its magnitude. There were too many dead men. Instant lobsters? No.

"Two things," Spargo said aloud.

"What?" Josef said. "Besides his lying?"

"Yes, he's lying about the lobsters. But the way I see it, the Japanese no longer think that he is important. In fact, they'd prefer that he wasn't around any longer. That ninja obviously meant to eliminate Vaughn."

"Why?"

"Because they either have his file, or know where they can get it. I doubt that Vaughn carries it with him, or that he will take it along on that scientific cruise."

"What are we going to do with the man who tried to eliminate him?"

"The tide will take him out."

When they walked the two hundred yards back to where the man had fallen, all that remained was the bloody black hood.

CHAPTER TWENTY-TWO

Harry Cleve did not look like an executioner, Pryor thought as he looked at him: Peaches-and-cream complexion, wavy blond hair, long, tapered sideburns, innocent china-blue eyes that looked out on the world much as those of a child, wide, curious, naive. Five-feet-ten, slender, he had the loose-limbed movements and flat-footed-ballet walk of a gymnast, the reflexes and the instincts of a weasel.

Pryor motioned Cleve to sit down. They had discovered him in Vietnam, working in the Phoenix program. He wasn't exactly insane, but there was a distorted lobe or two in his brain, the lobes that signaled remorse, sadness, right, wrong, joy. Harry Cleve had virtually no emotions about anything – except his craft of killing to order. He had been impressively efficient in eliminating Viet Cong who had been captured and questioned. One estimate was that he had, totally without remorse, killed three hundred and fifty men and women.

The Agency utilized talent wherever it could find and employ it. It had placed Harry Cleve on a retainer and used him mainly to terminate company agents who had become dangerous, his schoolboyish looks girding him in the armor of harmless anonymity.

Harry Cleve's weapon was a simple .22 pistol, a Ruger using long rifle cartridges. He carried it in a unique holster under his suit jacket in the hollow in the small of his back, the jacket constructed so that there was no bulge.

He was an emotional cripple, but a perfectly functioning assassin. Besides the .22 holstered on his back, he had another .22, designed to look exactly like a package of cigarettes.

In addition, he had an ingenious briefcase, with a .22 fastened inside, its exit hole fit snugly into a brass ring that also had an exit hole on the outside of the briefcase. There was an external trigger so Harry Cleve could fire at an unsuspecting victim.

For emergencies, and long-range use, he carried in that same briefcase a Smith and Wesson Model 57 .41 magnum. It was a unique weapon with the stock and cylinder designed so speedloads could be used. The speedloaders were plastic copies of the revolver's cylinder, holding the same number of cartridges, which made reloading simple and extremely swift. As spent shells were ejected, the speedloader fed new cartridges into the chamber with one fast motion, doing away with individual hand insertion of the cartridge.

The Teflon shells he used for the Smith and Wesson were so powerful and durable that they could drive through the engine block of an automobile.

He used silencers on all his weapons. As silencers actually are suppressors, distributing sound, and generally restricting the bullet's velocity and accuracy, Harry Cleve had his silencers made by a master gunsmith, who constructed them of titanium to aid velocity and accuracy.

Harry Cleve had one genuine emotion: He was proud of his skill. Once, when he had demonstrated his prowess at the Playhouse's target range, proving that he didn't necessarily have to fire at close range, his skill from a distance was so impressive, the range instructor said, "But it's a peashooter. Too much chance for a fireback if the twenty-two doesn't take 'em out."

Harry Cleve said, "A .22 long rifle has killed an elephant dead. One shot." The next day he brought a news clipping to prove his point.

But he really didn't have to prove his point; his record of no failed mission did that for him.

Now Pryor said, "I want you to accompany me on a job. Cape Cod."

Harry Cleve nodded. "Never been there."

"The target is a top professional. I doubt that you've ever faced opposition this good before. It won't be easy."

"Why not?"

"Because this man is super good."

"You said that about Lare. Kemp too. They were no trouble."

"True," Pryor said. "But you're going to prove yourself all over again on this one. It could be your most important mission. You may need an advantage to throw this man off. There's one word: Salwa."

"Salwa —"

Pryor nodded. "Remember it. S a l w a. Got it?"

Harry Cleve nodded.

"And put some good strong nylon rope in that killer's kit of yours."

Cleve grinned. "We going to hang someone?"

"Could be," Pryor said grimly.

CHAPTER TWENTY-NINE

Spargo's shoulder ached, with the sharpness and persistence of a toothache. Josef had taken out his medical kit and cleaned, disinfected, and dressed the wound. The razor-sharp *shuriken* had sliced off some flesh but hadn't severed a vein or an artery. This was the second time the weapon had been used against him.

He was happy to see that retirement hadn't dulled Josef's sharp edge. He was as fast, as skilled as ever. In fact, he had moved more quickly than Spargo. Knocking the chair over had been a clumsy move on Spargo's part. But he had been surprised by that ninja chain-weapon flashing in the moonlight.

It was clear: Japan was the adversary. Natural enough; they were the masters of industrial espionage. If anyone were on top of the situation it would be the Japanese.

As he drove to the Oceanographic Institute to pick up Harla Brownlee for the jogging date, Spargo noticed children playing in the sand, on the long, curving beach, drawing finger-pictures. There was an air of timeless peace about the scene; the mad world was someplace else.

The laboratory looked deserted. He had expected that Harla would be outside waiting for him, eager to get started on her jogging day.

As he entered the lab he immediately noticed that the purple buoy was missing. So what, he said to himself. Yet something kept buzzing in his head as he walked to the back of the lab where her office was. The door was open; Harla was at her desk, phone in hand. She waved him in.

It was a larger office than it appeared from outside, she sat at the far side, her desk against a bank of windows that faced the sea. She turned back to the phone and continued her conversation in a low voice. The buoy was propped against the wall not far from her desk. Spargo silently walked to it, picked it up. It was surprisingly light, as if made from feather-light balsa wood. He replaced it just as Harla swung around in her swivel chair, placing the phone on the cradle. Her look was cool, appraising.

She was dressed in the same light-blue jogging suit she had worn when he had first seen her at Mertz Hall, her ebony hair shining as if lacquered. A wide black leather belt was cinched around her slender waist; looped into it was an object that looked like a blackjack or a billy club. On the floor beside the desk was a bulging canvas pack. "I hope you haven't got jogger's jounce, or fallen arches," she said lightly. "I'm putting you through the paces today. It's a long run out there by the sea."

She looked at him critically. "But you look up to it. No gut to speak of. I think you'll do okay."

Spargo laughed. "Maybe I should have brought a beach buggy."

She led the way out. Opening the back door of the Aspen, she placed the pack on the seat, took the club out of her belt, and put it beside the pack. "Picnic and protection," she said, as she got in the front seat.

Spargo closed her door, got behind the

wheel. "I'd prefer to consider myself the protection. What's the club for?"

"We call it a 'rapejack'," she said. "Allan Vaughn made it for me. It's heavily leaded, every effective. Several girls have been attacked up here while jogging. So I stick that in my belt, just in case."

She said that they would drive north, leaving the tourist world behind, as they headed toward the National Seashore, preserved as a coastal wilderness, which occupied one-tenth of the entire peninsula.

The Cape itself, she said, reached out thirty-five miles into the ocean, narrowing, then curving abruptly around to the north for another thirty-five miles. "Our destination," she said.

As he drove, he found himself wondering if Allan Vaughn had slept with her during his hideout.

Strengthening his IRS cover, he asked her then about her work.

"I'm more or less the cleaning lady," she said cheerfully. "I maintain the proper water chemistry in the tanks. Subject the water to constant chemical analysis to make certain conditions are perfect for the lobsters and fish."

"How?" he said.

"Oh, using the equipment and techniques of chemistry, testing for nitrate buildup, and ammonia, which is toxic to fish in parts as minute as one part per million. We fight it also with bacteria that devours it, bacteria that we encourage to grow on the gravel in the filters at the bottom of each tank."

"But as a marine biologist you must do much more?"

"Oh, I help Allan. When he asks. Assisting in some tests — analytic, chemical, biologic, olfactory."

"All this to grow lobsters faster?" Spargo said. "It somehow seems misplaced dedication."

"Oh, I don't know!" she said with spirit. "It's America's favorite seafood, and with the farm plan we also bring down the price. You know what lobsters cost today?"

They were silent then, watching the traffic flow by, cars from about every state, few observing the speed limit. There was much darting in and out, much bad driving by both young and old. Holiday called for abandon.

"We'll be out of this soon," she said. "I'm getting so I hate the summer tourist season up here. The litter, the noise, the cheap commercialism —"

They drove another ten miles. Suddenly she said, "About one mile up on the left is a thick, rotting cedar post, and an unpaved road. It's bumpy, so take it easy."

The road coiled in *S* curves, so when they came upon the water, it was a dramatic sight. A deep blue-green, it lay like a gigantic sapphire melting in the sun.

"O-oo," Harla Brownlee gasped. "It's so beautiful I can't stand it."

She directed him to park in an area beside a sand dune that hid the car from the road. As they got out, she strapped on the knapsack.

"Let me carry it," Spargo offered.

"No, it's light, and part of my jogging. We jog from this point on," she said, putting the club in her belt loop.

Spargo had on chinos, a light denim shirt, and blue Adidas running shoes. They started off side by side in an easy, long jog.

There was a slight wind off the water, cooling.

They jogged in silence, expertly eating up the meters. There was not another person in sight. But there was a large residence of gulls, resting, heads under wings, standing one-legged, all along the shore, closer to the water.

"Those gulls," she said abruptly. "Did you know that they can actually drink salt water? Have a special gland that filters the salt."

"I didn't know. Those gull people have a lot going for them."

So did she. Harla Brownlee ran like an Indian, long, easy strides, feet coming down lightly, surely. Jogging was not a conversational sport, so they did not talk much, enjoying the sun warm on their heads, the seabreeze soft. It indeed was her private place, and Spargo thought then that he truly loved solitude.

"See that pair of big dunes ahead?" she suddenly said. "We'll stop there and picnic."

Harla took a pedometer from her pocket. "Would you believe it? We've run six miles. You're in good shape, man."

"I'd hate to race you. You run like a well-oiled machine."

"Practice. I do it often. Love it. Gets me away from the fish."

She put down her knapsack. "Hope you're hungry."

"Starved."

"And thirsty?"

"Like I've run fifty miles on the Sahara.

Water! Water!"

"What about wine?"

"Wine! Wine!"

They were stretched between the dunes, a sand hill behind them, the shimmering sea straight ahead. She began preparing the picnic, spreading a red cloth, with matching napkins, pulling out two thin, stemmed wine glasses, a bottle of Muscadet. She handed him a corkscrew and he yanked the cork and poured the wine, tilting a small amount into her glass first. "Madam?"

She sipped it tentatively, cocking her head. "Um. Bit corky, but let's not send it back."

He filled their glasses, and toasted, holding his glass high. "Jogging."

She waved her hand. "Sit down, please. This table okay, or would you rather have one by the window?"

"This one's fine. I always say it's the company, not the place."

She apologized for the paper plates and then proceeded to place items on them, two oblong pieces of meat, thickly sliced avocadoes, crisp, thin, unbuttered triangles of toast, long, slender white radishes.

They ate with their fingers. The meat was delicately flavored, delicious.

"A delight!" Spargo said. "What is it?"

"Pojarskis. Ground breast of chicken and loin of pork, browned, then simmered in heavy cream and fresh dill. It's supposed to be served hot with rice but I like it better this way. Cold. With ants." She brushed a bevy of black ants off her leg.

They sat silently and ate, savoring the sound of the gulls crying, the murmuring of the sea. A sound for lovers, Spargo thought.

"Look!" she cried, pointing at the sky. "Blue herons!"

The dozen birds floated like kites, long legs behind, lazily flapping until they were beyond their vision.

She lay back on the sand. "A quiet day. Funny, not even the sight of a boat."

"Suits me," Spargo said. "I've seen plenty of boats."

"Let's allow our picnic to settle," she said. "Then jog to a place where I like to swim. Okay by you?"

"Fine." He stretched back on the sand while she cleaned up, folding cloth and napkins, putting everything back into the knapsack, not leaving a scrap of paper.

"Too bad," she said. "I didn't figure you for a glutton. There's not a crumb left for the gulls."

They resumed their running until they reached her swim area. By now she was calling him Larsen and she had become easy, unstrained. She led them to an area where several dunes converged, forming almost a seaside cave.

Harla shrugged out of her knapsack, unbuckled her belt with her bludgeon, took off her running shoes and slipped out of the jogging suit. Her swimsuit was just bra and shorts, jet black, matching her hair and eyes.

Spargo caught his breath. Her legs were long, beautifully shaped, her breasts large, but wellformed, the nipples pushing firm and hard against the bra. She walked to the water in the graceful almost flat-footed walk of a ballet dancer; her buttocks, hard, moved with a controlled muscular motion.

It was as graceful and as natural as if she had been born in the sea, her swimming skillful as a dolphin. She was underwater as often as she was on top; she floated, she swam on her side, her back; she reveled in the water.

Then, abruptly, it was all over and she came wading from the sea, dripping water like a mermaid, her black hair tight against her head, smooth and shiny as sealskin, the bra and trunks molded to her body.

What happened next Spargo was to always remember as in a dream:

She took him by the hand, led him to her sand cave, took off her swim suit, her coppery body gleaming, its naked symmetry absolute perfection. She was as natural as a small child, naked on a seashore. The wind dried her quickly and she got into her jogging suit.

Attempting to quiet himself, Spargo pulled out his hammered silver cigarette case and took out a rolled cylinder of betel, putting it into his mouth.

"What is that?" she said huskily.

He quickly told her that one tenth of the human race chewed it, that it was a mixture of shell lime; dried, sliced areca nut, cardamon, aniseed and cloves, rolled tightly in a leaf from a betel vine called *pann*.

"A red paste made from the liquid of boiled chips from the catechu tree binds the ingredients together and gives color and flavor."

"What does it do?" she asked, her tongue slowly licking her lips.

"It's a masticatory exhilarant."

"Gives you a lift?"

"Small."

She held out her hand. He gave her one, watching her reaction as she chewed.

Her face flushed slightly. "I like it. It reaches you fast but gently."

Then in a quick, catlike movement, she stretched out on the sand, said, "Come here, Larsen."

As he approached, she reached up and pulled him on top of her. Her jogging suit was fully unzipped, her brown body gleaming. With skill, she unzipped him.

It was so natural, he thought, so unstrained, their motion matching the slow, stroking rhythm of the sea until it seemed that they were flowing into one another.

He could smell her scent, slightly musky, and suddenly thought of the words of Lewis' he had read in *The Lives of a Cell*, " 'At home, 4 P.M. today,' says one female moth, and releases a brief explosion of bombykol, a single molecule of which will tremble the hairs of any male within miles . . ."

Harla was releasing her own bombykol, writhing in a circular movement that excited him. She began moaning, eyes closed, her motion becoming faster, then slow again.

Spargo knew what the blow from behind was. A *yubi*, a thumb blow. It was aimed at his carotid artery. If it had landed on target with enough force it would have killed him.

It was skillful and powerful enough to hurl him sideways off Harla.

As he hit the sand, Spargo rolled, coiling, his feet pulled back as the man followed up, a long, slim knife in his right hand.

Spargo's double-footed blow caught him midsection, knocking him backward onto the beach. He was up immediately as if made of rubber. The man's hurled knife sliced skin off Spargo's right hand as he automatically raised it to deflect the flung knife.

Spargo's right-foot kick centered on the groin, the left the throat, the right again struck the man on the side of the head, spinning him to the sand.

He was still moving when Spargo stood over him, spearing his right foot to the center of the man's hyoid bone so powerfully that the bone snapped and the man flipped, face down.

He lay motionless, spread-eagled, face in the sand, the sea nibbling at his feet.

Spargo turned him over with the toe of his right foot, watching for reaction. But he was out; if he had been conscious he would have been gagging, trying to get oxygen in past the broken hyoid bone.

Spargo stood erect, breathing deeply.

He took a handkerchief from his pocket and

tied it tightly around the bleeding heel of his right hand. Harla watched anxiously.

He examined the would-be assassin. Young. Japanese. If he was a ninja, he would have come prepared with weapons other than his almost lethal hands.

Off to the right of the sand cave, Spargo saw a fishing rod and a metal chest. Good cover. Fisherman. In fishing country. Ninja technique.

He opened the metal chest, motioning to Harla.

Taking objects out of the chest, he identified them mentally one by one. He picked up the pointed, star-shaped weapon, *shuriken*, great for cutting the throat when thrown by an expert, the *fukiya*, a blow gun that throws poisoned darts; dirks, small throwing knives, probably also poisoned; *shuko*, brass knuckles with spikes.

He took out a red-and-black fountain pen, a small cardboard box taped to it. In the box were four capsules. Spargo smelled them. He put the cardboard box in his pocket, unscrewed the bottom of the fountain pen. It had a capsule inside. He screwed the bottom on again.

Near the fallen man on the beach a curious

young brown herring gull was getting bolder, cautiously approaching.

Moving carefully, Spargo walked toward the gull, one step at a time.

Twenty feet from the bird, he stopped and held up the fountain pen, aimed it like a pistol at the gull and pressed the bottom of the pen.

Hissing, then, in straight, true trajectory, a stream of vapor flew from the pen at the gull, striking it in the head. The gull jumped straight up, then fell and was still.

"I heard the Japanese had perfected this technique," Spargo said.

"What is it?" Harla seemed dazed.

"Hydrogen-cyanide. Its vapor kills instantly, causing what looks like a massive heart attack. Death is always diagnosed as cardiac failure. The Soviets used to use it often, but it had a blowback spray that made it dangerous to the operator. And it had a limited range. Only a couple of feet. The Japanese have developed it into a deadly weapon. This little fountain pen will kill at twenty feet. Obviously this guy meant business — and I don't think he was after the IRS. Whoever he mistook me for is in serious trouble."

Spargo clipped the fountain pen to his shirt pocket and walked over to the man in the sand.

Grabbing the Japanese by the hair, he dragged him into the surf.

When the water reached his chest, he released the man, then stood watching him slowly sink, face down, to the bottom.

Spargo stood silently until bubbles began to rise to the surface. Then he waded back to shore.

CHAPTER TWENTY-FOUR

Like Spargo, Josef kept himself in shape, practicing his *savate* routine as often as possible. Working with Spargo on this job had given him a new vigor, brought him out of his perpetual reveries of the old days when he taught at the Playhouse. He had been forced to retire because of a stupid, autocratic dictum that made no sense. Age improved instructors, he thought now, angrily.

Today he had found himself humming an old Hungarian folk song, feeling as he did when the students used to sit at his feet in admiration. Even Spargo.

But when he thought about his timing with the man who had tried to kill Alan Vaughn, he was not happy. His footwork should have been faster. And the knife? Not good either. He obviously had missed the heart, and the throw could not have had the power it should. The man had vanished. Where? Perhaps one of the dark bungalows?

Right now he was in his little rented car, a Vega. He was cruising, looking for an area where he could limber up, do a few dozen kicks, maybe even throw his knife a time or two, but it didn't look promising.

The place was crawling with tourists. It took him almost two hours to find what he was looking for.

Off a back road he found a school that looked as if it hadn't been in operation for years, two-storied, gray clapboard, large, overgrown with grass and weeds, but with an area behind it that apparently had been a football or baseball field. Surrounded by trees, it was barely visible from the road.

He drove in. Perfect. Old, unused schools are like carnival grounds in winter, sad, uncared for, memories of happy hours full of laughter, the ghosts of days that never will return.

Ah, Josef thought, nostalgic nonsense.

He hoped that it would remain deserted.

He'd work out for a half hour, forty-five minutes, go back to the motel, catch a quick nap and be ready to meet Spargo when he returned from jogging.

He went through a routine round of *savate*, kicking over his head with one foot, then the other; making a quick sidekick, one side, then the other; kicking straight backward, right foot, then left. Then he sparred, dancing lightly on his feet.

Feeling muscle tug, he stopped and stood swiveling his hips, bending his torso, then making deep bends, placing his hands flat on the ground without bending his knees.

"Kodály," a voice said softly.

Josef straightened and swung around.

Norikura stood there grinning at him.

The fucking Jap ape! Josef thought angrily.

"Norikura!" he said, faking a grin. "What are you doing here? You wouldn't be tailing me by any chance?"

"Chance is the correct word," Norikura said politely. "I come here myself to do exactly what you are doing. It is the only place in this section of the Cape where there is any privacy. I had to remain here for a few days on business, so I came here for exercise."

That, Norikura, Josef said to himself, is pure shit.

Aloud he said, "Quite a coincidence."

Both men were aware that they had never really liked each other. Jealousy might have been a factor; both had been popular instructors at the Playhouse, Josef with a slight edge because he taught a double bill: footwork and knife.

"Mind if I join you?" Norikura asked, bowing.

Josef shook his head. "No."

Norikura took a quick step forward. With forefinger and thumb, he clamped a viselike grip on the top of Josef's right shoulder.

It flamed in pain, then went completely numb.

"You won't be able to use that arm or shoulder for about two hours," Norikura said. "Thus you won't be able to bring your famous knife into play."

He whirled, striking Josef on the hip with a side thrusting kick, bowling him over. Josef was up again like a jack-in-the-box.

"Let us see, shall we, Kodály, if you can prevent me from killing you. Seems you are getting in the way up here —"

He blocked Josef's quick attempt at a throat-kick with a skillful counter-kick, and hit him hard with a *yubi*, a lightning-swift thumb blow to the area just above Josef's left kidney.

Grimacing with pain, Josef leaped high, hurling himself forward, striking Norikura in the chest with both feet, knocking him to the ground.

Approaching quickly, Josef threw a left foot at the fallen Norikura's jaw.

Norikura adeptly caught the descending foot, pulled Josef off balance; jumping erect he forcefully clapped Josef's ears simultaneously, almost breaking both eardrums, staggering him.

Norikura grabbed Josef's right arm, whirled him around, then smashed the heel of his foot into Josef's stomach, slamming him to the ground.

Josef avoided Norikura's *mae tobi geri* forward jump kick to his face, and grabbed the Japanese's left foot, spinning him onto his back.

Both men nimbly jumped to their feet. Norikura was grinning. He was playing cat-and-mouse with Josef. With his double skill, feet and hands, he was superior to Josef with only his *savate* defense.

Breathing hard, Josef said, "Norikura, in your

arrogance you overlooked one possibility."

"Yes?" Norikura hissed the word politely.

"Perhaps I can throw my 'famous' knife equally well with both hands —"

CHAPTER TWENTY-FIVE

Walking back along the beach to Spargo's Aspen parked behind a sand dune, they were followed and attacked by a swarm of biting insects.

Newborn, they were aswarm searching for food, black bodies, opaque grayish wings, antlike heads. They were a savage, biting, persistent host, buzzing into hair, eyes, crawling on the skin. They preferred dead flesh, but in their new earthborn innocence, they would take anything they could find.

As they tried to beat them off, Harla gasped, "What are they? They're millions!"

"How the hell do I know?" Spargo said. "I'm not a goddamned entomologist. All I know is

341

that lately the insects seem to be getting out of control."

"Allan Vaughn agrees. He says the insect population has tripled in the last two years. Pesticides are ineffectual."

She stopped walking, stood swatting the insects.

"You are right, Spargo. You are no goddamned entomologist. You are some kind of goddamned assassin!"

Batting at the insects, Spargo said, "That man who attacked me back there is not exactly a man. I'm alive only because he hadn't quite perfected *his* assassin's art. Probably an advanced ninja student winning his spurs. A skilled ninja probably would have simply cut my throat."

As they continued fighting the insects and began walking again, he told her about the ninja.

"They're not only expertly trained to kill in countless ways, they're bred and born to kill. I thought that the sect had been wiped out by Japanese authorities years ago. Obviously they've had a rebirth. That fellow back there in the sea would definitely have tried to correct his mistake with me, and probably have taken you out, too."

As they walked, flailing their arms like mad creatures, abruptly the swarm of insects gained altitude, then vanished.

"Thank God," Harla said. "I'm one big welt."

They were silent on the drive back to Jacob's Landing.

Spargo's mind was putting together the jigsaw of what had happened, and he didn't like the picture that was forming. He believed that he had already solved the puzzle of Allan Vaughn's accomplishment. The films he had seen, what Lewis had spelled out in *The Lives of a Cell*, plus the experience Paucek had with those seven lobsters pointed in one direction. He hadn't been able to pull the scientific parts together into one cogent whole, but he knew now why the file was important enough for industrial spies to commit murder to obtain it. Or thought he knew. Nothing was certain until he located the file itself. He also thought he knew where the file had been hidden.

It wasn't dark when they reached the laboratory, but night wasn't far off; stars were pinpricking the sky, the new moon shoving its horn through drifting clouds.

As they got out of the Aspen, Harla said, "I've had it. I'm going to the motel and bed."

"Don't you want to stop somewhere first and have a little supper? Piece of fresh fish or something?"

She shook her head. "Thanks."

He walked her to her Volkswagen (or was it Vaughn's?) and stood watching as it spurted up the road and onto the highway.

The laboratory door was simple to open. Not even a wire was necessary; two slide-throughs with a credit card did it.

He went directly to Harla's office, using a little pencil-flash he always carried. The buoy was still there, leaning against the wall near the desk. He picked it up, placed it on her desk, and tapped it. Hollow. He upended it and twisted the bottom section. It screwed off. He shook it. Out fell a rubber band and two paperclips.

"You're almost as smart as they said you were, Spargo."

He whirled around.

Harla. Gun in hand.

"Enter the villain. I don't believe this." Spargo carefully placed the buoy back on the desk.

"Believe it," she said softly. "I want you to go over and sit at the desk. Face me. Place your hands on the desk."

"You set me up. Why?"

"I was told to divert you. Separate you and Josef. You are the opposition."

"You're a Japanese plant. You finally found Vaughn's file."

"I've been working for the Japanese in marine industrial espionage for several years. We knew through Lundberg that Vaughn was getting close to a breakthrough. I arrived with excellent credentials. I enjoyed working with Vaughn. He's a nice overgrown boy."

"The file?"

"Accident. Knocked over the buoy. Heard it clunk."

"Waited for the arrival of Kim Dong Jo, the eminent Korean scientist, and delivered it to him as ordered. Why the Japs? Why not us or the British?"

She smiled. "Spargo, you're keen. But not keen enough. I'm Indian, as you may have guessed, but only half Indian. My father was an Apache. Chiricahua. My mother was Japanese."

"So you're not really American. You're part hate. Part snake."

"You forgot the other part. Upper hand."

"Of course. The gun. You'll use it?"

"We need time. Kim Dong Jo must have the

345

file examined by one of our men here. A marine scientist. It may be incomplete. A dummy file. I think it's the real thing. But my employers are most careful people."

"You'll shoot me?"

She sighed. "Spargo, I'm in a bind. I'm afraid there's another ninja in your future. This is a tranquilizer gun. Knocks a porpoise out in three seconds."

"Did they tell you about me? What I am? What I do?"

"Enough," she said sharply. "Why?"

Spargo slowly held up his right hand. Salwa glittered.

Harla drew a deep breath. The hand holding the gun trembled slightly.

"I promise you," Sargo said softly, "that I can put this knife in you before you can get a tranquilizer dart into me."

"We'll have to see, won't we," she said stonily.

Salwa flew like a bird suddenly released from a cage, striking Harla's right wrist, knocking the gun to the floor.

Spargo was at her side instantly.

He picked up the knife and the gun. "How long does the tranquilizer keep one out?"

"About two hours, I think." Harla was

sullen now, holding her wrist, standing as defiant as an Indian squaw facing a white rapist.

"Enough time," Spargo said. He shot her in the neck, the dart hanging there like a huge, obscene insect.

She went to the floor in stages, falling softly.

Spargo stood for an instant studying her. Then he walked over, removed the dart and made her comfortable. He picked up the telephone directory, found the Oceanographic Institute's information service, told the person who answered that he was just in from Korea and urgently needed to reach Professor Kim Dong Jo.

He was told that the professor was having dinner with the president of the Institute. He then asked where the professor was staying. The female voice said sweetly, "The Sea Dog Motel. Right here in Jacob's Landing."

The file wasn't in the motel. Working swiftly but carefully, Spargo examined everything in the room. It wasn't a complicated search. The room was the stereotyped motel room. Bed. Desk. Bedside stand. Bathroom. Shower. Nothing.

But as he moved the telephone on the stand beside the bed, a slip of paper was revealed. It had a name and a time: 7:45.

He checked his watch. It was 6:45. Again he dialed the information service of the Oceanographic Institute.

Professor Yoshiaki Hatsumi was one of Japan's most talented marine scientists. Today, he also was one of its most envious. He respected Dr. Allan Vaughn's multidisciplinary approach in his chemotaxis investigation. But mainly, he envied him for complete mastery of a subject that no one else had been able even to properly contemplate.

Yoshiaki was a top scientist, but he also had been expertly trained in industrial espionage by the master himself, Tokura. Tall, big-boned, with bushy black hair and piercing dark eyes without much of the Oriental slant, Yoshiaki Hatsumi would be a difficult man to identify immediately as Japanese. Actually, he was a direct descendant of notable samurai and arrogantly Japanese. He possessed a keen, analytical mind, was a consummate actor, dressed in high style, liked Caucasian women, and was one of the most effective industrial espionage agents of his country. He had delivered plans of marine innovations to Japan before the nations that had conceived them even knew they were missing. He, of course,

348

specialized in his own subject, the sea, and roved widely in his thieving. He was here at Jacob's Landing on direct orders from Tokura.

Yoshiaki had become especially proficient in the use of the Nambu 7 mm. Made only for Japan's elite officer's corps, it had a grip slant designed for natural pointing, for quick shooting at close range. It propelled a .32-inch bullet weighing 100 grams, with a muzzle velocity of 860 feet a second. It also had a silencer.

He hadn't found it necessary to use it often; guile was still better than force. But it reposed beside the Vaughn file in his desk drawer, a safety factor that gave him a feeling of confidence.

Scowling now, he was annoyed because the Indian woman, not he, had delivered the file. He had been here for a year, the Harla woman only five months, and yet she had reached the target first.

Tokura was very pleased with her. She had placed the file in his hands, claiming that it was genuine. But Tokura, careful as always, wanted Yoshiaki's expert opinion.

"It could be a deception," Tokura said. "A dummy to delay us. Vaughn is no fool. He could have planted this and have the real file with him. I want you to go through it word by word. I'll be here at seven forty-five for your decision. We will not use the telephone. We will do this person to person."

It was the real sea file. No doubt about it. A spectacular accomplishment. As he sat in sour meditation, the telephone shrilled.

He lifted the phone off the cradle, said softly, "Professor Hatsumi." He listened. "Of course. I shall be here."

Brewster, Director and President of Jacob's Landing Oceanographic Institute, was sending his male secretary over to have another of those forms signed, a form that renewed his stay as an exchange associate professor. He had signed one like it last week.

He sighed. An American weakness. They buried themselves in an avalanche of useless paper.

In less than ten minutes, the knock came. A timid knock? But then, weren't male secretaries lesser people?

"Enter," the professor said in an authoritative tone.

The secretary wore horn-rimmed glasses, carried a paper in one hand, a fountain pen in the other.

"Good afternoon," the professor said. "Or

should I say evening? You're working late."

The man sighed. "Yes, sir. My days are long ones . . ."

As the man held the pen toward him, Professor Yoshiaki Hatsumi suddenly remembered that President Brewster's male secretary was a slender, bald man.

He reached for the Nambu in the desk drawer. But he was too late.

The stream of vapor from the fountain pen caught him full in the face.

He coughed, tried to get up from the desk. Then he slumped, face forward in the chair.

Spargo lifted the file in its briefcase out of the deep desk drawer, unclasped and quickly examined it. He closed it, pushed the drawer shut.

Then he shoved the professor back in his chair in a position so that it looked like he was cat-napping, chin on chest.

CHAPTER TWENTY-SIX

His shoulder still pained from the wound made by the *shuriken*. He was weary, but his curiosity forced him to pull into a parking area and look at Allan Vaughn's file.

He was stunned by what he read. Man had been dreaming for years about attempting to do what Allan Vaughn had accomplished. It was incredible. Impossible to project what it would mean to mankind.

No wonder Japan had made such a determined try for the file. Lives were cheap wagered against obtaining the answer to that scientific secret, locked in the sea since the beginning of time.

What would the group represented by Carson do with the file when he presented it to them? Actually, who did Carson represent? The CIA? A new secret force as he claimed? Was he really in government or acting for the private sector?

Spargo had learned a long time ago that men were rarely what they seemed. But he had been well paid to do a job and he had done it.

That had always been his motivation: Accomplish a mission successfully. Receive a proper reward.

But with this one, somehow that wasn't enough. He was disturbed by the magnitude of Allan Vaughn's discovery.

Thinking again of those seven giant lobsters that had been strangely drawn to Harry Paucek's lobster pots, he was pleased that he had partially solved the secret of Vaughn's sea file, even before Harla Brownlee confronted him in her office.

He should have been quicker in putting the whole complex business together. The Japanese obviously had been. But then they had had the advantage of an early start, plus name and direction, probably supplied by Lundberg. Planting Harla had been sheer brilliance. At the very elbow of the source itself.

Actually, he should have seen immediately that the key to the entire solution had been those seven lobsters, one of the last tests Allan Vaughn had made. But it was all too far-fetched, had a dreamlike, otherworld quality to it that defeated logical thinking and natural progression of events.

Ahead, as he drove, was the flicker of the lights of Falmouth. He wiped the thoughts from his mind and made himself contemplate simple things, a Boodles martini, a good dinner, a long talk with Josef. He wondered what Josef had done today. A miser with time, Josef always had to do something constructive. Spargo was happy now that he had brought Josef into this. He had performed well and was a rock — always solid support.

He pulled into his parking slot at the Beachcomber, noting that Josef's Vega was not in front of his room.

The pond was illuminated by a spotlight, permitting the guests to agitate the Pekin ducks and the swan all night if they chose.

He unlocked his door and went into the motel room, snapped on the light, the switch to the left of the door.

"Good evening, Spargo." The voice arrived with the light.

Sitting in the plastic chair was Carson, his heavy helmet of white hair gleaming in the unshaded overhead light. On the bed sat a young blond man in a denim leisure suit. A long-barreled .22 pistol lay on the bed beside him.

"Carson," Spargo said quietly. "If I unbuttoned my shirt my heart would fall out."

Carson chuckled "Surprised? We were up this way and thought we'd drop in to see if you'd made any progress."

He nodded toward the blond. "Meet Harry Cleve."

"Howdy," Cleve said.

Spargo ignored him.

"You've saved me a trip, Carson," Spargo said, placing the briefcase on the small desk.

"That it?" Pryor said softly.

Spargo nodded.

"Worth the effort?"

"Vaughn's really done it."

Pryor got up and went to the desk, opened the briefcase and took out a bound, 8½-by-11, three-inch-thick, blue paper-covered book.

He read aloud, "*Chemotaxis. Control of the Sea.* Allan Stanley Vaughn, B.S., M.S., Ph.D."

"What's '*Chemotaxis*?'"

"Involved. You'll have to read it."

" '*Control of the Sea.*' Is that a fact?"

"Yes."

Pryor slid the book back into the briefcase. "This is the complete file of all of his successful experiments?"

"Yes. This is what you were looking for."

Pryor smiled. "Spargo, I do believe that you are as good as they said you were. Congratulations. Now do us a favor. Lie face down."

"Salwa!" Harry Cleve snapped, picking up his .22.

As Spargo's head swung toward Cleve in surprise, Pryor whipped a .32 Smith and Wesson revolver from a belt holster.

"The knife on your right arm," Pryor said sharply. "Don't take it out. Unbuckle the sheath. Drop the whole business on the floor."

" 'Salwa.' Where did your robot get that name?"

"First, the knife."

Spargo slowly pulled up the sleeve of his seersucker jacket, unbuckled the knife sheath and let it fall.

No eye followed the knife. He had no chance. Both men were too far away for him to use his feet.

"I want an answer."

"First, on the floor!" Pryor said harshly. "Harry!"

The .22 thudded.

Spargo felt his right foot jerk. Cleve had shot off the heel of his shoe.

He lay face down on the floor.

"Salwa," Pryor said in a musing tone. "Yes, I knew your Jew agent girlfriend. I didn't realize then who you were. I traded her identity to the Arabs for about a half million barrels of crude and Arab goodwill, which was more valuable. Or, rather, the U.S. did. I was only a spokesman. I admit they didn't have to be so messy about it. Cutting her horse's throat. All that blood. But Arabs, as you know, all are somewhat crazy."

As he lay, face on the rug, Spargo felt cold fury uncoiling, the rage almost nauseating him.

"Tie him up, Harry," Pryor said. "Tightly. He's a tiger. Tie him so that his hands are in front, where I can see them. Don't try to prove how good you are, Spargo. I'll have this S and W one foot from your head. No matter how fast you are, the law of velocity is against you."

Working swiftly, expertly, Cleve trussed Spargo with nylon rope.

"I owe you an explanation for a job well

done," Pryor said. "My name isn't Carson. It's Pryor. What I am is a bit complicated."

He went on to tell Spargo that he worked for two masters, the Director of the CIA, and the President of the United States; that he had been in the Agency first and the President had offered him a proposition. He was to secretly assemble major evidence against the CIA, which would topple the already tottering Agency.

"When our people discovered that Vaughn had perhaps developed a spectacular scientific breakthrough, we needed someone to pick up on that. It was the lever we needed."

He stopped. "My, look at the hate in those gold-flecked eyes." He turned to Harry Cleve. "Those knots better be tight."

"Houdini himself couldn't get out of that truss-up," Cleve said.

"If we sent some of our own people, there was every possibility they would fuck up," Pryor continued. "That's what the Agency has been noted for lately. So I got you. Your reputation is that you are a 'never-fail' guy."

Pryor went back and sat in the plastic chair, where Spargo himself had sat one night that now seemed so long ago, to read *The Lives of a Cell*. "It's simple," Pryor said smugly. "I deliver this file to the President personally. As promised, he makes me head of his new force. We pat the CIA on the head, tell them to behave themselves and we'll let the few good men stay in long enough to get their pensions."

He got up from the chair. "One problem. You. The CIA wants you dead. Reasons are somewhat complicated. The President would like to see that you are properly compensated if you complete the mission successfully. Incidentally, he knows your name. I had to tell him. I would like the President to believe that I alone am finally responsible for obtaining this all-important Vaughn formula. That means you are out. I don't want this to be messy, so I've worked out a neat method to accomplish this, and prove out a new Agency gimmick —"

A noise at the door, the knob slowly turning.

Pryor quickly placed his foot on Spargo's mouth, pressing down. Spargo's gurgle wasn't loud enough.

Harry Cleve moved soft and quick as a leopard and stood to the left of the door.

It opened and Josef entered. "Spargo, sorry I'm late. But Norikura and I had a —"

"Well, look who we have here," Pryor said

359

cheerfully. "Mr. Fancy Feet himself. Welcome. Come right in. Harry —"

Gun in hand, Harry stepped out from behind the door.

Josef made a swift downward movement with his right arm. Cleve's gun thudded, the bullet socking the flesh of Josef's right arm.

Josef stiffened, grasping his arm, glaring at Cleve.

"Mr. Pryor," Harry Cleve said. "Let me take both of these guys right now. Save us a lot of trouble. This gun doesn't make any more noise than a good fart. We'll have no problems."

Pryor shook his head. "No, here's what we'll do."

He went on to say that one of the big drug companies had developed an instant-exposure drug for the CIA, so effective that a minute amount caused hallucinations. When a stronger amount was used it made the recipient as responsive as a robot.

"We'll introduce a much stronger dose to both Spargo and his pal, Josef, take them down to the sea and instruct them to walk to Europe —"

A sound distracted him. He looked at Spargo on the floor.

"That sounded like a bone snapping, Harry, I do believe that you tied those knots too tightly."

Spargo rolled over face-down.

Pryor turned him over.

Spargo sat up quickly, a fountain pen in his right hand; he was still bound, but loosely enough now so he had wiggled the fingers of his right hand into the inside breast pocket of his jacket.

The vapor stream from the pen struck the bent-over Pryor in the face.

Pryor toppled, coughing.

Cleve swung around for an instant.

Josef kicked the gun out of his hand, speared him in the groin. As Cleve bent, groaning, he kicked him full-force in the throat.

Cleve gargled, retched, then went over backward, striking the floor hard.

"Untie me," Spargo said.

Using his good left hand, Josef loosened the knots so Spargo could finish untying himself.

Spargo went over and looked down at Harry Cleve. "I've heard about him," he said to Josef. "They wind him up, turn him in the direction of erring agents, and he terminates them."

He took the fountain pen out of his pocket, held it close to Cleve, pressed it.

"Cardiac failure. Big killer these days. They'll be driving a car with D.C. plates. We'll put it up here, drunk-walk them out in the dark into their car. Park it in the public lot.

"First, let's attend to your arm. Must be hurting like hell."

"In a minute," Josef said gruffly. "How'd you get out of that truss?"

"A Japanese escape technique. Norikura spent two weeks showing me how to dislocate joints. It's the old Harry Houdini trick. They'd tie him up, put him a sealed box, out he'd pop. It wasn't too difficult. All I had to do was throw a joint out so I could loosen the rope enough to get that pen —"

"Spargo," Josef said quietly, "I am so sorry to tell you that your friend Norikura who probably saved both our lives has departed for that big geishaland in the sky —"

CHAPTER TWENTY-SEVEN

Spargo came through the west wing entrance, past the guards, carrying the briefcase, past the Secret Service, past scurrying secretary after secretary.

The magic of his name cleared all security. He was not searched, his briefcase was not touched, doors were opened before he could touch them.

The President sat on his Exercycle watching him as he came into the Oval Office.

"Spargo?" the President said.

"Yes, sir."

"Any difficulty getting in here?"

"No, sir."

"Good. I hoped I had cleared the way. But

orders aren't always carried out."

The President got off the Exercycle, walked over to Spargo and shook his hand.

"There are few men I climb off that bike to meet," he said. "Come over and sit down." He motioned to the chair in front of his desk.

Spargo remembered that Walter Cronkite had described him as "a little man with a big presence." Cronkite was right.

As he sank in the chair behind the desk, the President pointed at the briefcase. "That it?"

"Yes, sir."

"Important?"

"Yes, sir."

"World shaking?"

"Yes, sir."

Spargo placed the briefcase on the desk; the President opened it, took out the blue-jacketed document and opened it.

"Are you familiar with this file?"

"Yes, sir. I've read it several times."

"Good. Then perhaps you can answer questions."

He read from the title page. " '*Chemotaxis*,' what exactly is that?"

"It's a complex chemical communications system of the creatures of the sea that has puzzled scientists for centuries."

"No more, I take it?"

"No. Dr. Allan Vaughn has solved it. He not only understands the language of sea creatures but can reproduce it. He has actually synthesized the chemical pheromones with which they communicate. In one of his last conclusive tests he placed seven male lobsters in the sea, ten miles apart, then summoned them to a single man's lobster pots, using a female lobster's sex pheromone, which he duplicated."

"Pheromone?"

"You'll have to get most of this from Vaughn himself, if you can drag him back from the marine expedition he's on. Best I can put it is that they are small, simple molecules, active in extremely small chemical concentrations. They do the talking."

"Am I to understand, then, that by using these pheromones, which Vaughn can actually manufacture, he can talk with sea creatures, get them to cooperate?"

"Any fish, shellfish, lobster, whatever, can be pulled by its own sex or other pheromone whenever and wherever Vaughn wants."

"He can actually do this?"

"It's all spelled out in his file."

The President got up from his desk, walked

slowly to the west window and looked out at the Rose Garden. The sun fell on his head, glinting on his glasses. Many flowers had faded and fallen, but there were still a few flaming American Beauties and some delicate yellow tea roses in bloom. The President hated to see the roses die and exhorted the gardeners daily to keep them blooming as long as possible.

"Have you made any speculations on the ramifications of all this?" the President finally asked.

"Yes. But I'm sure you'll do much better as soon as you have a chance to study the file . . ."

"Perhaps. But let's hear what you've come up with."

"Well, Vaughn could control migratory fish, use chemical signals to selectively harvest them. His chemical beacons could attract entire schools. Those fish could be stripped of their eggs and sperm for culture purposes, adults marketed —"

"Anything else?" the President said tensely.

"Vaughn himself, of course, has conclusions. Those young fish from the adults captured by chemicals could easy be hatched by artificial means. Imprinted with the chemical language to control them. Then released into the ocean to grow. No care, no cost. They then, as adults, could be brought back to their place of birth, through the final phases of migration, by those imprint chemical signals which could be released in coastal waters."

"Harnessed by chemotaxis, so to speak. Led wherever we want them." The President was now excitedly pacing. Suddenly he stopped and stared at Spargo.

"You haven't top clearance, but because of what you've done, I'll let you in on a secret that makes this file of Vaughn's doubly important. I expect your complete silence on this."

He walked back across the room to his desk and sat. "We are facing world famine. Certain. In the last part of this decade."

Spargo sat stunned. "Why?"

"The goddamned bugs have beat us. We can no longer control them. They're literally eating us out of house and home."

He sat up straight, fiddling his fingers on the desk. "I just have a thought regarding Vaughn's ability to communicate with the sea creatures. Why wouldn't it be possible to develop ocean fish ranches? Each owner having his own chemical brand? Bringing in only his own schools of fish to his ranches along the sea?"

"Vaughn himself suggests that," Spargo said. "When you study the sea file you'll come up with your own valuable suggestions. Opportunities are limitless —"

"Yes, yes," the President said excitedly. "Now, for the first time in many years we, as a country, have the whip hand. The oil exporting countries will no longer have us over their barrel. The Japanese will come crawling. They can't live without fish. The Soviets —"

He leaped from his chair and went again to the window. "Spargo, we've been dealt a straight flush. I'm going to enjoy playing political poker with the pricks that have been trying to back us into a corner. That also includes England, Canada, France, all the rest of the countries that have been hedging or ganging up on us lately —"

"Mr. President," Spargo interrupted. "Allan Vaughn has done something else to help us. He has experimented outside the sea. There is a small section titled 'Insect damage' —"

The President straightened.

"Vaughn has duplicated the sex pheromone of the destructive potato tuber worm. By synthesizing the sex pheromone of the female, he has trapped and destroyed as many as ten thousand male moths in a single night. In addition, he claims that the synthetic pheromone maintained its activity under field conditions for more than one year."

The President was calculating now, his banker's personality taking over. "If Vaughn has already done this, we're a big step ahead. The problem was that our scientists in that field say it could be another ten or even fifteen years before we can biologically even attempt to control the insects. If Vaughn has accomplished this with one species already, why not with the rest?"

He chuckled. "Let's not let this run away with us. It's an astounding feat Dr. Vaughn has performed. What can I say to you for what you have done? If this were the Middle Ages, I'd knight you. As soon as possible, I want to hear the entire story. After I have studied the file. I also want Vaughn back here. Now. I'll get my special people on that. Where did his expedition ship depart from?"

"Jacob's Landing. Cape Cod. Apparently a foreign registry."

"We shouldn't have much trouble with that. We can radio the ship. I'll send a helicopter. Dr. Vaughn will be conscripted in the national interest. Any idea of what his reaction might be?"

"I think he'll cooperate. He's dedicated. I have an idea that he's been afraid that some other country would take his findings and run with them. I suspect that he's interested in getting the Nobel for this."

"He should! Spargo, one question. Why did you come to me with Dr. Vaughn's sea file? Why didn't you go to your old outfit, the CIA? No longer loyal?"

"No question of loyalties. I have an idea you can handle something this important to our country better than anyone else."

The President gave him a long, probing look. "Thanks for that. I'll do my best to play this fair. For everybody. I thank God that Japan didn't outplay us on it."

The President returned to his desk. "I won't keep you any longer, Spargo. We'll get together soon. I want the entire picture from you. Lunch or dinner. Either one that is convenient for you. By the way, did you run across one of my most able men while you were putting this all together? Pryor?"

"Yes," Spargo said curtly. "That will be part of the picture you'll get from me."

"Very well," the President said. "I'll be in touch."

As Spargo reached the door, the President said, "Incidentally, I have something in mind for you that may prove interesting. And challenging."

"Maybe you better make that dinner, Mr. President," Spargo said softly. "We're going to be talking late into the night."